Scars of You

AMITY

MADI DANIELLE

Cover Design: Kimberly from @kbg.designs_

Cover Models: Kristin Travis (@Kristin.travis) & Daniel Jackson

Photographer: Bree Marie (@breemariephotography)

Map Illustration: Chesreadsromance

Editing: KMorton Editing Services

For those that have found yourselves in the darkest times. I'm proud of you. You did it.

Content Trigger Warnings

This book has many fun moments, however does deal with some heavy topics. These do contain spoilers so, but if you have triggers please take care of yourself.

Triggers include:

- Mention of suicide
- Suicidal ideation
- PTSD
- cPTSD
- Depression
- Mention of childhood abuse
- Mention of substance abuse

National Suicide Prevention Hotline

If you ever feel the need for additional support call the National Suicide Prevention Hotline.

Call or text **988** for help.

Playlist

Siren sounds - Tate McRae
Heart Attack (Rock Version) - Demi Lovato
Mr. Anxiety - Iris Grey
I Like It - We The Kings
So It Goes... - Taylor Swift
Skin - Rihanna
Say Less - Chandler Leighton
Battle Scars - Lupe Fiasco & Guy Sebastian
Sports Car - Tate McRae
Dancing With Our Hands Ties - Taylor Swift
Angels Like You - Miley Cyrus
Fix What You Didn't Break - Nate Smith

Hardware Store
GROCERIES
Food Mart
JAMESON'S HOUSE
Roasted Bean Coffee
Barkin Pups
Grooming
AMITY
Fire Co.
MAIN STREET
SUTTON'S HOUSE
SCENIC DRIVE
AMITY
WES'S HOUSE
BAILEY'S HOUSE

CHAPTER 1

Bailey

"COLLEE, as in Brent Collee? The hockey player?" the cashier asks, looking up from my ID.

I give a close lipped smile and fight the urge to roll my eyes. "Yup."

"That's so cool," she gushes, and I nod in response, just wanting to get my things and go.

Thankfully, she finishes ringing me up, and I'm able to take the two bags of groceries and leave. It's so interesting to me that back in Ohio, the name Collee was equated to trash. Everyone in that small town knew who we were, and about our parents. Yet none of them stepped in to do anything about the shitty situation we were in.

We only had each other.

My three older brothers, my younger sister, and me.

Now, the name Collee has another meaning, thanks to my

oldest brother, Brent, being a professional hockey player. I've considered changing my last name, not wanting to associate with my past or be linked with someone considered famous.

All I want is to do is live my life under the radar, with no one bothering me.

That's the reason I moved around so much, traveling to find the right spot. I finally settled on this small town bordered by the mountains, and ocean, Amity, Washington.

I was lucky enough to get a job here as a barista in a small drive up coffee stand, Roasted Bean. I'm no stranger to doing odd jobs here and there as I moved around and when I was growing up, I always had to figure it out.

Our parents were useless, and though my siblings and I all did what we could for each other, my three oldest brothers all left eventually. Which just left Brynn and me. Until we were able to get out ourselves and never look back.

Now, I own that same coffee stand I worked at when I first moved here because the owner was retiring and liked me enough to work out a deal for me to buy it. I never thought about what my life would look like. Some people grow up having dreams, picturing exactly what they'll do, the person they'll marry, the kids they'll have.

Not me.

I couldn't see past the day I was currently living because I didn't know what the next day would look like. Sometimes I still struggle with that, but I'm trying to be better about it.

For the first time ever I have friends. Real ones that aren't just using me because they think it will get them closer to my brother. It won't; I hardly talk to him. No, my friends, Sutton and Lily, don't even know about Brent and neither has mentioned hockey so it's been a nice reprieve.

Sutton's my neighbor, but she's about to get married to her fiancé, Jameson, and they're moving in together. I offered to help, but Jameson refused, saying I didn't need to. I insisted right back that I wanted to, and was sent to get some dinner and drinks, for the small house warming they're having tonight.

Lily's in town on summer break before she goes back to college for her senior year and is sure to be there. I wasn't too sure about her when we first met; I'm quiet, she's...not. But the more I've been around her and Sutton the more I feel myself opening up.

But only to them.

They still don't know the extent of my family history or everything I've been through. That's something I keep locked up tight. All they know is I hardly talk to anyone in my family, and that I have some siblings. That's it.

I pull up to Jameson's property, driving past the main house and following the directions Sutton gave me to get to the house further back on the property. They're working on adding to the place because apparently it's fairly small, but they couldn't wait to move in together.

They're disgustingly in love, and that's something I've never experienced and doubt I ever will. Which is fine by me. I don't think I could handle having someone around in my space all the time. No thank you, I like my independence.

Cutting the engine, I manage to balance the pizza and drinks I'm bringing, while also closing my car door before making my way up to the front of the house. See, *independent.*

Using my foot to knock on the door, I almost lose a pizza box, but I move to catch it, smiling at my success. But as soon as the door opens, that smile drops and is replaced with a grimace.

"What're you doing here?" I ask the huge man standing in the doorway of a house that is clearly *not* his.

"I'm here because Jameson is my friend and asked me to help Sutton move her things. What are *you* doing here?" Wes, my neighbor, and the bane of my existence asks right back. He also doesn't make a single move to help take anything from my arms.

I push past him into the house to set everything down before I end up dropping it all and head to the porch with pizza and beer.

"I bring sustenance," I say, slipping the pizzas onto the table. "But you don't get any," I sneer up at Wes behind me.

There aren't many people in my life that are taller than me, men included. I'm six-feet, and everyone in my family was supposedly "blessed" with height. My brothers are all at least six-foot-four while my little sister Brynn is the shortest at only five-foot-nine. While she's gotten shit for it from our brothers for her whole life, I'm a little jealous. I stand out in a crowd with my height when I would much rather blend in.

Wes stands around six foot six, with biceps the size of my head. Anyone who doesn't know him would be intimidated. But to me, he's just annoying and has been since I found out he's my neighbor.

Unfortunately, I found out *after* we had already slept together. It was supposed to be one of my usual hookups. My first night in town with a hot guy I found at a bar. Too bad it's been years since that night and I can still remember the way it felt when he touched me.

We've never talked about that night, and I'm not even sure if he remembers it. But then there's times like this when he chooses to fuck with me and I'm sure he does. Because he still doesn't move to help me, but he does crowd in behind my back, his face close enough I can feel his breath on my skin, causing a shiver I try to suppress.

"You don't make the rules, Angel."

My knees buckle at the nickname because that's the same thing he called me that night, and I'm suddenly glad there's a chair to brace myself on. I turn to glare at him, but he's already walking past me.

Blowing my hair out of my eyes, I mentally prepare to get through this. Hopefully without completely losing it.

CHAPTER 2

Wes

I DON'T LIKE big group settings. Especially when I don't know very many people. Though, this isn't exactly a *big* group, I still feel uncomfortable only knowing Jameson. He's cool, nice even. I kind of know his fiancé, Sutton, but I tend to try not to go out of my way to talk to very many people. I prefer keeping to myself.

Then there's Bailey.

My neighbor, who I fucked years ago and have yet to forget about. It would've been nice to keep that up, but I knew it would be a bad idea. Feelings could get involved and then it's awkward. I don't do commitments, so instead I just pretended like it never happened.

And made her hate me.

To be fair, that wasn't exactly my intention, I was just going to pretend like I didn't know her to avoid the awkwardness. But ever since then, it seems as though everything I do pisses her off. And when she and I get into it, I can actually feel something, so I continue to do it.

Like right now, at Jameson and Sutton's house, I didn't help her even though I could tell she was struggling to carry everything. She's made it a point to ignore me, focusing all her attention on her friends: Sutton and I think the younger girl is named Lily.

I lean against a wall because I refuse to have my back open. Even if I'm in a place that's supposed to be safe, nothing ever feels safe enough. Even my own house doesn't feel secure enough at times.

Across the room, Jameson is talking to his friends, who coincidentally work at the fire station with him. There's a younger guy named Parker, an older guy named Dave, and a woman named Jo. I watch all of them as they're talking, and notice the way Parker keeps looking over at Lily. How Jameson finds any excuse to touch Sutton. And the glares Bailey sends in my direction.

Those make me smile, and I try to hide it behind the beer I bring to my lips.

"What about you, Wes?" Jameson asks, and while I'm always aware of my surroundings, I'm not always aware of the conversations happening around me because I'm so focused on *what* is happening.

"What about me?" I ask nonchalantly.

"Any plans for the rest of the summer?"

I shake my head. "Just your wedding."

"You guys are boring," Parker scoffs.

"Not all of us are twenty-one and stupid," Jo mumbles.

"I'm twenty-two in a *week*. God forbid I do something to celebrate my birthday," Parker argues.

I finish off my beer and debate getting another one but decide against it since I should head home soon. I'm starting to feel suffocated in the small space with all these people around. My eyes catch on Bailey, noting how she has her arm around her body, holding her opposite elbow, a tight expression on her face and somehow I can tell she's feeling something similar to me. Though, she would probably rather gnaw off a limb than admit that.

"I think I'm going to take off," I announce, loud enough I'm sure she can hear me.

"You sure?" Jameson questions.

"Yeah, I'm pretty tired." *I'm not. I can barely sleep most days.*

"Alright, thanks for your help today."

"All good. I'll be by tomorrow," I tell him. We both know I come by to help with the horses, but I don't ever talk about *why*.

Because talking about why would lead to questions and I don't want those. I can't even admit to myself the things going on in my mind. The nightmares remind me enough, which is why I avoid them by avoiding as much sleep as I can.

It's fucked up, but it's how it has to be.

I walk outside and over to my Aston Martin DB11, I parked it where I usually do when I come down here and away from the horses so I don't scare them when the engine roars to life. Though, the distance doesn't seem to matter because I still feel my phone signal a text before I'm off the property and I smirk when I look at the screen.

Bailey: You don't have to announce yourself with that stupid car every chance you get, you know?

Wes: I don't? How else would I make sure you know my every move?

I toss my phone onto my passenger seat and pull out onto the main road, letting the car take off underneath me. I'm finally able to breathe out fully as I lay on the throttle. This is what driving does for me—it's the best therapy. I had to do quite a bit after I got out of the Army, but still, nothing beats the way I feel when I'm out on the open road with no end in sight, no time limits, just me and the car.

That's why when I can't sleep, I take a drive. But Bailey seems to have superhuman hearing and she gets frustrated hearing my car in the middle of the night or in the early morning hours. I try to keep it down, but I like nice cars, *sue me.*

I don't go directly home; it's not like there's anything or anyone waiting for me there. Instead, I take my time driving through the forested roads that I know like the back of my hand. I don't even pay attention to the time, I just turn up the music and drive.

When I finally get back to my house, I feel like I might be tired enough to get a couple hours of sleep. Bailey's car is in her driveway, and I find myself wondering how long she's been back.

I get inside, and go directly to my room because if I get caught up doing anything else I know any chance I have to actually go to sleep will slip through my fingers. Though, that's exactly what happens when I see the light on in the window across from mine.

The window that I know leads to Bailey's bedroom.

Her curtains are drawn so I can't see in. But since I know she's not sleeping, I pat my pockets for my phone, pulling it out to tease her just a little bit more.

Wes: Can't sleep? I know something that can help with that.

Bailey: Listening to you talk? Because I can't think of anything more boring.

Wes: One day you're going to eat your words.

Bailey: I'm so scared.

I can practically hear her monotone voice say the three words, and yet it makes me smile. She's not scared, she likes it. One day maybe both of us will get to learn just how much.

I can still see that tattoo on her ass, the image of her face down on that hotel bed, her ass on display for me. How it felt in my hands and those two words inked into it.

Bite me.

Fuck, I wanted to.

And her mouth challenging me, we both know the type she is. It's exactly the same type I like to handle into submission. The type that likes to be put there, right where I want her.

Shit, now I'm hard just thinking about the possibilities with her if we would just give in. I look over at her window, the curtains still drawn, and then back down to my phone.

Wes: I'll come over and see just how true that is.

I watch for any movement, hoping she'll tug the curtains aside, open the window and yell at me. Because at least when we're arguing back and forth, I feel *something*.

The curtains sway and she peeks out, clearly trying to be subtle about it. I tilt my head and raise an eyebrow. She disappears from my view immediately knowing she's been caught.

I wait to see if my phone will light up again, but it doesn't. Oh well, probably for the best anyway. Though, when I try to go to bed, sleep eludes me, always staying just out of reach.

CHAPTER 3

Bailey

LILY WAS in the middle of one of her outrageous stories when I noticed Wes leaving last night. All my attention focused on him. Even when the words "leash" and "man" were used in the same sentence, I wasn't able to focus on what Lily was saying because I was glaring at the back of my neighbor.

I tried to stay and enjoy myself, but eventually ended up leaving because my social battery felt almost completely depleted. I do enjoy being around them, and even Jameson and his friends were nice, but I'm an introvert to my core. When I do venture out to a bar or something, I'm not social. If I'm looking to go home with someone, I don't need pleasantries and they're the sole focus of my attention.

Sometimes I don't even need a name, or I forget it. Like the night with Wes. I'm pretty sure he didn't remember mine either since he kept calling me angel.

I heard him come home last night, and it wasn't long before I had a text from him. He didn't have my number for the longest time, but Sutton "accidentally" gave it to him, supposedly. She's been on me for awhile, questioning if there's something between. She had some excuse as to why she gave it to him, but I think it was some failed attempt at trying to play matchmaker.

That will never happen between us.

Now he has my number and uses it to his advantage more often than I would like. The grump sure as shit stays to himself, and I try to as much as possible. You'd think we could live in peace, never speaking to each other, but that's just not the case.

I left him on read last night because his threat to show up at my house was a little too tempting. It's been a while since I've had an orgasm that I didn't give myself, and unfortunately for me I remember exactly how easy it was for him to pull the pleasure from my body.

And I'm sure there's more where that comes from.

I did get a text from Sutton this morning sending an SOS because she needs caffeine and left her coffee at home, apparently. I was working on inventory, but told her I would be her savior. Luckily, Amity is extremely small; we only have one stoplight and the grooming salon where she works is less than a mile down the road from my coffee stand so it won't take me long to get over there.

She always orders the same thing, an iced vanilla latte with almond milk, so I put it together quickly, and let Jenn, one of my employees, know I'll be right back.

I could easily walk to the grooming salon next to the fire station, but I opt for the faster option of driving. When I walk in I'm greeted with a bark that definitely did not come from a dog.

"Shut up, Vern!" the shop's cockatoo, Jerry Lee, announces like he always does. No one here is named Vern, and no one really knows where that came from, but he has lots of interesting phrases he's learned over the years.

"Jizz! Hot guy, Jameson!"

Like those.

"Jerry Lee, I swear to God I will pluck your feathers out one by—Oh hi!" Sutton greets and I laugh, handing over her drink. "Thank you so much. I owe you my life, or my first born."

"Keep any child you have to yourself, you don't owe me anything."

"Wait, why are we offering children?" Lily steps out into the entryway. "Hold on, where's mine?"

Sutton clutches the drink tightly to her chest, as though she's trying to conceal it.

"This isn't fair," Lily pouts.

"You didn't ask, she did. Sorry." I shrug.

"See if I do anything for you two ever again." She looks between us with a glare before storming off.

Sutton smirks before calling out, "Parker's outside."

"He's not on shift today," Lily calls back, and Sutton slaps her hand over her mouth, stifling her laughter. "I didn't say that, I don't know anything about him or his schedule and I hate you both."

Standing between them, I'm a little lost in their banter. I know Parker is a firefighter who works with Jameson, and that he and Lily have a past. I'm not one to bring up anyone's histories, considering mine with my neighbor, so I stay quiet like usual.

Lily's head peeks around the corner. "I'm kidding. You know I love you both, but also you're mean." Then she's gone again.

"Anyway, I should head back to work. Lily," I call out, "do you want me to bring you anything?"

"It's too late for you to try and buy my love now, this ship has sailed!" she yells from the other room, and Sutton just shrugs.

"Okay then, I'll see you later."

"*Bitch!*" the bird squawks.

"That's a new one," I comment.

"Yeah, take one guess where it came from." Sutton points her thumb in the direction where Lily disappeared.

I smile, shaking my head and saying goodbye before I turn and head back to work.

ONE THING I've always loved about my job has been the hours. I prefer waking up early so I can be done before the day is over. Call me crazy but it's my preference. However, I don't like it when I've been woken up in the middle of the night. Especially by Wes's damn sports car roaring to life, then tearing out of here to wherever the fuck he goes at all hours.

I can only imagine it's some woman's house or something. He never has anyone over to his place, and other than annoying me, he hasn't attempted to get me into bed again. Though, he doesn't seem like the commitment type, so I'm sure whoever the poor girl is will get her heart broken. Or girls, I'm sure there's multiple when it comes to him.

No judging here, he can do whatever he wants and break all the hearts he wants.

It just will never be mine.

I am, however, tempted to break something of his when I'm awoken for the second time tonight. *Yet again,* I look at the clock and see it's a little after two in the morning. Everything is silent so I can hear when he shuts the car door, and I debate storming over there to yell at him.

I hang on to my composure, but just barely. Though, when I'm unable to fall asleep after several minutes, I grab my phone again and type an angry text I may not even send.

Fuck it.

> Bailey: I don't know what or who you're out doing all the time but either stay out or get a quieter fucking car.

> Wes: You sound jealous.

I scowl at the screen even though he can't see me.

> Bailey: What's there to be jealous of? Two seconds of mediocre dicking? I'm good.

I swear our street is so quiet I can hear his bark of laughter from next door. But there's also a high probability that I'm just hallucinating because I'm half asleep and pissed off.

Wes: You and I both know I last a lot longer than that, and that it's anything but mediocre. Go to bed.

Bailey: You don't tell me what to do.

Wes: Watch me.

I toss my phone down and stare at the ceiling.

It's times like this I can't but think about the night we had together. Does he remember? Has he remembered this entire time? I feel like I'm going crazy and any chance I had of going to sleep tonight is now completely obliterated because he's fucking with my head.

And the worst part is, I think that's exactly what he's wanting to do.

CHAPTER 4

Bailey

ALTHOUGH JAMESON and Sutton didn't plan many events for their wedding, they are throwing a small engagement party. It's been about two weeks since Sutton moved in, and it feels like the wedding quickly approaching. They didn't want a long engagement, but they still wanted to take time to celebrate.

Or maybe it was his mom that still wanted to celebrate. She's recently gone into remission from the cancer that brought Jameson back to Amity. With that and losing her husband a little over a year ago, Sutton said she'd been waiting to see Jameson get married for so long, that now she wants to celebrate every little moment.

However, Sutton has drawn the line at a bachelorette party. Lily tried to convince her that we should all go to Vegas and go crazy. That was shot down very quickly by both Sutton and I. Nothing sounds worse to me than Las Vegas with a slightly insane twenty-one year old.

I normally don't dress up beyond jeans and a nice shirt, but for this event, I put on one of the few dresses that I own. And for that, my friend should be thankful. I even curled the ends of my long hair, and put on a little bit of makeup.

When I look in the mirror, I almost don't recognize myself. For some reason seeing myself like this reminds me of my younger sister, Brynn. She's always been the one that enjoyed wearing nice clothes and makeup. She's always been known as the "prettiest." It's not like I was ever called ugly. The bullies had plenty of other things to pick on without needing to attack my looks.

But right now I can see the resemblance between us, and it causes a pang in my chest because I haven't spoken to her in a long time. She tries, but I don't respond. Both her and my oldest brother, Brent, try to reach out, and sometimes I give them a short response.

But most times, I leave them on read.

I never know what to say without spiraling into memories of our childhood and the trauma it left behind. So instead, I chose to run away. To distance myself from that place and the people—my family—and start over fresh.

Even if it hurts.

But there are times like these when I find myself missing them. Texts I almost send. Calls I almost make.

I just never do.

My other brother, Bryson, never reaches out, though I know he talks to them a bit more. After our brother, Brandon, died, something shifted between all of us, and we all chose to cope in our own ways. Mine was to isolate.

The sound of my phone ringing pulls me from my thoughts and away from the mirror, so I can stop seeing the image of my sister staring back at me. Part of me expects to see her name on my screen, as though I willed her into calling me, but instead it's Lily's name I see.

"Hello?" I answer because she never calls me. We have a group chat with Sutton and that's her most common form of communication. I'm not a big phone talker, and I'm not the best texter.

"Hey, have you left to go to Sutton's?"

"No, what's up?"

"Can you give me a ride? My car is dead."

"What do you mean dead?"

"I dunno, it won't turn on. Will you just come get me? Pretty please?"

"Yeah, did you call a tow truck or anything?"

"Nah, that's a later problem."

I sigh, looking up at the ceiling, not liking that she's going to be without a car. Everyone needs to have a way to leave if they need to. I don't think she has any issues at home, but I can't help my own thoughts of feeling trapped without a car.

Then I remember who I live next to and grimace.

"If I can get someone to help you out, would that be okay?"

"Yeah, I guess." Her tone is so nonchalant I wonder how

someone can be so calm about something going so wrong in their day.

"I'll be over soon."

We hang up, and I take in a deep breath before walking next door. I raise my fist to knock, but hesitate. I don't think Lily would care if I didn't follow through on the offer. But I don't like how it would feel. She shouldn't be stuck. I'm sure she's going to need to get to work. And maybe go see Parker, even though she insists there's nothing going on there.

I inwardly groan, knocking on Wes's door. Rocking back on my heels, I feel like he's taking forever. Maybe he's not even home, but his car is in the driveway. I'm about to walk away and pretend like I never showed up, when the door swings open.

Wes is standing there looking more put together than I thought was possible. He's in black slacks, a black button up, and his dark hair is styled...nicely. Not a hair out of place. The worst part is his sleeves are rolled up to his elbows, showing his thick forearms, his veins are prominent and make my mouth water when it shouldn't.

I hide any other response my body has to seeing him like this by narrowing my eyes in his direction and folding my arms across my chest. Which is clearly a mistake because the way his eyes drop down to my chest makes goosebumps break out across my skin. Everything is made so much worse because I know exactly what it feels like when he's holding me down and doing whatever he wants to me.

"You know things about cars," I blurt, because my mind needs something else to latch onto, that isn't how good he looks, and how good I know he feels.

He smirks, his eyes moving back up to mine. "Sure, and you hate mine."

"I do, but my friend is having some issues with hers. I was wondering if you would take a look at it."

"I'm not a mechanic, but I can try."

"Obviously not right now, you're clearly about to go somewhere."

"So are you, and I think it's the same place."

I choose to forget that he's friends with my friends, but I know he's right.

"Well, I have to go pick up Lily since her car is dead, but then I'm going to the party."

"I'll follow you there and take a look," he says easily, almost too easily.

"No, you don't have to do that," I insist.

"I'm going to."

"You're annoying."

"So you've said."

I walk back over to my house, grabbing my keys while convincing myself he's not actually going to follow me to Lily's. But when I come out, he's already in his car, and when I pull out of my driveway he's right behind me.

I hardly pay attention to the road; I'm so focused on him, and wondering why he would do something nice for me. It's unlike him and makes me feel like there's a catch. I'm just worried about what that may be. Or maybe he's just nice... *no way.*

The drive to Lily's isn't a long one, and she's standing outside leaning against her front door. She waves at me as I pull up, then looks at Wes when he parks, cocking her head to the side with a smirk aimed in my direction.

"What's he doing here?" she asks as I step out of my car.

"He's going to look at your car." I shrug. "I told him not to worry about it today, but he insisted."

She grins. "Probably wanted some time with you."

I roll my eyes just as Wes walks up.

"What's the problem?" he asks, and while his gruff voice makes him seem rude, Lily doesn't seem fazed.

"It won't turn on," she answers simply.

"Keys?" he grunts out and I narrow my eyes at him. He could at least *try* to be personable. It's not like I forced him to come here and yet he's acting like he's being held against his will.

Lily hands over her keys, and I hold back my chuckle at seeing the giant man with arms that look like they could lift the car in question holding keys with a bright pink puff ball on them.

Wes immediately opens the door, and pops the hood like he's

a professional and I can't deny that it's hot to watch, but I'm trying to manage my facial expressions. And my body's reaction.

Lily bumps into me as Wes leans over and out of our view.

"He's hot," she murmurs.

"He's a dick."

"The hot ones usually are."

"I can't stand him."

"We love a good hate fuck."

"I wouldn't touch him with a ten foot pole." *Again.*

"Well he would, and I bet he knows his way around the clit."

I choke on my own spit, also pretty sure she said that loud enough that Wes heard her, but he doesn't react as far as I can tell.

"I think I know what your issue is," Wes calls out and I jump at the sound of his voice. "Pretty sure it's just your battery, but you may have a starter issue as well."

"Great, so that's going to cost me a bunch of money I assume," Lily complains.

"If you get a battery, I'll install it for you."

"That's nice of you." Lily looks at me for some reason.

"Yeah, super nice." I roll my eyes, still feeling like there's some sort of catch here.

"I'm done with this, let's go party." Lily bounces toward my car, and I don't have a chance to tell her I don't think it's the type of party she's probably used to. At least from the stories I've heard.

"Thanks," I grumble.

"Yeah, well, you could say I know my way around a car." I hear the slight humor in his voice and I scoff, walking off. "Bailey."

I turn around to face him, placing my hands on my hips.

"Roll your eyes at me again and see what happens."

He climbs into his black sports car and I stand there dumbfounded for a few moments before the loud blaring noise of my horn goes off. I see Lily reaching over into the driver's seat and shake my head as I climb in.

"You're so fucked." She laughs.

"I don't know what you're talking about."

She just laughs harder as I drive us to the party.

CHAPTER 5

Wes

SOMETIMES I'M NOT sure why I became friends with Jameson. He's a cool guy, and I like helping around his family's property and working with the horses. He calls it equine therapy, but I don't like to think of it as therapy because then I feel like it takes some of the enjoyment out of it for me.

I do it because I want to, not because something is wrong with me.

However, I'm questioning this friendship because this is the second get together in a short amount of time. And then we still have his wedding coming up. I offered to officiate, though I'm somewhat regretting that now.

The only thing I'm not regretting is how much I'm getting to see Bailey and watching how she interacts with others. Every time I'm involved she scowls at me or has some sort of snarky comment or remark to say. Both of which I enjoy more than I should.

But it's also interesting to watch how she is with her friends and even with strangers. There's something about her, a darkness behind her eyes. She doesn't smile a lot and I don't know much about her as a person but I can tell she hides from most everyone, even those closest to her.

I recognize it because I'm the same way.

I would never tell her that, and I'm sure she would rather chop my balls off than hear we have something in common. Except maybe our preferences in the bedroom. Those seem to be a perfect match, if our one night together is any indication. I'd love to see if a second time would be just as good or even better.

"You going to join everyone else, Wes?" a soft voice asks, and I look down to see Jameson's mom, Emily, smiling up at me. She's the only person around here that knows even a fraction of my story.

I don't have my own parents to talk to about anything, not that I would anyway, but Emily's presence is so peaceful and calming that she managed to get me to share a couple of things. Though, it felt like I was talking to the horses more than to her, but even then she never seemed to pity me. She didn't say a word, just listened.

"I'm just observing," I tell her honestly, leaning against the wall as I nurse my now lukewarm beer. The people around me often feel like too much. I find myself more comfortable observing and hidden in the background. Interacting too much can drain me, but sitting back and watching gives me breathing room.

"I see that. You could talk to her instead of standing here staring like a creep?"

I scoff. "I'm not staring like a creep."

"I raised a stubborn boy already, you know."

"I'm just trying to stay out of the way."

"You don't need to. As much as you'd like that wall to suck you in, it's not going to. Try to enjoy yourself." Emily walks over to Jameson, squeezing his arm before walking over to Sutton who pulls her in for a hug.

I watch Bailey's face as she observes these two women who clearly have a close bond smile as they say something to each other. Bailey looks uncomfortable, shifting on her feet and looking around as though she's trying to avoid watching them. Her gaze lands on mine, and just like it always does, her eyes narrow.

She mouths, *"What?"*

I just shake my head, bringing the rim of the bottle to my lips for a drink while she keeps glaring at me. It's enough to have me pushing off the wall and walking toward her, and I see the questioning look on her face as I do. The other people she was standing with, including Lily and Sutton, don't seem to notice her start to inch away as I get closer.

"You like something you see? Because you keep staring." My voice is low so others can't hear me.

"Just wondering what you're even doing here; vampires usually can't come out during daylight."

"You've seen me outside in the sun, clearly not a vampire."

"I'm still not convinced."

"I willingly helped your friend and I've yet to hear a thank you from you." I move a little closer to her, my shoulder brushing hers.

"Nobody forced you to help."

"No, knowing you owe me something is enough."

She rears back slightly. "I don't owe you anything."

The corner of my lip quirks up slightly. "Don't worry, I'll make sure to cash in soon."

I don't give her a chance to retort before I'm walking away and joining the small group of people, even though it makes my skin itch trying to be social. I push through because I know I'm getting under Bailey's skin and it only makes it worse when she can't do anything about it.

To some, my job as an Apache pilot is unreal, a lot of people really don't think about what we do. To me, it's just another day's work. We lift off into the air, the heavy machinery moves easily under my control as we navigate the sky.

We're preparing to do just that, the anticipation always gets to me while we inspect the choppers before heading out.

There's a loud booming sound.

"What the fuck?" my copilot, Chris, exclaims.

I'm looking around, searching for the threat.

A flash of light.

Another booming sound.

There's yelling to take cover. But I try to grab anyone I see to take them with me. Chris drags me down, stopping me from running out toward anyone else.

More booms, more explosions, there's dirt, debris, and metal pieces flying everywhere. There's no time for emotion, all we have is pure adrenaline. We do everything we can to remain calm as the world around us explodes and we're unable to do anything to stop it.

There's another boom even closer, this one makes my ears ring. There's a pain in my leg that's so bad I'm blinded by it. Then everything goes black.

I jolt awake, heart racing and drenched in sweat. My breaths come in sharp, uneven gasps as I struggle to orient myself in the darkness. The scar on my leg pulses with a deep, familiar ache. A reminder of the metal buried beneath the skin, fused to me since the surgery. I'm wide awake now, tangled in the sheets. Dropping my head into my hands, I try to calm myself as the memories from that day assault me.

We all understand what we might experience the day we sign up for the military, but nothing prepares you for it actually happening. I know sleep is going to evade me for the rest of the night. Needing to distract myself, I throw on some clothes, grab my keys, and drive out into the night.

By the time I get back home, the sun is rising, haloing the trees in a soft glow. I cut the engine and just sit in silence. I wait for the exhaustion to hit me, wait to feel anything, but the numbness has taken over. It always does. It's never *if*, it just depends on how long it takes to get here.

There's a pounding on my window and I immediately go into defense mode. When I see it's Bailey standing there, my shoulders relax. Instead of rolling down the window, I open the door and step out. She's tall for a woman, and it's one of the things I liked about her from the start, but right now as I tower over her with the half a foot I have on her, the numbness begins to fade away.

Even while she scowls at me, I feel myself drawn to her even more.

"What's the problem, Angel?"

The nickname only makes her scowl deepen, which also has my dick hardening. It may be inconvenient, but another outlet when I feel this way has been sex. Until that stopped helping and started to leave me feeling worse afterwards.

Except when it was with her. That one time felt different. And nothing has felt the same since.

"You waking up the entire street this early is my fucking problem."

I look down and notice she already looks dressed and ready for the day in jeans and a basic shirt, her unofficial uniform for work.

"Looks like you were already awake."

"That doesn't mean everyone else is."

"Are you the neighborhood noise police?" I step closer to her and she doesn't back away from me at all.

"No, it's called being a decent person."

"Hm," I hum, making a point to look down her entire body in an exaggerated way one more time. "You and I both know you're not as decent as you want everyone else to think."

She rolls her eyes, and I wrap my hand around the back of her neck, hauling her even closer to me as she gasps.

"What did I tell you about rolling your eyes at me?"

She swallows roughly, then shrugs, but I don't miss the way she tamps down the smile that threatens to appear.

"Don't test me, Angel. Next time I might not be able to let you walk away."

I hear her sharp intake of breath and for a second, I don't think she wants me to let her go. I think she may even fight it and beg me to close the small distance between us.

But she doesn't.

Instead, my grip loosens on her and she backs away looking surprised with herself, shaking her head. "You can't make me do anything."

My jaw tightens as I watch her get in her car to leave. The numbness from before is long gone, replaced by the fire under my skin. I'm dying to touch her, to make her deal with the situation she caused. The one that is making my pants feel impossibly tight.

One day, I'm sure I'll feel Bailey Collee again. And she's going to see how much I was holding back that first night. The one and only time I will.

CHAPTER 6

Bailey

I FEEL like my feet have been swept out from underneath me. Dealing with Wes always throws me off, but doing it first thing in the morning is a whole other level. Add in his body being so close to mine, the things he said. *The way he said it.*

His growly tone shot right between my thighs. It brought me right back to that night, once again. The night it seems I can never escape, no matter how much I want to.

"Look at you, Angel. You like what you see?"

"I'm far from an angel."

"Good. I don't want you to be a good girl. Get on your stomach."

"Make me."

"Hey Bailey, we're almost out of whole milk." Jenn's voice pulls me away from the inappropriate memories my brain is choosing to replay a lot more lately. You'd think after three years since that night, they wouldn't be so vivid. But it seems like the more time passes the clearer they get.

"Dammit, it should've been included in the last delivery." I shake my head, both trying to physically shake away the thoughts in my mind and at my disappointment in the company we've been using. This isn't the first time something has been missing from the order. "Is there anything else we need? I'll run to the store."

Luckily, we're past the busiest part of our morning rush, so we're able to check through our delivery to see if there's anything else they left out. I'll also be having a really angry phone call later with the supplier who thinks they can fuck me over.

Once I'm back from the store, I'm struggling to carry in all the gallons of milk, really hoping I don't drop any. That would be a huge problem since I bought the last several they had. Jenn notices my struggle and quickly jumps in to help me. As we're filling the fridge, a car pulls up. I'm closer to the front so I offer to help the customer.

The low rumbling engine should have clued me in on who would be waiting there. It's not like sleek sports cars are common around here. I don't even bother pasting on a fake smile as I go to greet him. Not while my body is still humming from our interaction hours ago.

"What can I get you?" I ask without any pleasantries.

"What's good here?" he looks me up and down and I bite back my reaction.

"Depends what you like."

"I like a lot of things. What is it that *you* like?"

It's probably due to our run in this morning, or maybe it's from the lack of bedroom attention I've gotten recently. Or maybe I'm just so screwed up in the head that I'm reading into his words like an innuendo. He could just be messing with me because he knows it gets under my skin. Knowing that's probably what it is, I do my best to hide any sort of reaction.

"I'm an Americano person, generally don't like things too sweet," I answer.

Wes smirks. "Sounds perfect, I don't really do sweet. I like when things have a little *bite* to them."

My hand slips on the counter where I had it resting. The way he just said that four letter word, the one I have tattooed on my ass. The one I'm *sure* he didn't see, has me questioning several things about him, and about myself.

"Great, coming right up." I turn away, and hope I didn't sound too breathy when I said "coming."

For fuck's sake I'm losing my mind.

"You okay?" Jenn calls out from the back of the small coffee stand.

"Yeah, would you ring him out for me?" I don't want to face him again. I don't think I can continue to keep my cool any more today.

Jenn charges him, and I hand her the finished drink without showing my face out that window any more. Jenn doesn't question my need to escape and I continue to busy myself for the remainder of the day.

It's not until I get home that I check my phone for the first time today and instantly wish I didn't. Not only do I see a text Wes sent me earlier, right after he got his drink. But there's a text waiting from my oldest brother, Brent.

He doesn't reach out much, and both him and Brynn have started to try less and less, but I don't think they'll stop completely. Not like Bryson who I'm pretty sure is so caught up in his own bullshit to think about anyone other than himself.

> Brent: You're going to have another niece, thought you may want to know.

I sigh. The urge to say something is strong, but the fear of being pulled back into the repressed memories and screwing up the happy life he's clearly building holds me back. I know he's with a woman named Chandler, who he apparently shares with two other guys on his hockey team. I don't judge, but damn do I want to ask some questions about *how* and *why*.

They had a daughter a couple of years ago, and as I scroll up in the text thread there's a picture of a tiny baby wrapped in a pink blanket with the name "Evie" on a round wooden sign resting next to her.

My niece. One I haven't met before, and now I guess I'm going to have another one. I'm not surprised Brent is having kids, he's probably a good dad. He did what he could to raise all of us, even though he left and couldn't protect us from the daily abuse we endured. I don't blame him for it.

I did what I could to protect Brynn from most of it. I learned no one was coming to save us, all we had was each other. But as we grew up, I only ever had myself because I refused to drag anyone down in the depths of my mind. Not with the memories and trauma constantly threatening to pull me under at any given moment.

Like right now, when I can hear the yelling again.

Brandon, my second oldest brother, slamming doors on cabinets and drawers looking for something. He's always looking for something. I don't know what it is, but when Brent was still here he would stop him and kick him out.

But Brent's gone. He's playing hockey. He said he would get us money and help, but right now I just wish he was here.

"Should we help him look?" Brynn's little voice asks.

I shake my head. "No, we should stay here."

I quickly go to the bedroom door, making sure it's locked so he won't come in. Whatever he's looking for isn't in here with us. Bryson yells again, and I can hardly even understand the two of them, it's just raised voices and slamming objects.

Our parents aren't here, but that's usual, I don't know where they go. If they aren't gone, they're passed out. Brynn sniffles, and I pull her into me, wrapping my arms around her head trying to muffle the noise.

Doing that for her makes it so I can't cover my own ears. I try to use my shoulders to help myself, but it doesn't work. I'm not sure how long it goes on before the noises finally stop. As soon as I get the chance to leave this place, I'm never looking back.

This is the reason I'm not replying to Brent. I won't be pulled back in. Brandon is gone. He died, and he can't ruin my life any longer. But I could ruin theirs if I'm allowed in.

I exit out of the text thread and see Wes's text. The distraction seems nice, and part of me wishes I could just give in. Let him use my body like he did that night and give me a distraction I so desperately need. But I know it isn't worth it, and it will only leave me feeling worse the next day.

> Wes: Didn't even say goodbye to me. That's another strike, Angel.

I can't even come up with a witty comeback with my mind swimming in the sea of trauma that I don't think I'll ever get out of. I lock my screen, toss the phone onto the couch and go to the freezer, pulling out a bottle of vodka to pour myself a drink. I try to limit myself when I'm like this, knowing our family history with drugs and alcohol.

It nay not have been alcohol that took my brother's life, but it was an addiction and I don't ever want to battle with that myself. I vow this will be my one for today, even with a heavy pour and the juice I mix in. The cold liquid burns my throat on the way down, but helps my muscles loosen and my mind calm. At least for now.

CHAPTER 7

Wes

"HAVE you ever thought about getting a dog?" Jameson asks as I'm sweeping the aisle of his barn.

"A dog?" I question looking at him, then down at the two other sets of eyes staring up at me. One is a giant black and white fluffy dog named Bennet, and I know he was Sutton's before she moved here. The other is a blue nose Pit Bull named Duke. I like dogs, I've never owned one, but I get along when them fine, especially these two.

"Yeah, you know, maybe you'd be less lonely," he ribs.

"I'm not lonely, I have plenty of women keeping me entertained." *I used to. Not anymore. The one I want refuses to give into what we clearly have.*

"I'm sure you do, but you can never have too many friends." He shrugs, and the dogs follow.

I consider what he's saying, and I know service dogs have been offered to several other veterans I've known over the years. I've just never seen the need for myself. I don't need any service a dog can offer, but for some reason his words stick with me this time.

Maybe I'll go to the shelter and walk the dogs sometime. I do need distractions to fill my days, which is why I'm here with the horses so often. I don't have a job, nor would I know what I would even do if I did. Due to the circumstances of my discharge, how long I served, and the money I inherited from my parents after they died I don't have to work for an income. I like to do things that I want to do, not just for a paycheck.

I don't need much, my car is the nicest thing I own. I have no interest filling my space with useless junk I'll never use. But maybe spending time with dogs could help fill more of my days.

Animals are peaceful, and they don't talk back which is probably my favorite part about them. I don't have to say anything to them, they don't have to say anything to me. There's a mutual understanding and it's nice.

That's how I ended up at the local animal shelter. The older woman working there looked at me wide eyed, which isn't exactly new for me. I'm a big guy, a lot of people stare when I walk in somewhere and instantly think I'm scarier than I really am.

"How can I volunteer?" I ask, though I recognize I think it sounded more like a grunt than I meant.

"Y-you want to volunteer?" she stutters.

I nod, once.

"Yeah, okay, of course. Great. I'll get you the paperwork to get started." She starts rummaging around.

I shift, looking around at the small office area. "I just want to walk them."

"That's more than okay, we need all the help we can get, and sometimes they just want a little extra attention." She pulls out a couple pieces of paper, scanning them and then sliding them over to me.

"It's just general liability info." She waves her hand around like it's no big deal.

"As long as I'm not signing away my soul or something." My tone remains even, but she barks out a loud laugh like I told her the greatest joke possible.

"No, no it's nothing like that," she says through her laughter, and I still think she's laughing way too hard over my non-joke.

I don't even crack a smile, looking down at the papers and signing my name on the line and handing them over.

"Perfect, you can come by any time we're open." She smiles widely.

"I'm free now if that's okay?"

"Oh yeah, of course, please. There're so many dogs, I'm sure will be happy to stretch their legs a bit."

Nodding, she leads me back toward the kennels, and introduces me to some of the dogs. Some look so scared cowering in the back of the cage, some are laying under the cot bed they're provided. Others are sitting up front, wagging their tail just hoping they'll get an ounce of attention.

It's a German Shepherd that catches my eye. He's curled up as small as he can be, face turned away and I can feel his sadness from here. "That's Bruno, he's been shy ever since his previous family dropped him off here about a month ago."

My stomach sinks. "Why would they do that?"

She sighs. "It happens a lot more than you think and there's always a different reason. Moving, a new baby, change in lifestyle, and sometimes, they just don't want them anymore."

"None of those seem like good enough reasons to get rid of a dog," I grumble.

"I agree, but other people don't."

"That's fucked up," I murmur.

She hums in agreement. "Want to take him out?"

I nod, and she grabs a leash hanging on the side of the kennels before unlocking the door. She hands me the thin fabric, and Bruno doesn't even stir from his spot. I kneel down. "Hey bud."

His ear perks slightly, but he still doesn't move.

"Want to go on a walk?" He moves a little, just the smallest swish of his tail.

I don't push him, opting to just wait. He must realize I'm not leaving because his head lifts up a bit and he looks at me. Even his big brown eyes look sad as he stares at me. I lift up the leash to show him and he starts to stand. It's slow, and he keeps his head low as he approaches me.

"Wow," the woman sighs. "This is the first time I've seen him get up for anyone."

I want to feel proud of that, but it just makes my chest hurt even more. My leg aches from the way I'm kneeling on the hard floor, but I refuse to move. I don't want to scare him and ruin the little bit of trust I've somehow built.

He nudges my hand, and I pet his soft fur; he looks at me a little more, and gets closer. I lift the leash higher,. "Walk?"

He lets me slip it around his neck and I'm finally able to stand, my legs protesting as they stretch. The woman looks at me in awe as I lead Bruno out. The shelter isn't near a busy road, and has walking paths throughout the forest around the property.

Not wanting to rush the dog, I let him take in his surroundings as slow as he wants. He walks with his head low, but his ears aren't completely pinned back so I know that's a good sign.

I don't try to talk to him, instead enjoying the peaceful quiet as we walk. I think about the few things I need to take care of at home, which then leads me to thinking of what else is at home, or more so who's next door. She'll probably be home by the time I get back, not that I'll get to see her since she holes up in her house just as much as I do.

Bruno stops lifting his head slightly.

"What is it?"

Listening intently, I try to hear what he does, but there's nothing other than the leaves rustling in the slight breeze. Bruno doesn't move, just looks off in the distance at something I can't see while hearing something I can't hear.

He's on alert, just like I am in almost every situation. I didn't know I could relate to a dog more than I do in this moment. He finally relaxes subtly, dropping his head again and leading us down the path.

When we're done with the walk, I don't want to put him back in the kennel. Especially when I see the way he resists walking in. Again, I don't force him, but I do ask for some treats to help. Though, as the kennel is closed on him I want to rip the metal apart and take him out again. To take him away from here and never bring him back.

But I can't do that. I don't know how to take care of a dog or if I would even be good at it. Plus all the animals here need homes, and I can't bring home every single one just because I feel bad, no matter how much I want to.

"I'll be back tomorrow," I promise because if I can't bring him home, I'll certainly take him out every day until someone else comes along to give him his forever home. Everyone deserves the opportunity to get a second chance at life.

At least that's what I've been told, even if I think it's bullshit for myself. I got my second chance, and I'll never understand why. I also feel like I'm completely wasting it, so this is the least I can do.

CHAPTER 8

Bailey

SUTTON SHUT down Lily's suggestion for a bachelorette party almost immediately. However, just like everything with her, she didn't let it go right away. Somehow, she convinced Sutton for a lowkey girls night instead of the Las Vegas showdown she was hoping for. And *somehow*, that girls night ended up being at my house, without my say in the matter. Lily insisted that it can't be at her house since she stays with her mom during the summer. And it can't be at Sutton's house because she lives with Jameson.

Apparently suggesting that he have his own guys night out is not enough for her, and that's how Sutton and Lily ended up here. I don't necessarily mind, it's just hard to let people into my space sometimes. It feels vulnerable, like they can see things I don't want to share. Despite the fact that they're my friends.

"Shot time!" Lily announces holding up a bottle she brought.

"What game are you going to make us play this time?" Sutton sighs, dropping back against my couch.

"No games necessary. Just drinking, we're celebrating Sutton no longer being a single woman," she declares.

"I mean I technically haven't been single for awhile but—"

"Single. Woman." She cuts her off and I shake my head.

"Alright, no game, then pour the drinks."

She does, and my phone dings reminding me to put it on silent, and then I look down rolling my eyes at who it is.

Wes: You have company? Damn, that ruins the plans I had for us tonight.

Bailey: We had no plans. We will never have plans.

Wes: I have plans for us.

Bailey: You can enjoy those, alone.

Wes: No, my plans can't be done alone.

Bailey: Then find another unwilling participant.

"Up for another?" Lily asks, grabbing my attention away from my phone. I switch it to silent and set it face down so my two nosy friends don't catch sight of Wes's name on the screen and decide to hit me with the third degree.

Or worse, because I wouldn't put it past Lily to go over to his house, and spin some insane story that I need him to come bone me.

I'VE LOST track of how many shots in we are. We have music playing and are laughing while Lily shares more ridiculous stories. And there's a lot of them. Sutton's biggest addition is the fact that her dad and her best friend were having an affair and she caught them—while her mom was in the room.

She starts laughing over it once again, which is probably thanks to the alcohol. My confession sure is because I never share anything about my childhood, but I find myself sharing a small detail.

"Yeah, well mine was an abusive piece of shit." I throw back another shot.

Lily looks between the two of us. "Am I the only one here with a normal dad?"

Sutton and I both shrug, answering at the same time, "Yup."

We all burst out into laughter which is interrupted by a knock at the door.

I look between the two of them. "Did you guys order something?"

They both shake their heads. I stand up, swaying slightly because once I'm on my feet, the alcohol really seems to hit me. My head is spinning as I walk the short distance, that feels a lot longer right now, to my front door. When it opens, the light-headed feeling I have fades into annoyance.

"What're you doing here?" I demand, folding my arms, but quickly reach out to steady myself on the wall.

"I think you need to turn down the music. It's getting a little loud."

"Are you fucking kidding me?" I snap at my giant neighbor. "You're not allowed to complain about noise."

He's about to say something, but Lily appears like the little chaos fairy I swear she is. Her five-foot-one frame looks even shorter when we're standing next to one another, and her blonde hair sways as she swings her head around me.

"Who ordered the stripper gram? Take it off!" she exclaims and I redirect my eyes, shooting daggers toward her instead of Wes.

"He's not a stripper, he's leaving," I tell her, nudging her out of the way.

"Boo you're no fun! I want to see some *abs*. Maybe a dick!" My face flames as she walks away, but then she calls out, "Oh I know! We can put on some porn." And I go to slam the door in Wes's face.

He stops it with his lightning quick reflexes, leaning forward with a smirk on his ruggedly handsome face. I hate that he's attractive. I hate that he looks even better right now while my brain is foggy. I *really* hate that right now I remember what it felt like to fuck him, and how my body is begging for it to happen again.

Bad. No desiring assholes.

"I assume I'm the asshole."

Fuck, I didn't mean to say that out loud.

"I figured you didn't."

Goddammit.

His smirk turns into what I think is his version of a smile. "When your friends leave and you still want to know about the plans I have for us, let me know."

"I already told you, there are no plans. Get the fuck over yourself," I slur, raising my hand to wave him off, but he's quick, grabbing it and pulling me into him so hard our chests crash together and I gasp.

I don't try to push him away, but I'm going to blame the fog in my head and not the fact that it feels good to feel his muscles against me. It takes every single bit of restraint I have to not run my hand down him and feel every indent I know is there.

"I certainly have plans, and they all have to do with you. Face down, on my bed. Your hands and legs restrained so you can't fight back while I spank this perky little ass of yours." I gulp and my breathing quickens as he continues. "I'd make you apologize for every little thing you've said and every time you've rolled these green eyes at me. I'd wait until your face is soaked with tears and your pussy soaked from how badly you need something to fill it."

Said pussy clenches, and I know it has to do with how drunk I am because there's not a chance in hell I'm this turned on by Wes. I refuse.

"And maybe you'd get what you want. Or maybe I would leave you like that all night. Needy and begging while I made you watch me jerk my cock off as many times as I want while you remain wet and desperate."

I squeak, lacking the words to say how I'm feeling.

"Go back inside, Bailey." He lets go of me, and backs up. It's not cold, but my body feels like it is from the loss of him being so close to me. My skin is on fire, and my body is humming. "Turn the music down."

He turns away and walks over to his house. I close the door and have to compose myself before facing my friends again.

When I do I'm glad to see they haven't put on porn, but I am faced with two very smug looking girls.

"What?" I ask, hoping my voice sounds normal.

"Lily's right, you're fucked." Sutton smiles.

"Haha, you both are hilarious," I deadpan.

A couple of hours later there's another knock at the door, and I refuse to answer it this time. "Not it," I call out. I know that if it's Wes again, I can't be held responsible for my actions, so I'm not about to risk it.

"It's Jameson." Sutton giggles, struggling to stay steady as she stands up and bounds toward the door.

"I really hope they drop me off before they start to feel each other up," Lily tells me.

"You'll be fine," I insist. The two of them don't really seem like the exhibitionist type, but what do I know.

They all leave and my house instantly feels quieter. Lily originally suggested a sleepover, but I can't bring myself to open my space like that. I never had a sleepover growing up, and never as an adult either. Not even with hook ups.

That includes the man that turned out to live next door.

The one I need to stop thinking about and definitely need to stop having run-ins with. I groan, standing up and walking up to my bedroom, because I need to go to sleep to hopefully ward off the hangover I'm sure I'm going to experience in the morning.

There's a light on in the window that mine faces. I can't help but step closer to see if he's in there. That's when I see he's reclined on his bed, not looking in my direction. I know my next actions are fueled by the drinks I've had and not my rational brain, but I don't care.

His words from earlier are ringing in my head, and I only have so much self control it seems. That's why I stay facing the window as I start stripping my clothes, slowly. Just knowing he could possibly see me is enough to have me continue. It doesn't take long before he looks over. His face doesn't give away how he's feeling, it never does.

But his dark brown eyes look even darker in the low light in his room as he watches me so intently. My heart rate increases, but I try to keep my face passive as well. Even as I hook my thumbs in the waistband of my pants, bending at my waist as I push them down.

Wes stands up, and moves closer to the window. I hide the hitch in my breath as my pants hit the floor. My eyes remain locked on his through the glass of our windows. I'm only in my bra and underwear, even though it feels like I'm more exposed than I am with the way he's watching me. I could walk away. I could end this right now. But for some unknown reason my mind tells me to keep going. So I do.

Sliding my hand down my stomach, I tease my middle finger just below the trim of my panties, my eyes not daring to look anywhere else. Wes tilts his head, the only indication he's thinking anything at all. His face remains just as passive, which pisses me off because I want a reaction. I want to see how much he wants me. I want to know what he would do if he was in this room with me instead of separated by a few feet and two panes of glass.

I dip my hand lower, grazing my clit and my mouth drops on a gasp. Wes clenches his jaw and he shakes his head. I stop my movement, narrowing my eyes at him. He folds his arms across his broad chest and raises his eyebrow like he's challenging me.

My hand moves again, dipping lower, feeling how wet I am from this teasing and he shakes his head more firmly, then pulls out his phone. He types without looking at the screen and mine goes off.

He nods and I don't want to move, but I want to know what he said. Removing my hand from my underwear, I grab my phone and read the message.

Wes: Don't continue that unless you want me to finish it.

But what if I do? What if that's exactly what I want?

I can't, though. I'm not in my right mind and know I'll regret it in the morning. The smallest piece of my rational brain kicks in, and I go back to the window, closing the blinds and letting go of the breath I was holding.

My phone goes off in my hand again.

Wes: Thanks for the show, I'll remember this.

I hope I won't.

CHAPTER 9

Wes

NOT THAT I was planning on sleeping anyway, but after what Bailey pulled in the window there's no way I'll be able to now. The temptation to go over there and make her show me how she touches herself right there on her bed is so strong. I stop myself, just barely. I bet she would let me, but that's not how I want her again.

The longer I stay here the harder it'll be to fight the temptation to not go over there, and bang on her door. So I grab my keys and leave. Not even trying to keep my car quiet as I drive down the street. I hope it pisses her off because I would love nothing more than to get even more of a rise out of her.

The small gym in town is open twenty-four hours, so I head there first, needing to push my body to the point of exhaustion. I need the burn, the sweat—anything to distract me and take the edge off the erection that's been tormenting me ever since I saw her pull her shirt off.

Though the image is still playing on repeat in my mind— especially when she slipped her fingers out of view—touching herself just barely. I know it's not enough for her. She needs it rougher, harder.

And I can give it to her, if only she would let me.

❋

WHEN I'M DONE at the gym, I drive around aimlessly for hours. The roads are quiet and the sun is starting to appear. I feel like I may be able to fall asleep, but head to Jameson's instead to help out with the morning chores before going home and attempting to sleep.

My muscles ache from being overworked at the gym, but I like the pain as I feed the horses. I'm standing up in the hay loft, dropping flakes down in the stalls when my name is called. I look over to see Jameson's mom, Emily, standing at the entrance of the barn.

"What're you doing here so early?"

"Just wanted to help out, couldn't sleep. Like usual," I answer, dropping down the last flakes of hay into Juniper's stall.

"That's not good for you, you know?" Emily scolds, and I can't help but smirk at her motherly tone. I know she's not my mom, but since I haven't had mine around in a long time it's kind of nice.

I climb down, and see she has her arms folded while looking at me with a raised eyebrow. "I know, but I've tried basically everything else and nothing seems to help."

"Hm," she hums. "Well, if coming here to do farm chores

helps, then I won't tell you no. Though, I'm sure Jameson has argued with you about it."

"Eh, he can get over it."

She chuckles. "He will. I appreciate your help, if there's anything we can do for you please let me know."

"No need for anything, I'm happy to help."

"You're a good man, Wes."

I don't always feel that way, but I'm not about to argue with her about it, or spill all the not so good thoughts that run rampant in my mind every waking moment. The same ones that keep me awake at night.

I give her a small smile, and nod. "Thank you, ma'am."

"Now go home and get some sleep. I could use the bags under your eyes as suitcases."

That makes me chuckle lightly, shaking my head. "Thanks, Mrs. Turner."

"Go," she encourages.

I'm not about to argue with the woman, so I head home. When I get there, I somehow manage to fall asleep within only a couple of minutes after my head hits my pillow and my eyes fall shut.

Bruno perks up his head as I approach his kennel with a leash. "Ready to go on another walk with me?" I ask quietly, opening the door.

His tail wags once as he approaches me slowly. I slip the leash on him and let him lead the way. It's completely obvious that he's taking the exact same trail we did the last time. It's almost like his paws are taking the same steps he took before. His head stays low, but he seems more sure in his movements, or maybe he's just more sure of me.

And that feels pretty good.

We walk for a while, because just like before I don't want to bring him back to that cage. I push it off as long as I can, but when he's panting and clearly needing water, I know I can't put it off any longer.

He sulks back into the kennel and immediately starts drinking the water, but I don't want to leave him just yet.

"He seems to like you," the woman, who I learned is named Gloria, says as she approaches.

"Has anyone been interested in him?"

She shakes her head. "Not unless you're wanting to take him home."

I sigh, looking back at Bruno who's now curling up once again in the same spot he seems to always be.

"I don't think I would be good enough for him."

She's quiet for a second. "Dogs don't need us to be perfect. They just want to feel safe and loved."

As much as I wish I could do that for him, it's unfair to give him a life he's going to continue to be sad in. Because how can I give him something I don't even have myself?

"It's just not a good idea," I tell her.

"What about fostering him?"

"What does that mean?"

She brightens. "You'd take him home and care for him while he waits for his forever home in a place that's more comfortable."

"How can anyone meet him if he's living at my house?"

"We still let people know about adoptable dogs that are being fostered. If they're interested you'd bring him here to meet them."

I'm still not sure. It seems like so many things could still go wrong. I've never had a dog, and I don't know what to do with one. What if I make his life worse than it already is? What if I fail him?

But when I look over at the brown and black dog curled up, trying to be as small as possible, I know I can't keep leaving him here like this.

"What do I need to do?"

BRUNO WON'T HAVE to spend another night alone in that kennel because he's now in my home. He was nervous when we went to the pet store to get him the supplies he needed. Gloria offered to send me home with some, but he deserves new things that I'll make sure goes with him whenever he gets adopted.

I'm not sure if a dog needs a memory foam bed, but that's what I got for him. It's actually pretty comfortable. I know because I'm sitting on it. Even as my leg protests the pressure, I keep it stretched out in front of me trying to ease the ache. It doesn't do much, but I stay there anyway.

Bruno is looking at me, still unsure and nervous.

"I'm sorry. I don't know what I'm doing, but I do think this bed is pretty comfortable," I tell him, patting the mattress.

He steps forward slowly, then sits next to me. I pat his head, and he leans into me, just barely.

"We can go visit a friend tomorrow and maybe get some advice so you can be comfortable while you're here." I swear I feel his tail wag. It's small and subtle, but I'll take it as a good sign.

The next morning, I'm surprised to find that I actually got a couple of hours of sleep. When I go into the kitchen, Bruno perks up from his spot on his new bed. He already seems more relaxed here, and it makes me feel better about my somewhat impulsive decision. But today, we're going to see Sutton, because she'll know what I need to do with him.

He gets into my car easily, the passenger seat already coated in his fur from when I brought him home yesterday, but it doesn't bother me like I thought it would.

Because she can't ever seem to escape me, Bailey is pulling into her driveway, and immediately furrows her brow when she sees me as she steps out of her car.

I don't say anything, just look at her, waiting to see if she'll try to pick a fight with me. I hope she does. I'm dying to put her over my knee and give us both what we're wanting. But her eyes move past me, and she looks surprised.

"Did you get a dog?"

"Not exactly."

She looks at Bruno, then back to me, and narrows her eyes. "Who is that, then? A family member?"

"Yeah, my brother."

"Makes sense. Always thought you were a dog."

I almost laugh, but I just smirk. "Just give in, Angel, it'll be easier for both of us."

"I don't know what you're talking about."

"Your show the other night says differently."

Her jaw drops, but she shuts it quickly and storms away. I climb into my car, and Bruno looks at me like he has so many thoughts. Like he knows so much more than he can let on.

"Don't worry, she likes it. It's only a matter of time before she admits it." I make sure to be extra loud as I take off, driving the short distance it takes to get to the dog grooming salon, Barkin' Pups.

Bruno is nervous once again as we walk in. I regret bringing him to another new place, but this is somewhere dogs go, so it would make sense, I think.

"Hi bitch!"

I rear back, wondering who would greet someone like that before I come face to face with a white bird who starts barking at me and I quickly realize it was him.

"Jerry Lee, you're fired," Sutton says right before she appears. "Wes, hey. What are you doing here?"

"I have a new..." I pause, he's not my dog so it's not fair to claim he is. "I'm fostering a dog."

"Aw, that's so sweet." Sutton drops down, and stretches her hand toward Bruno. "You're so cute, what's your name?"

"Bruno," I answer because he clearly won't.

He sniffs her hand, and then steps closer allowing her to pet him.

"What a sweet boy," she coos.

"Do you want to adopt him?" I offer.

She chuckles lightly. "I would adopt every single dog if I could. Why don't you?"

"I don't know what I'm doing with him, which is actually why I'm here."

"Oh." She stands up again. "Do you need help with something? Is he okay?"

"Yeah, he's okay I think. I know he needs to be walked and fed and I got him a bed, but what else does he need?"

She bites back a smile, and shakes her head. "There isn't some big secret handbook on taking care of a dog. Just give them attention, love, food, and a safe place to stay."

It really can't be that simple, can it? That's kind of what Gloria said too and I don't believe it.

"What about bringing him here for...this."

Again, I see her stifle a smile. "You should talk to Jameson about your lack of dog grooming knowledge. You two can bond over it."

"Hot guy, Jameson!" the bird squawks.

"Do you like your feathers, Jerry Lee? Because I'll start plucking!" she threatens.

"So he doesn't need to come here?" I clarify.

"He can get a bath, maybe deshedding, and his nails trimmed every six to eight weeks."

"Deshedding? Like you shave him?"

Now she really laughs. "No, definitely not. It just helps get his undercoat out."

"Will that help him not coat my car in his fur?"

She nods.

I look down at him, and he still seems so nervous. "Maybe we should do that, but I just brought him home yesterday. I could bring him back in a couple days, though."

"Whenever you want, just let me know."

"I'm sure whoever ends up adopting him will like him to be clean and all that too."

"Mhm."

"Should he play with other dogs or anything?"

"If he's friendly, sure. Bennet and Duke get along with everyone if you ever want to try."

"Maybe."

"Just let Jameson or me know, and he can come with you to the ranch if you'd like."

I nod, and we start to head out, I tell her I'll bring him back in a couple days. The bird screams out, *"Shut up, Vern!"* as I leave, and I hear more threats from Sutton, wondering what kind of a mad house that place is.

When I get back home, Bailey's car is gone again, and I can't help but be a little disappointed. At least now I have Bruno to fill my days while he's living with me.

CHAPTER 10

Bailey

I'VE BEEN AVOIDING Wes like the plague since the night of Sutton's "bachelorette party." I hoped that maybe everything that happened through the window was just an illusion or some insane dream. Unfortunately, realizing it was very much real had me wanting to hide away for the foreseeable future.

Since that's not possible, I'm doing the next best thing and just avoiding the one and only person who bore witness to my moment of weakness and insanity. I try to be out of the house early and quickly before work, and when I get home, I race from my car inside as fast as I can.

It's worked for a couple days since I saw him with his new dog, but I know it's going to end sooner rather than later. Especially since Jameson and Sutton's wedding is quickly approaching. The rehearsal is tomorrow and I'm sure *he who shall not be named* will be there.

"Before you even ask, yes, Wes is going to be there tomorrow. And no you can't skip. But yes, you're not sitting next to each other," Sutton says like she can read my mind as I help her put together the bouquets for the wedding.

I groan while Lily chuckles behind some leaves.

"You," Sutton focuses on her, "on the other hand *do* have to sit next to Parker."

"What? Why?" Lily complains, throwing the flowers down on the table.

"Because that's how it is."

"But Mo-om," Lily groans.

"Don't 'Mom' me, I'm only five years older than you. If anyone is Mom here, it's Bailey."

"Whoa, don't bring me into this like I'm the one making the seating arrangements." I raise my hands up.

"Maybe you should be. You wouldn't put me next to my arch nemesis," Lily says.

Sutton just rolls her eyes with a scoff.

"That's a little dramatic. You dated him for how long?" I give her a pointed look.

"Exactly, that's even worse! He's my ex *and* my arch nemesis." Lily looks back at Sutton again. "Put her next to Wes so she can see how it feels."

"He really *is* my arch nemesis, so no let's not."

"*Yeah okay,*" Lily mocks in a deep voice. "Have you seen the way you two look at each other? The sexual tension is so strong it practically makes *my* clothes fall off."

"She does have a point." Sutton shrugs.

"Now whose side are you on?" I narrow my eyes.

"The one where you both get over yourselves and admit you like the guys."

"Never," I state firmly.

"Not gonna happen," Lily says at the same time as me.

"Fine." Sutton sighs. "But the seating chart stays how it is."

Lily grumbles something under her breath, and we continue working on the arrangements. Then, Sutton speaks up again and I'm pretty sure it's purely to cause more chaos.

"Though Wes did look really cute with that dog of his."

"Oh my God." I shake my head. "I'm just waiting for the dog to realize who it's living with and start to pee in his shoes."

"That reminds me of this stray cat I took in." Lily perks up, and I brace myself for some insane story because that seems to be how she is. I'm not sure how so many crazy things happen to one person, but apparently she's just lucky in that regard. "My dad did *not* want us to keep the cat, and I think she knew that which is why she would make sure to pee on his ties he laid out for work. Every. Single. Day."

That is probably one of the tamest stories I've heard her tell.

And shortest.

"Did you keep the cat?" Sutton asks.

"Of course we did, her name is Petunia."

"Does she still pee on your dad's ties?" I clarify.

"No, he learned to not lay them out anymore."

I'm still waiting for more to the story, but she goes back to arranging flowers, and I think that may actually be it.

"Oh that reminds me, when I came back from class one day and learned my roommate was a furry."

There it is.

✽

Brynn: I miss you.

I SIGH, looking at the text for way longer than necessary before scrolling up through the dozens of unanswered texts from my sister. I used to give her simple responses, but when she mentioned she was going to be in Washington and wanted to meet up, I just couldn't do it.

And I haven't answered her since.

I don't want to throw her life off balance. I don't want to go back to the dark place we both escaped from. I don't want to be the reason any more of my siblings lose their lives because they remember where we came from. It's just best if I stay away.

That's why, even though I want to answer her and tell her I miss her too, I don't.

It's better this way for all of us, even if she doesn't see it. She's always seen the best in people. She's positive and bubbly. She just wants us all to be together again, but that's something that can't happen.

I lock my phone and finish getting ready to go to the rehearsal dinner, hoping the smile I paste on my face is believable and that no one around knows how deep and dark my thoughts can go. Tonight, I'll be the Bailey that stays quiet and is happy for her friend before I slip away to my quiet, lonely house once again where the thoughts can swallow me whole.

As SOON AS I walk into the large farmhouse, Lily's voice is the first I hear. "I just don't understand why the males always have to be the pretty ones." That sentiment has me shaking my head and forgetting about everything else for a little while.

"Because we're all just naturally better looking, obviously." Parker stands up straighter and flexes his arms which has Lily loudly groaning and dramatically rolling her eyes at him.

"You look like a rat dragged you out of the gutter after you passed out there for two years," Lily retorts and I really question how she comes up with the things she says.

"Why would a rat drag me out of the gutter? Wouldn't it want to keep me there?" Parker smirks, folding his arms across his chest.

"I wouldn't know, I don't speak to rats like you do."

"Aw, come on, Lil. You miss slumming it with me, don't even lie."

"Having fun?" A deep voice comes up behind me, and I hide my small jump at the sudden appearance of the man I've been desperately trying to ignore.

"I was." I turn my head to the side slightly. "And then you appeared."

Wes crowds my back, and I look around to see who's paying attention, but when I try to step away he clamps a strong hand on my hip, stopping me. His mouth dips close to my ear, his hot breath tickling my skin as he speaks.

"This is your last warning, Angel. The next time you give me attitude I'm going to punish you, and trust me when I say it's not going to be fun."

My jaw drops. I'm not able to say anything before he's walking over to Jameson, and I'm being surrounded by Sutton and Lily, who's apparently no longer engaged in her face off with Parker.

"You okay?" Sutton asks, and I do my best to school my expression.

"Yeah, of course. Why wouldn't I be?"

"Because your face is so red it looks like you're sunburnt," Lily adds unhelpfully.

"Maybe I am."

"No, I think it has to do with whatever Wes just said to you." Lily smirks.

"Are there drinks here?" I look around, trying to completely divert all attention from me and my supposedly red face.

"You think alcohol will save you?" Lily teases and I ignore her because I know she's just trying to goad me.

"Of course we do, come on." Sutton leads me into the kitchen where I'm able to pour myself a drink.

Emily announces we're going to run through the ceremony. We all make our way behind the house to where a beautiful floral arch is set up at the end of a small aisle flanked by a couple rows of chairs.

Jameson and Wes are instructed to stand by the arch while Lily and I are paired up with Jameson's coworkers, Parker and Dave, and told when to walk down the aisle together.

"Trade me." Lily nudges my arm.

"I don't think it works that way," I tell her.

"I don't want this one," she insists.

"I can hear you," Parker whisper-yells.

"Good because I wanted you to," she whisper-yells back.

"Everyone ready?" Emily announces.

Dave and I nod while Parker and Lily continue to bicker

behind us. We're instructed on when to start walking with the timing of the song that's playing. Even though we start several feet before the other two, I swear I can hear their quiet arguing the entire time before they finally separate to stand on opposite sides of the altar.

Sutton and Emily walk together, and I watch Jameson the whole time. The way his eyes never leave his fiancée, the way the love between them is so palpable it's almost hard to watch. The way they smile at each other, lost in their own little world where no one else even exists.

"Then we do the ceremony and everyone lives happily ever after." Emily smiles. "You guys will pair up again to walk out after Jameson and Sutton."

"Do I have to or can I walk out solo? Actually, can I change jobs and be a flower girl or something?" Lily asks.

"No, actually, I think she should have to jump on my back or I'll just fireman carry her out," Parker adds.

"If you try to lift me, I will drop-kick your ass."

"Think you can? I'll give you a free shot to try, Lil."

"I think we got it down, who's hungry?" Jameson cuts off their bickering.

We all end up inside at the dining table, and I wish I could say it's a peaceful dinner, but it seems nothing with this group ever is. Throughout the entire meal, I focus on not paying attention to Wes, but when my eyes accidentally look over, I find he's already looking at me.

I want to say something snarky and antagonize him like I usually do, but then I remember his threat from earlier and bite my tongue, holding back. He tilts his head like he knows I want to say something.

"I swear to God, Parker, if you keep trying to play footsies with me I'm going to jam one of my heels into your big toe," Lily threatens and it's enough to pull my attention away.

As the night continues, Wes's threat lingers in my mind, and I struggle to figure out if it's even a threat at all. Or if it's exactly what I want to happen.

CHAPTER 11

Wes

I CAN'T TAKE my eyes off Bailey the entire dinner. I'm waiting and hoping she gives me attitude. I'm practically silently pleading for it to happen because I want nothing more than to punish her. There's so many ways I could do it. So many ways I've fantasized about it, and I would love nothing more than to make them a reality.

I'll make her scream, plead, and beg for my cock until she's a mess. Then I'll deny her. I'll push her to her absolute limit and it's going to make up for the years of attitude she's given me. She'll make such a pretty mess, I already know it. If she gives into this thing between us.

I can see her holding back the entire dinner, just trying not to do or say anything to me. That's okay, I can be patient. I know it's only a matter of time.

She's quick to leave once dinner is done, but I'm not far behind. I left Bruno at home because I'm not sure how he would be around other people when he's still getting used to me.

Once I get home, I notice Bailey's car is already parked and most of her lights are off, probably anticipating me coming home shortly after her. I let Bruno out in the backyard and lean against the doorframe, facing her house watching for any movement.

It's subtle, but the curtains in her bedroom move, and I know she's watching. I step outside, staring up at where I know she is, knowing she can see me. I raise an eyebrow, but say nothing. She doesn't move, just watches.

Bruno walks inside, and I wait an extra moment to see if Bailey will step away from the window first, but she doesn't. I walk inside, grab my phone off the counter, and send a single text before setting it back down and going upstairs.

> Wes: Were you expecting a show? The only one that does that is you, Angel.

I do my best to get some sleep knowing tomorrow is a big day, and it's one of the few where I need to be well rested.

I'VE BEEN a part of several weddings for friends, but I think Jameson is the calmest groom I've ever seen. No one I know has ever been as sure of who they are marrying as he is. There's not even a hint of hesitance as he finishes getting his suit on. Parker's already started pouring drinks, but other than him, no one else is drinking.

I'm not sure that's going to help him and Lily get along, but I'm not here to parent anyone.

When it's time to start, Jameson and I walk out to where the small crowd of guests are already seated. He greets several of them by name as we head down the aisle. I don't know anyone so I just make my way to the front and take my position, folding my hands in front of me as I stand, just waiting to begin.

The same song they played at the rehearsal yesterday starts and I watch Bailey walk down the aisle with Dave. Even though it's completely innocent, the way her hand rests on his arm has me clenching my jaw. She isn't looking at me, and that only makes me more pissed off, but I do my best to hold it together.

Parker and Lily are behind them, surprisingly not arguing, though I'm sure it's killing them both not to be trying to get under each other's skin.

Finally, Bennet and Duke walk down, meeting up with Bailey and Lily before Sutton and Emily make their way down the aisle. I can't see Jameson's face, but I'm sure he's smiling and completely focused on his future wife making her way toward him.

They meet in front of me, whispering to each other, and acting like they're the only two people here.

I clear my throat. "Are you ready to start?"

There's a scoff off to the side, and Bailey mumbles, "Don't be a mood killer."

Guess she made her decision.

I do my absolute best to get through the quick ceremony without focusing on when or how I'm going to get Bailey alone. And what exactly I'm going to do with her once I do. She doesn't seem fazed as I finish up; even with a small interruption from a bird, we manage to get through the ceremony easily.

I can hardly focus on anything that isn't the tall woman that's about to learn how serious I am about following through when I say something. I keep her in my sights as the night goes on. They all do pictures, there's dinner, and when the music gets louder and everyone starts to let loose a bit, I know I'm done waiting.

Bailey separates herself from her friends. A rare small smile is on her face as she tells them she's heading inside for a few. I don't even bother to hide the fact that I'm following her. Everyone is so preoccupied, no one's going to care what we're doing. And I don't care even if they do.

She walks toward a bathroom downstairs, and before she can shut the door, I push it open, forcing my way inside, shutting and locking it behind me.

"What the fuck are you doing?" she snaps.

I crowd her against the wall in the small space. "What did I tell you?"

"You've said a lot of stupid stuff. Get out."

"No, you know what I'm talking about. What did I say to you yesterday?"

I see the moment she realizes what I'm talking about, and what this means. I can't help the smile that appears on my lips.

"Yeah, Angel." I step forward so her back is forced against the wall and our chests graze with each heavy breath she takes. "I'm going to tell you what's about to happen. You're going to listen, and if you really don't want to play, this is your last chance. But just know that if this starts, there's no playing games without consequences. You'll get a safe word and the only way it ends is if you say that word."

"What's the word?" she squeaks.

I glance around, noticing the one decoration that's made its way in here is a small bouquet of flowers. My eyes lock on hers once again. "Sunflower."

Her face scrunches, and I wait for her to say the word immediately, but she doesn't.

"You say it, everything stops. For good."

She swallows roughly. "And if I don't?"

"Then you're mine to play with until you do."

I count to five, waiting to see what she's going to do. When she doesn't do or say anything, I move quickly, not giving her anymore time to change her mind. I grab her hips, turning her around. She braces her hands on the wall, as I cage her in, covering her body with mine.

Pulling up her dress, I kick her feet apart and snake my hand between her thighs. She gasps when I make it to the wet fabric between them and tsk. "Don't even try to deny how turned on you are when I can feel how dripping wet your cunt is for me."

She whimpers quietly as I apply a small amount of pressure. I'm already impossibly hard. I press myself against her ass so she can feel me before moving the soaked fabric to the side, and slide my finger through her wetness, groaning into her ear.

"So soft, Angel, just like I remember."

"Get off me," she protests weakly. She knows how to make

this stop, she knows the single word she has to say, but she doesn't.

"Aw, you don't want me to touch your needy pussy? Don't want me to make you feel as good as I did that first night?" I graze her clit lightly. "Tell me something, has anyone ever made you come like you did for me?"

"Don't flatter yourself," she tries to sass, but the way her hips move against my hand, seeking more pressure, I can't help but chuckle.

"Answer the question. I feel how badly you want to grind against my hand, but I'm not giving you anything unless you answer me."

She lets out a frustrated cry. "No."

I hum, dropping my mouth to where her neck meets her shoulder, sinking my teeth into the exposed skin there at the same time I thrust a finger into her, and she cries out. I clamp my hand over her mouth, muffling the noise so no one can hear us.

"Do you want to be caught? Because if you keep making noises like that someone is going to catch us. Bet they would love to see how hard you want to fuck yourself on my hand."

She says something against my hand, but I can't understand the muffled words.

"What's that?" I taunt. "Do you need more?"

Without giving her a chance to respond, I push a second finger in alongside the first and she cries out again, rubbing her hips against me.

"Do you have something else you want to say, Angel?" I take her earlobe between my teeth. She moans against my palm as my fingers fuck her, creating wet noises that sound so loud over the pounding in my ears.

I want to take my hand off her mouth and make her scream as loud as I know she can, not giving a shit about anyone in the house hearing her. Part of me wants them all to hear her, and know that it was me that got her there. That way when she decides to try and deny things with me, everyone can know the truth.

I already do. Especially the way she's moving against me, there's no denying how badly she wants this.

Wants me.

"You seem close. Are you going to come all over my hand?"

She nods, and I press my palm harder against her clit while pumping my fingers, bringing her closer and closer to the edge. When she tightens around me, I know she's right there, and she's also about to learn what this means to be mine to play with.

I pull my hand away, flattening her against the wall completely, plastering my body to hers while she cries in protest against my hand still covering her mouth. I switch hands, so she can feel the wetness coating my fingers against her skin. So she can feel how badly she wanted my touch.

"You thought you were going to get to come? You think you deserve a reward with the way you've been acting?" I laugh darkly. "Brats get punished. Now you get to go through the rest of the night needy, wet, and unsatisfied."

She nips the skin of my palm, and I thrust against her ass once again. She huffs out a breath when her chest collides with the wall.

"Oh Angel, that's not how you get what you want. Maybe if you behave the rest of the night I'll come over and let you come before you go to bed tonight." I move back, slowly taking my body away from hers. "Or maybe, I'll leave you even more desperate."

Once my hand is off her mouth and I step closer to the door she speaks up.

"I'll just finish myself."

I let out a small laugh. "No you won't, because you know it won't be enough for you."

I walk out before she has a chance to respond because there's nothing she can say. We both know I'm right.

CHAPTER 12

Bailey

I'M PISSED OFF.

Partly because the way Wes cornered me in the bathroom was stupid and reckless. But mostly because I'm wet and throbbing all thanks to him. I know I could have said the safe word and he would've stopped, but I didn't. I'm trying not to read into why I didn't say it, but right now the last thing I want to do is anything for him.

The party doesn't look like it missed a beat while we were gone. Even though I feel like my entire being has shifted, nothing else has changed. I feel like I have a sign flashing above my head that I was just fingered in the bathroom by the giant grumpy asshole currently standing against a wall and scowling at everyone. I do everything I can to avoid eye contact with him as I find anyone else I know to distract me.

Lily seems to be on the same mission as me because as soon as she sees me, I'm grabbed and pulled onto the dance floor. It takes me a moment to start to move in a way that resembles dancing, but in my defense I feel like my brain was just completely scrambled. And I'm still fighting with myself over if I should beg Wes to finish what he started, or find a new place to live and never step foot in this town again.

The problem with the second option is that I don't want to run away again. I like it here. I've actually built a life here, and one that is mine. I own a business I enjoy. I have friends for the first time. I feel comfortable. It's rare anyone brings up my brother, and no one knows my past or the reputation the Collee name carries.

I'm just Bailey, and I don't want to have to start over again.

"What's wrong?" Lily asks over the music.

"Nothing."

She looks me up and down, and that sign I feel like I have on my head feels like it's neon and flashing, especially to her. If anyone can sniff something out, it's Lily. Her eyes narrow on me.

"You sure about that?"

"What about you? You yanked me out here like you were trying to escape," I divert, though I'm sure she catches on.

"I am. Parker won't leave me alone and I don't want to start a fight at Sutton's wedding. That would be rude."

"I'm sure she appreciates that."

"So, whatever is going on has nothing to do with the fact that Wes is staring at you like he wants to take a bite out of you?" Lily smirks.

"Who's that?"

"Ah, I see how it is. Okay, we're playing that game? Alright."

She moves around me, dancing dramatically, and I follow so she doesn't end up behind me because I don't know what she would do. This has me facing Wes, and I refuse to look up and see whatever look Lily supposedly sees.

"Just know," she speaks up again. "The next time you want to try to play dumb, at least make sure to hide the bite mark a little better."

I gasp, pulling my hair over my shoulders, doing what I can to cover whatever mark Wes left on me. That fucking asshole.

Lily throws her head back laughing. "Oh, you're so fucked."

❋

IT'S EXTREMELY LATE by the time I get home. Wes left before me, and as I pull in the driveway I refuse to look at his house. His car is there, but I don't want to see if there are any lights on, see any movement, or even hear him in the yard with his dog. I don't want to give him any more of my attention or time.

Especially not tonight while my body is still thrumming from his touch, desperate to find that release he took away from me. The worst part is he's right. If I were to take care of it myself, it wouldn't be even close to the same.

But I won't give in. I won't go over there, and I won't contact him.

I refuse to give him that.

I get in the shower, washing the night off me, including the memories of Wes's hands on me. When I get out and wipe the steam from the mirror, I see my reflection including the small mark on my skin from his teeth. The throbbing between my thighs is back at the sight alone. I groan, stepping away, not wanting to feed into his mind games anymore for the night.

Once I'm dressed, I crawl into bed and refuse to look at my phone to see if Wes has said anything to me. One of the biggest flaws with this house is the fact that my bedroom window faces his. Right now, while my room is dark, it makes the light currently on in his room shine directly in here.

I pull my blanket over my face to block it out. Closing my eyes I try to fall asleep, knowing it's futile. Especially when the only thing I can see behind my closed eyelids is the wall I was pressed against.

The only thing I can feel is Wes's hands on me, covering my mouth, roughly touching between my thighs.

The only thing I can hear are his growled words, the tone of his voice, and the way his filthy words only made me more desperate to erupt.

I let out a frustrated groan, throwing the blanket back so I can just stare at the ceiling. My hand finds its way down my shorts, and I close my eyes, letting the thoughts take over once again, but this time trying to give into them. Letting them guide me as my fingers roam where Wes's were just hours before.

It's not the same.

As much as I try to focus, to bring myself to the brink and

send myself over, it's just not the same. I cry out again, so unbelievably annoyed that I can't even orgasm by myself at all because my stupid neighbor touched me, and got in my head.

I look up, and see that his light is still on. For a split second I think about doing something I shouldn't.

My phone goes off, and I look at it like it's a bomb about to explode. If I pick it up, I don't know what I'll do.

Then it goes off again, and I give in.

> Wes: Do you think you were good enough for a reward?

> Wes: Or bad enough for another punishment?

> > Bailey: Neither.

> Wes: Sounds like you're choosing punishment. It's too bad, you cry so pretty when you come, but it seems like you don't want that to happen.

> > Bailey: I don't need you for that.

> Wes: No? How's that working out for you right now?

I slam my phone down, and cover my face with my hands. I feel like I'm going insane, and who knows, maybe I am.

The fact that I'm considering letting him into my house only proves that I most definitely am. I close my eyes once again, trying to pretend like it'll help make everything go away, but my phone goes off again.

I'm not going to look at it. Nope, I refuse.

I'm not even going to open my eyes, I'm going to force myself to sleep and tomorrow I'll wake up in my right mind once again.

I squeeze my eyes shut so hard light starts to dance behind my eyelids, but I continue to refuse to open them or to even think about Wes anymore.

After several hours that I'm sure in reality was only five minutes, I let out a frustrated cry, grabbing my phone and giving in to see what he said.

> Wes: Just say the word and I'll be at your door.

No. No way.

> Bailey: I could say another word to make you stop.

> Wes: You could.

> Wes: But you won't.

The worst part is he's right. I won't. At least not yet because as much as I want to deny the things my body is feeling, they're evident. And he's the only one that's made me feel like this in... ever.

He reads my body in a way I've never experienced before. My ex, who in hindsight was a real asshole, shamed me for my desires when I finally shared the things I wanted with him.

Put me in my place.

Give me a little pain.

He thought he was trying, but pulling my hair and spanking my ass was not enough.

Wes has already made me feel more in the two times he's touched me than Jake did in the entire year we were together. And that was without me needing to say a single thing about what I want.

My eyes swing toward his window, and I wait to see if he's going to appear. It's like I can feel his eyes on me, even though I don't even think he's standing there. Then his light turns off, and I sit up to get a better look. I wait to see what's going to happen, but nothing does. The room is silent, dark and suffocating.

The ding from my phone sounds louder than usual, the noise ricocheting off the walls. I pick it up and my annoyance is back full force at the two words staring at me on the screen.

Wes: Goodnight, Bailey.

This motherfucker.

He knows exactly what he's doing. He wants me to come to him, but it's not going to happen.

CHAPTER 13

Wes

"DO you actually want to ride any of them one of these days or just do the dirty work?" Jameson asks, entering the barn as I bring back the wheelbarrow I used to clean out the horse stall.

"I think they like thinking I'm their bitch."

"They don't think that. They're probably wondering why you sneak them treats but don't do anything else with them."

"I clean up their stalls and brush them."

"Next step is riding."

I look over at the biggest horse, Juniper, remembering she was Jameson's barrel racing horse for a while. She's large with black and white spots, which I've been told is called an Appaloosa.

"She would take good care of you if you wanted to give it a try," Jameson encourages.

"Maybe one day." I look over at him. "Aren't you supposed to be holed up with your new wife?"

He huffs out a laugh. "I tried, and she insisted she had to work today. But I'll be whisking her away for our honeymoon in a couple of days. Would you mind coming by here to check on everything while we're gone?"

"Not a problem."

"Thanks, man, and if you need anything from me let me know."

I shake my head. "You're good."

"No, I owe you. If anything comes up that you need from me, please let me know."

"You don't owe me anything. Don't worry about it," I insist.

He just shakes his head, but doesn't try to stop me as I head out. I go right to the animal shelter because even though I've taken Bruno in for the time being, I still want to check in and help out. Gloria said she would call if anyone comes in with interest for Bruno, but I also want to check in person, just in case.

She gives me a big smile when I walk through the door but it's one I don't match, I just give her a head nod in greeting.

"How's Bruno doing?" she asks brightly.

"Good, he seems to be comfortable. Has anyone shown any interest in him?"

She shakes her head. "Not yet."

"Is it because he's living with me? I don't want to hold him back."

"No, not at all. He's still on the website, and I'm sure he's much happier at your house than he was here."

I nod, knowing he is, but I feel bad having him get too comfortable when he's going to end up going to another home at some point.

"I got a good one for you to walk today if you want," Gloria offers brightly.

I nod again, not saying anything as she leads me to the kennels and up to a chocolate Lab who wags his tail as soon as he sees us.

"This sweet boy is Maverick," she introduces. "He was picked up the other day and I think he has a family looking for him, so we're doing what we can to find them."

I take the leash off the hook and lead him out. He's a lot more energetic than Bruno, which I don't mind. He sniffs the ground, going to several bushes and trees on our walk, but just like with any dog, my favorite thing is that we don't have to talk.

Part of me wants to talk about the situation with Bailey that I can feel it escalating. Or at this point it's escalated past the point of no return because touching her again made me realize I'm not going to be able to stop.

She likes the sound of it too, I know she does. If she wants to act like a brat and be treated like one, then she'll get punished like one. But when she behaves she'll get rewarded, even though she may enjoy the punishments I have planned with the way she keeps testing me.

My phone goes off in my pocket, and I think for a moment it might be Bailey, but when I pull it out, I'm met with a message from someone I didn't expect.

Chris: Hey.

Chris and I served together for years. He was my copilot the day that changed our lives. We talk every once in a while, but at least for me, every time we talk I feel the memories surface. They're so much worse, than the pain radiating in my leg, a physical reminder of that day.

Wes: How's it going?

He doesn't respond right away, and it's slightly concerning that he's reaching out, and I can't help but wonder why. I feel like I only hear from my fellow soldiers when I'm being told someone else has died.

I've witnessed and experienced so much death, it's easy to be numb to it, but it also makes me question many things about my own life. Like when I wonder why I'm still here yet they aren't.

Apparently it's survivors' guilt. At least that's what I've been told. I don't really care what it is. I can't help that it takes over my thoughts at times like this. Just like I can't help when the memories of that day assault my mind. Or the funerals. Or anything else from my past.

When my arm is yanked I realize I stopped walking, and Maverick is clearly not happy about it.

We continue down the trail, and I wait for Chris to reply. He doesn't live near me, and the last I heard he was somewhere in the Midwest. But I think the last time we spoke was over a year ago, so he could be living anywhere now.

Chris: How you been?

I furrow my brow at the screen. I remember him being similar to me when we worked together. Not a big talker, so this seems even weirder that he's just wanting to have a conversation out of the blue.

Wes: Fine, I guess. You?

Chris: Fine. Been thinking about that day a lot.

I stop dead in my tracks once again. Maverick busies himself with a bush, and I stare at the screen. One thing we never talked about was that day. It's been ten years, and there's nothing more that could really be said about it.

We went through it. Our lives were changed. End of story.

What else is there to talk about?

Chris: Do you?

I don't want to respond. I don't know where he's going with this conversation, but I don't want to be a part of it. There's a small voice in the back of my head that tells me I should at least say something, but I'm not going to entertain an in-depth conversation about the worst day of my life.

The day that completely altered who I was as a person.

Wes: I try not to.

Chris: Ok.

His response throws me off, but I don't know what else to say. I lock my phone and put it back in my pocket, trying to do anything I can to take my mind off the odd exchange. Maverick and his adventurous nature helps with that.

But I know what distraction I really want.

The tall, gorgeous woman that lives next to me and enjoys driving me insane is exactly what I would like right now.

Actually, that may be exactly what I need. More-so, it may be just what she needs too.

I left her exactly how I wanted to, wet and needy. I thought she may actually give in that night, but she's too proud. And she's had years to convince herself that she hates me, which is fine, it makes it a little more fun for me.

It'll make it even better once I finally break her down. She'll crawl, beg, cry, and do whatever I want because she wants how I can make her feel.

The best part is, her body can crave me, but there's no risk of her developing feelings for me. If there's one thing I know about Bailey Collee, it's that she isn't one to fall in love. Neither am I, which is why it would be perfect if we can enjoy each other's company and move on with our lives.

I bring Maverick back to his kennel, his food dish is full so he's happy to go back in and start eating, which makes me feel better about having to lock him in the cage.

On my way out, I give Gloria a small wave, then pull my phone out to text my little distraction.

Wes: Ready to play, Angel?

CHAPTER 14

Bailey

I'M CLOSING up the coffee stand by myself because I sent Jenn home since we weren't very busy for the last couple of hours.

My phone goes off, and I look at it without thinking about who it could be. The second I realize it's Wes I freeze. This man is haunting me, the ghost of his touch specifically. I should end it all right here and now. And then move, because I clearly can't be trusted.

Wes: Ready to play, Angel?

Bailey: Whatever game you're trying to play I'm not interested.

Wes: Say the word to end this then.

My fingers hover over the screen, right over the S and U. But I can't bring myself to type the word. Instead of saying anything, I lock the screen, tucking my phone in my back pocket while I finish cleaning up so I can leave for the day.

Of course, when I pull up to my house I see Wes's car in his driveway, so I quickly run inside hoping to avoid getting caught by him. I let out a sigh of relief as I close and lock my front door. It's ridiculous that I feel like I need to do this. It seems so silly to be running and hiding in my house just because an attractive man wants to drive me crazy, especially because my entire childhood was spent running and hiding for safety.

The yelling starts. First it's my parents, and then Brandon starts yelling back. I freeze in the chair I'm sitting in at the overflowing dining table as I try to eat my cereal. My stomach is growling. I managed to find some stale cereal that doesn't taste very good, but it will have to do. We didn't have any milk, so I have to eat it dry.

"Bailey." Bryson steps in front of me, blocking the view of my screaming family members. "Go join Brynn in the bedroom."

"But I'm hungry," I whine.

"Take it with you." He grabs the bowl, and pulls me from my seat, though I try to protest as he drags me to the bedroom where Brynn is already sitting on the bed with her hands over her ears.

I want to ask where Brent is because he always helps us, and he isn't mean about it. I think he's at practice; he's been doing that a lot lately. Hockey has become his life, and we don't matter as much anymore. Bryson slams the door after pushing my bowl into my hand and I struggle to hold onto it. I want to go out there and scream at all of them, especially when I see Brynn press her hands harder against her ears and the single tear that rolls down her cheek.

With a sigh, I climb onto the bed next to my sister, and share my cereal with her while I hug her against me.

"I just want them to stop," she cries.

The yelling is getting worse and I hear something crash, so I hold Brynn even tighter.

"Me too," I say quietly. Probably too quiet for her to hear, but I'm sure she knows. We all want it to stop. We all want to just be normal, but that's not the world for the Collee kids. We were born to struggle.

The pounding on my door pulls me out of the memory, and makes my heart race. My fight or flight reflexes kick in while I try to bring myself back to the present. Where I'm safe and no one knows where I am to find me. Not that they would even care to.

There's another harsh knock. I furrow my brow, turning toward the front door and opening it where I'm greeted with a sight I did not expect.

Wes stands there, tall, imposing, and intimidating with that permanent scowl on his face while he looks at me like I've pissed him off already when I've hardly done anything. The way he's glaring at me immediately has me on guard. Especially when he pushes past me without a single word.

"What the fuck? I did not say you could come in," I snap.

"I'm not a vampire that needs to be invited in."

"You are breaking and entering, though. Get out."

"Angel, you don't make the rules here. Until you say the word, you're agreeing to my terms and to my rules."

I clench my jaw, wanting to argue, but the hum between my thighs at his harsh tone has me questioning several things about myself at this moment. Just like every other time we're together apparently and my body responds in ways it shouldn't.

I get a whiff of a scent that has my nose scrunching. "You smell like a horse farm."

"Probably because I did some work at one earlier."

"Didn't take you for a cowboy."

"I'm not one."

"Great, well you smell. Leave."

Wes looks around, and then smirks. "You have a shower."

"And you're not welcome in it."

He steps toward me, and I narrow my eyes at him even more, but don't step back.

"You don't make the rules. You can join me, or you can wait for me to be done. Up to you." He walks past me, further into my house. I know he knows where the bathroom is because his house is the same floor plan as mine from what I can tell online. Not that I've looked, of course.

Part of me doesn't think he's actually going to do it. But when I hear his heavy steps on my stairs followed by the sound of the water turning on in my bathroom I realize he really means it.

Somehow, I find myself following in his footsteps. It's like I'm in a trance as I reach the top of the stairs, and move toward the bathroom. The door is wide open, and I'm standing in the door-frame as Wes reaches behind his neck and pulls his shirt over his head revealing his toned back. The way his muscles move as he goes to undo his pants. I can't look away.

His back is facing me, but I know he can tell I'm here. Neither of us say anything as the water pelts against the tiles of my shower, and my neighbor strips completely in front of me.

I'm frozen, but can't look away. Definitely not when he pushes his jeans down. I follow his hands with my eyes. They catch on the long line of marred skin on his leg. There's clearly a story there. I don't know much about his past other than he's a veteran. Whatever happened looks like it was really bad. I look away and back up, seeing he's completely naked and stepping into my shower.

I hold back a gasp.

All the memories from that first and only night together come roaring back as I remember how it felt to have his strong body on mine. The same body that's now in my shower with the water coating his skin.

"You better join me, Angel." His voice is deep, gruff and it makes me want to argue with his tone.

I scoff. "I'll pass."

He turns around, and I bite back my reaction to seeing him fully. His muscled chest is honed over years of hard work, and tattoos cover one arm completely. His dick isn't even fully hard and yet I can see his size. I can remember how it felt, and how I've never felt more full than I did when he was inside me.

His face is passive as he looks at me, but his tone is serious when he speaks again. "Get in here. On your knees."

"Clothed?" I respond sarcastically.

He looks me up and down, shrugs, then turns back around.

I want to do it just to spite him. But I remember his text from earlier.

Ready to play, Angel?

This has to be a part of his game, and maybe, just this once, I want to see what would happen.

I start to strip my own clothes off, fighting the little voice in my head that's yelling at me for giving in. I'm sure I'll fight with myself about this later. Right now, I step into the steamed up space, completely naked with a man I swore I wouldn't touch again.

Wes turns around, looking me over, but doesn't say anything other than, "I said on your knees."

I look down at the tile, not missing the way his dick is standing at attention and I smirk. My knees are preemptively protesting about the hard surface, but I look back up to Wes's deep brown eyes, keeping them there as I sink down.

"So fucking pretty when you listen to me," he praises, and my mouth twists.

"Don't make me regret it."

"Still such a brat, though. It's almost like you *want* to be punished."

"Bite me." I smile sarcastically.

"With pleasure." He steps closer to me, his cock less than an inch from my face. "But right now you're going to put your mouth to good use. Take what I give you and maybe this time I'll let you come. If you deserve it."

I want to squeak out a protest, but the throbbing between my thighs and the way my mouth waters at the sight in front of me stops any words from coming out.

Instead, I drop my jaw, sticking my tongue out while keeping my eyes on him.

"Now that's a good girl."

He closes the last little bit of distance, sliding his fingers through my hair, tangling them at the back of my head, and guiding my open mouth onto his length. I moan as the weight of him hits my tongue, and his grip in my hair tightens at the same time.

The mist and steam from the warm water surrounds us while Wes blocks most of the spray with his large body. I keep my eyes up, watching the way his stomach tenses, how his muscles bunch and I clench my thighs together at the sight.

This towering, intimidating man holding onto me roughly while I lick the underside of his dick has my body reacting, begging to touch myself.

I squirm, sliding my hand between my thighs while wrapping the other around the base of his length where my mouth can't reach.

"Aw look at you, Angel. Your little pussy getting wet from this?"

I hum, pulling back slightly before pushing further to get more of him into my throat.

"You can touch yourself, but you can only come when I say you can."

I narrow my eyes up at him, and he yanks me off him by the grip he's got on my hair. I pant at the loss, my mouth watering as he bends over to bring our faces closer together.

"Don't give me attitude or I won't let you come at all. Now, if you listen and do what you're told, then maybe you'll get what you want."

I run my tongue along my bottom lip to tease him, and he watches the movement intently. I almost think he's going to close the distance between our mouths. It's one of the few things we haven't done, even that first night together. His mouth has been on other parts of my body, but we have yet to kiss.

Instead of changing that now, he stands up again, roughly guiding my mouth back onto his erection. I go willingly, wanting to do what he asks because the desire to come is clouding my mind.

"Touch yourself, Angel. Show me how wet you are from having your mouth so full of me."

I let out a small whimper, dipping my hand between my legs, then lifting my fingers up to do what he asked. To show him exactly what he wants to see. I could play it off and pretend like my body isn't screaming for release, or that he's not the cause of it. But I want to see what will happen if I give in. Just this once.

Wes grabs my wrist, thrusting forward, pushing himself deeper into my throat making me gag, but he pulls back. I gasp for air right before he sucks my fingers into his mouth, licking my arousal from them.

"Fuck, I hope you decide to be good so I can taste more of you again."

Something about the way he growls the words, or the way he grips my hair, thrusting into my mouth has me seriously concerned about spontaneous combustion.

"Make your pretty little pussy feel good," he grinds out, and I'm not about to question anything.

I hold onto Wes as he uses my mouth, all while I rub myself. Normally I want the teasing, but not this time. I like the way he's using me. I don't know how long he'll allow me to touch myself and I'm not about to waste it because I need to come more than I need air.

"That's it, Angel. So good," he groans.

I moan around him, my orgasm dancing just out of reach. I want more, rougher, harder. I want everything else to fade. The air's thick with steam as the hot water continues to fall around us. It's getting harder to breathe, which only makes me chase the release even more.

Wes continues to grind out praises, even as my mind becomes fuzzy. I'm so close, and all I want is to come. My eyes slam closed as I push a single finger into myself at the same time Wes yanks my hair so tight it burns, and it's enough to send me over the edge. The bite of pain, pressure from my fingers, the rough way he's taking my mouth, and the lack of oxygen is what does it.

Wes pulls my mouth off him and I gasp as the orgasm racks through me while I faintly feel warmth hit my chest. When I start to recognize what's going on around me, I see it's cum. Wes's cum. Coating my chest, falling onto my nipples, and the fact that it only makes me want this to continue should probably be a sign that I need to be evaluated.

I look up at him, my knees aching, but I don't dare to stand up yet because I don't trust my legs to hold me up. He's looking down at me with a self satisfied smirk on his face. He looks even bigger from down here, more imposing, almost scary, and hot as fuck.

"See how nice it is when you listen?"

I fight the urge to say something snarky back because the spot between my legs is begging for more. Instead of asking if he can handle going again I say, "Does that mean you're going to fuck me?"

He lets out a humorless laugh, and I narrow my eyes at him. He moves some of the hair that's fallen in my eyes away. "You may have been good, Angel, but you haven't earned that yet."

Before I'm able to protest, he turns off the water, and leaves the shower while I gape at him. And when I blink, he's gone.

CHAPTER 15

Wes

LEARNING to fly was the best part of training for me. It's nothing like driving a car. Something about being in control of the helicopter as it lifts in the air with the sky like an unpaved road. It's freeing, and while there should be an element of danger, I don't feel any of it.

Up in the sky, I'm able to breathe better than I do while my feet are planted firmly on the ground.

It doesn't matter where we are. The fact that we're in a war zone, and that danger is around us doesn't change things. The sky feels different. I'm in control up here.

"Anderson," Chris says through our headphones, getting my attention. "What're you looking forward to most when we get out?"

Our tour is over in three months, and I know a lot of the guys are getting antsy since it's the end of several of their contracts. Many of them, Chris included, have a wife and family to get to. Not me. Which is why I fully intend on signing on for more, though no one knows that yet.

"Some good food from home," I joke. Chris chuckles, shaking his head while we continue to fly around.

"I'm looking forward to becoming a dad," he says seriously.

I nod, but can't say I relate to that feeling. I've never been interested in kids. Maybe a wife, but no one I've dated has ever made me see a future with them.

This isn't the first time Chris has brought this up. He's talked to some of the other guys in our battalion about it, especially those that have pregnant wives and girlfriends back home.

"I know Isla is really hoping for a girl, but I think I want a boy."

"And I don't think you get to choose," I deadpan.

"No shit, but I have to keep looking forward to something to keep me sane in this mess."

"We'll be going home soon."

"Then what're you going to do besides eat?"

I shrug.

"You're reenlisting, aren't you?"

This shouldn't come as a shock. I'm sure it doesn't, but maybe he thought I would change my mind. "This is a career for me, man. I'm in for life."

"You're just built different." He shakes his head, focusing ahead once again.

I never saw myself doing anything else. I knew this was going to be my job, and as soon as I flew an Apache for the first time I knew there was no going back. This is my life. Nothing else could ever compare.

Except that choice was taken from me, and I didn't get to make it my career or my life. Everything I ever thought I would have was snatched away in a single moment. Now, here I am, no clear direction, filling my days with anything that gives me some semblance of feeling.

All while the vision for my life remains unfocused because the only thing I ever saw was shattered.

Somehow the only thing that's given me any sort of feeling lately has been Bailey.

The control she gives me, and the way she doesn't give it easily. The way I'm able to go to a different space in my mind with her. It's something that makes me *feel* for the first time in a long while.

My mind is distracted from the flashback of one of the good times from the Army, but it doesn't make it any easier to sleep. Especially thinking about how Bailey looked when I left and the restraint I had to walk out that door.

Leaving her house, while she was naked, wet, kneeling, and covered in my cum was one of the hardest things I've ever had to do. But I want her even more desperate. This game we're playing feels a lot like playing with fire, and despite the fact that we might both go up in flames, I'm not afraid of being burned.

She makes me want to push both our limits, which is exactly what I intend to do. My relationships aren't always...conventional. And while we haven't discussed limits or boundaries outside of a safe word, I can tell Bailey likes *this*.

She wants to continue to push my buttons. To get punished and I want to give it to her. When she deserves it she will get rewarded. But I'll enjoy every step along the way.

Her lights are off right now. I could go over there, see how she reacts and what other punishments I could inflict. Maybe next time I'll let her come so many times she can't see straight, until she's begging me to *stop*.

She's going to drive me out of my mind with everything I want to do to her and with her. My dick is hard in my boxers, but I don't touch it. Not unless she's here to watch. Maybe tied up to my bed, helpless to do anything but look. She could beg, plead, and try to move but I'd just ignore her. I'd make her watch as I brought myself to another release.

I drag a hand down my face, needing a distraction. Anything to pull my mind away from the thing I can't have right now. I need to shift into safer territory that won't send me spiraling into the weight of old memories.

I pull on sweatpants and a T-shirt before grabbing my keys and heading out. I keep my eye on Bailey's house as I turn my car on, waiting to see if she'll appear and yell at me for the loud engine. If she does, I don't think I could stop myself from getting out, bending her over the hood, and giving her exactly what she deserves.

Nothing happens, and I'm not going to sit here forever, so I take off driving to nowhere in particular.

While I'll never fly again, this is the closest I can get to feeling free. Empty roads, windows down, music blaring. It's almost good enough. *Almost.* It's enough to keep the booming sounds from that tragic day at bay. Enough to keep me from thinking about the burning sensation in my leg. Enough to drown out the yells from the people around me.

It's all just enough.

But like always, it comes back. It always does, because nothing about that day ever truly goes away. It never will. No matter how badly I want to forget about it, it lingers—etched into me— because I live with the aftermath every single day.

All while people I knew—friends—don't get to live at all.

JAMESON AND SUTTON are on their honeymoon, so I'm helping out with his property like he asked. Honestly, it's got me thinking maybe I should get some land and a few farm animals of my own. It would keep me busy and I could use that.

Bruno came with me, and he sticks close by my side. At first, I was worried he would try to run off, but it's the exact opposite. It's like he's afraid to get more than a few feet from my hip. The farthest he went was into the barn. He approached one of the horses, the large spotted one named Juniper. Everything seemed okay until she let out a puff of air through her nose, and Bruno jumped back, pressing his side against my leg.

I pet his head. "It's okay. I don't think she'll hurt you, but we can tell Gloria not to let you go to a home with horses."

I make sure all the animals are fed, and the horses are brought out to the pasture for the day, when I hear another car approaching. Bruno follows behind me as I exit the barn, and I recognize the white SUV pulling up. I can't help the small smirk that appears on my lips while I fold my arms across my chest and lean against the entrance, waiting for her to notice me.

She's not looking up right away. I see the moment she notices me while stepping out of the car, pausing before she shuts the door. Her eyes narrow, while mine remain still.

"What're you doing here?" Her tone is accusing.

"Helping Jameson, like he asked. What're you doing here?"

"Helping Sutton, like she asked." She sounds unsure, looking around and I want to laugh, but keep my face completely still. "Do you think they did this on purpose?"

I shrug. "Have you ever taken care of a ranch before?"

She folds her arms to match my posture. "Have you?"

I don't answer, just keep looking at her, waiting for her to say something else because I know she will.

"My bad, didn't realize you were such a cowboy. I guess that's why you showed up to my house smelling like you rolled in horse shit," she sasses, and I love that she's being feisty like this again.

Submissive Bailey is fun. Bratty Bailey is entertaining. Bailey coming is beautiful. And the thought of turning her ass red from a paddle is magnificent.

Either way it's a win-win for the both of us, and she knows it whether she wants to admit it or not.

"You're too late anyway." I push off the frame of the barn, and step toward her. She doesn't move from where she's standing as I approach. "I already took care of everything."

"Well some of us have a job."

"Some of us don't need one."

"A cowboy and a trust fund baby, I'm learning so much about you," she says condescendingly.

I scoff. "You can have my cock in your throat, but are so wrong about knowing things about me."

"The feeling is mutual because you don't know shit about me either."

"Don't I?"

Her jaw snaps shut so hard I hear her teeth click. I notice Bruno starting to approach her, and it catches my attention for a brief moment that he doesn't seem afraid of her. He allows her to pet his head. Maybe she wants to adopt him, then he can stay close by.

She stands up once again, and I continue to tell her exactly *how much* I know about her.

"I know you have a tattoo on that perky little ass of yours," I state easily, and her jaw clenches. I step closer to her. "I know what you look like when you come." Another step. "I know that you like a little pain." Another step. "I know that you want a repeat of that first night we had together, and maybe if you behave you'll get exactly that."

She adjusts her stance, steeling her spine and standing up straight. Her green eyes glare directly into mine as she opens her pouty lips to speak. "Knowing my sexual preferences is not the same as knowing anything about me. And you'll never know any more than that."

Bailey gets in her car, the door slamming shut, punctuating the end to her statement dramatically. I watch her drive away, continuing to smirk in her direction as she leaves. She may be right that knowing that information isn't knowing her, but she's wrong that I won't know more, because now I'm determined to know everything there is to know about Bailey Collee.

CHAPTER 16

Bailey

I'M plopped down on my couch as soon as I get home, folding my arms across my chest before pulling my phone out to text Sutton. I know I shouldn't since she's on her honeymoon, but if she wants to meddle, then I'm going to bother her.

> **Bailey:** Was your plan to try and get Wes and me alone?

> **Sutton:** I have no idea what you're talking about?

> **Bailey:** No? You didn't know Jameson asked Wes to help at your house while you asked me?

> **Sutton:** …Maybe

> **Bailey:** I thought we were friends!

> **Sutton:** We are, which is exactly why I did it!

> **Bailey:** I'm all for you pulling this stuff with Lily, but her situation is different than mine.

Sutton: Lily went back to school so it has to be you for now. And I'm not even sorry about it.

Bailey: Give it up. Wes and I are neighbors, we see enough of each other without needing to be caught up in whatever scheme you two have cooked up.

Sutton: Whatever you say. *smiling emoji*

Bailey: I mean it.

Sutton: Of course you do. *smiling emoji*

Bailey: Seriously, Sutton.

Sutton: See you when we get back. *smiling emoji*

Tossing my phone down, I shake my head, knowing she's brainstorming some sort of plan. Little does she know that I need to stay away from Wes, because I don't trust myself around him anymore.

I was able to push away the memories of how he feels for years, but now that we're playing this game with each other, I can't stay away. Even though I should. I don't want a relationship. I doubt he does either. And sleeping together while we're just neighbors seems like a recipe for disaster.

There's just no way this ends well for either of us, which is why it should stop right now before anything else can happen. Before I can lose any more of myself with him. He's already seen pieces of me that others haven't.

I let out an annoyed sound and grabbed the remote to turn on the TV to drown out my runaway thoughts before I can spiral too far.

I forgot the last thing I had on was the sports channel. Sometimes I watch to see if there are any updates in the hockey world. The season is about a month out from starting. My attention is pulled to Brent's headshot being shown with the Denver Dragons team logo next to him. I turn up the volume, and am a little surprised to hear what's being said.

"Brent Collee, the captain of the Denver Dragons, has announced his retirement going into this season. Who do you think will take over as captain or will the Dragons go without one for now?"

Another voice chimes in while the camera shows four men sitting at a giant glass desk. "Do you think they will ask Matt McQuaid? His temper has been better in recent seasons."

"Hardly," another man scoffs. "McQuaid doesn't have what it takes to be team captain. They might consider Vince Dumont or Charlie Mann for the spot."

"Mann and Dumont aren't captain material either. What about Wheeler? He's shown improvement both in his gameplay and attitude."

The first man speaks again. "I think no matter who they choose, it will be an adjustment. They're losing a great captain and a great player."

I mute the TV while they continue to talk about the future of my brother's, soon to be previous, hockey team. It's weird, even though I don't really talk to him, but the thought of him not playing hockey isn't something I've ever thought about.

He's Brent. My big brother, the hockey player. And now he's

just not going to anymore? Sometimes I would find myself turning on his games for a glimpse of him. Although hockey is so fast paced and it's not like I could really see him, it was enough to know he was okay. As ridiculous as it seems, that was enough to justify not needing to reach out and check in on him.

Brynn texts me enough for me to know she's okay.

Bryson is probably out screwing half the population and updates his social media enough for me to know he's okay.

Brandon lost his battle with addiction, and none of us talk about it. We didn't even have a funeral for him.

I chew on my bottom lip, staring at my phone laying face down next to me. I debate for several minutes, but finally pick it up and type out a quick text to my brother.

Bailey: You're retiring?

Part of me doesn't expect him to reply, especially not so quickly, but my phone dings in my hand and I fumble with it for a second, almost dropping it on the floor as I open the text.

Brent: I am. It's time since there's about to be two babies around. I don't want to be on the road as much.

Brent: I'm surprised you heard.

Bailey: Apparently losing you from the team is a pretty big deal.

Brent: They'll be fine. How're you doing?

Bailey: I'm fine.

Brent: Fine enough to come visit sometime? Chandler wants to meet you. Brynn misses you.

I sigh. I know my sister misses me, and I would like to meet the woman my brother is with. The woman who is strong enough to be with three men—three hockey players at that.

But just the thought of facing two of my siblings has panic surging in my chest. What if the moment we all see each other the thoughts from the past consume me and I can't pull myself out?

What if it's the same for them, and we all regress when we've all finally managed to build our lives up to be how they are? It wouldn't be fair to them.

Yet, I can't bring myself to say no, just like always, because I don't want to explain why.

Bailey: Maybe one of these days.

I'm sure he knows the true meaning behind my words, but instead of calling me out on it his reply is simple.

Brent: I hope so.

I'M TOSSING AND TURNING, which isn't totally unusual for me, though this time it isn't because I'm struggling with memories from the past. I'm not thinking about my siblings or the hell we went through. I truly have no real explanation for my restlessness except the fact that I know Wes is home.

It's insane. I've lived here for years. Lived next to the same annoying man the entire time, and he's never been the reason I've struggled to fall asleep. But right now, the only thing I can think of is if I asked him to come over, or showed up at his door. The things he could do to make my body sing over and over. And I'm sure it would lead me to a completely peaceful sleep.

But that's not going to happen.

I continue to toss and turn, trying to find a comfortable position when I start to rationalize going over there and how it wouldn't be giving in. *Really it would be empowering because I would be the one in control of our interaction.* It wouldn't be a moment of weakness, but really a moment of strength.

Yeah, that's it, I can do it.

I toss my legs over the side of my bed, when I hear a loud noise. One I recognize well as the sound of his car starting up. I go to the window facing the front of the house and watch his black car drive off.

Guess that takes the choice away. He probably got a better offer since I'm convinced that's where he races off to in the middle of the night.

I flop back onto my bed, burying my face in my pillow, I just hope that knowing he's no longer close by will help me fall asleep.

Still I struggle. It's not until the sun starts to peek through that my eyes finally grow heavy enough to pull me under. And, of course, just before sleep takes me, I realize I never heard Wes come back.

CHAPTER 17

Wes

WORKING on Jameson's family ranch has me seriously considering getting my own. Maybe not this big, but a small one. It's a good way to fill my time and the work distracts my mind. Bruno seems to like it too, other than the horses which he's still unsure about.

If I had a place like this I might be able to keep him. Maybe he would have enough freedom to be happy since I can't give him enough of myself as it is. Just like with everyone else.

I swing another hay bale around to the spot in the hay loft, making it easier to grab the flakes and feed the horses. As I drop some food down to the animals below, I hear the sound of footsteps entering the barn. I look down to see Emily petting Bruno, so I climb down to see her.

"Good morning, Wes," she greets, cheerfully.

"Good morning, Mrs. Turner." I wipe my hands on my jeans, though the ache from where the baling twine dug into my skin is still there.

"All of you like to be so respectful." She waves her hand around like it's ridiculous. "I hope these ladies aren't giving you too much trouble."

I huff out a small laugh. "They've been on their best behavior."

There's only one lady in my life giving me any sort of trouble, but I like it.

"Good. The dogs are currently running my house, but if Bruno wants to come visit he's more than welcome."

I shake my head. "No, that's okay. I don't want to add more onto your plate. Your hands are clearly already full."

"I like being busy. Jameson acts like I need to sit around all the time, even now."

"It's probably just because he cares."

"I know he does." She smiles softly. "Now, please tell me you've officially adopted this sweet boy."

Bruno wags his tail once, it's the one thing he does to show excitement. He doesn't run around, jump, or act overly excited like I've seen Bennet and Duke do. Bruno's more reserved. Nervous but still sweet.

"No, I haven't, we're still waiting for the perfect home for him."

"Hm," she hums, bending down to pet the German Shepherd. "And why don't you think you're the perfect home for him?"

"He needs more than I can give him."

She hums again, and I can tell she wants to say something else. I raise an eyebrow waiting to see if she will.

"You can give him more than you think, but what do I know I'm just an old woman." She shrugs, and I let out a small laugh. "I'll leave you to this and deal with the hellions back at my house. I may make them a nice meal, just don't tell my son."

"Your secret is safe with me."

"What about you? Any secrets you want to share? I'm a vault." She smiles widely and I shake my head. Emily is nice, and I can see where Jameson gets his sense of humor from. Even after she lost her husband last year she seems to be doing well. Not that I'm any sort of professional when it comes to grief and coping.

We all have our own way of handling it. Mine is avoidance. There's no point in dwelling on things you can't do anything about.

I think about what she's asking. If there are any secrets I want to share. I debate bringing up Bailey for a moment. It's not like my mom is around to talk to, I'm not sure I would even if she were. I never talked to her about much anyway, but that was just the nature of our family. Everything felt so surface level with both my parents.

I shake my head, not even sure what to say. "No secrets."

"If that changes, I'm here. Or you tell the horses, they never share anything I tell them."

"I'll remember that."

She heads back to her house, and Bruno joins me as I feed all the other animals around the property, sticking close to my side just like he always does. None of the other animals get close enough to him that he freaks out like he does with the horses.

After I'm done, I make sure to say goodbye to Emily so she knows I'm leaving before driving away.

On my way home, I pass Bailey's coffee shop and decide to stop by. I've never been much of a coffee drinker, but I won't give up the perfect chance to see her. To remind her I'm around before the next time either of us decides to cross that line again.

Which may be sooner than later for me. She's always there, so close. Just right next door. I can see her movements through her window. I know when she leaves for work, when she comes home. I know she watches me, too. I can feel when she's got her eyes on me. I'm always overly aware of my surroundings. I've had to be with my history in the military, so even when she thinks she's being sneaky, I know she's watching.

I pull up to the window, and her back is turned, but when she faces me her expression instantly hardens. Her dark blonde hair is pulled up in a ponytail that tempts me to wrap my fist around it, and yank her head back while I bury myself in her heat.

Her mouth parts in surprise before she quickly closes it, and my eyes can't help but fall to those pink lips that were wrapped around me just days ago. With the way she let me take full control, I know that's exactly what she wants. She wants to fight and be a brat, but at the end of the day, she wants to be at my mercy.

"What're you doing here?" she snaps, folding her arms across her chest.

"Getting a coffee, is that a crime?"

"You're actually on our banned list, so you can just move along."

I smirk. "What did I do to get on the banned list?"

"I'd go get my list, but it's long and neither of us have the time it'd take for me to go through the whole thing."

I sit back, adjusting in my seat. While I love having a sleek sports car, I'm a big guy and it doesn't leave a whole lot of room. "I've got all the time in the world. What else are you doing today?"

"Working, and doing anything else that isn't talking to you."

"Right. You prefer to do other things with me that aren't talking. Last time we were together your mouth was a little full."

Her face flames and she drops her gaze, looking around like she's trying to busy herself.

"That is one of the reasons you're banned," she mumbles.

"Fine. Is Bruno banned, too?"

"Of course not."

"Great, then he will get a large Americano."

"Dogs can't have coffee."

"Are you a vet?"

"Don't need to be, I'm just not an idiot."

"Are you saying I'm an idiot?" I lean out the window.

She shrugs.

I press my tongue to the inside of my cheek, biting back a smile and shaking my head. "Damn, Angel, you really are asking for a punishment, aren't you?"

"And that's another reason," she murmurs, as she works on getting the coffee. I also notice her grab a smaller cup and fill it with whipped cream.

She hands me the small cup, and nods toward Bruno. "He can have a pup cup. And you can fuck off."

I let out a chuckle, taking the cup from her, covering her hand with my own, and pull, making her gasp as our eyes lock on each other's.

"Keep testing me, Angel. You know the consequences. I'll be waiting for you when you're done here."

I take the cup, and hold it in front of Bruno as he sniffs and takes a tentative lick from the top.

When I turn, I see she's handing me the large coffee, and I trade it for more cash than I know it costs. Before she's able to give me change, I pull away and drive the short distance home. When I get there I pull out my phone to send her a text.

Wes: Come to my house when you're done. Don't even try to hide in your room. It'll only make things worse for you.

She knows exactly what she's doing, and I know exactly how she wants to be handled.

CHAPTER 18

Bailey

I DEBATE RUNNING AWAY ONCE AGAIN.

I've done it before, and I'm sure I could do it again. It's a pain in the ass, but I could manage. I always do. The only thing tying me here is my business. Roasted Bean is my pride and joy, but I could sell it. I'd be sad to let it go, but it would be okay.

I'd miss Sutton, I think. She's one of the first real friends I've ever had and not having her around might be disappointing.

Lily too, I guess. But she's away at college and who knows what she'll be doing once she graduates. Maybe she won't even come back here. I'm not exactly sure what degree she's settled on because last she said she's been bouncing around majors all the way from philosophy to business.

I don't think she knows exactly what she's going to do and I don't blame her. She's young and has plenty of time to figure it out.

I, on the other hand, have spent the entire thirty-one years of my life just trying to survive, escaping when I felt trapped or unsafe. And right now, that feeling is starting to appear again, but not because I feel like Wes is going to hurt me. I'm afraid I'm in over my head and while we haven't had the most peaceful time living next to each other, I've managed to do my best to avoid him.

Until now.

I watch him drive away, his words are still replaying in my mind. Five minutes later, once I've finally managed to push them from my thoughts, my phone signals a text, and the words on my screen almost make me drop the device.

> Wes: Come to my house when you're done. Don't even try to hide in your room. It'll only make things worse for you.

That smug bastard.

I want to scream, but someone pulls up to the window to order. I know it won't look great if they see me losing my shit in here just because my neighbor is determined to send me spiraling.

After only a couple more hours, I'm closing up and my phone goes off again. I glare at it like it's a bomb about to detonate. I don't want to see what could be waiting on there for me because lately, it hasn't been great.

Threats I want to challenge and demands I'm tempted to follow. That is not what I should be feeling. *None* of what's been happening should have my mind so scrambled. Somehow, my life has turned into some weird alternate reality where Wes is trying to get into my pants, and I kind of want to let him.

I dare a glance at my phone, and see that it appears to be safe because it's a text from Lily in the group chat. She's not addressing me specifically, but I still read the message. If you don't want it read by everyone, you don't put it in the group chat.

Lily: Sutton! How's the honeymoon going? Hope you're having a good time *winking emoji*

Sutton: We are, actually. It's nice to be up in the mountains relaxing.

Lily: I bet you are relaxing…relaxing on your new husband's pecker.

Sutton: Do not call it a pecker. I'm leaving.

SUTTON HAS LEFT THE CHAT.
LILY HAS ADDED SUTTON TO THE CHAT.

Lily: Bailey, where are you? Back me up.

Bailey: I'm not backing up you using the word "pecker."

Lily: Is it because you haven't gotten to relax on a certain neighbor's pecker? *side eye emoji*

Bailey: Now I'm leaving.

BAILEY HAS LEFT THE CHAT.
LILY HAS ADDED BAILEY TO THE CHAT.

Lily: You bitches don't get to leave me that easily, now someone better tell me something interesting. I'm bored out of my mind here.

Sutton: You first! Have you heard from Parker or anything to do with his pecker recently?

Lily: That was just rude.

LILY HAS LEFT THE CHAT.

Bailey: Should we even add her back?

Sutton: Let her sweat it out for a minute.

Bailey: She's relentless.

Sutton: No kidding. I love her, but she's a lot.
Be thankful you weren't around for the jelly
bean story.

Bailey: ...I don't even want to know.

Sutton: No, you really don't.

Sutton: Think enough time has passed?

Bailey: Yeah, probably.

SUTTON HAS ADDED LILY TO THE CHAT.

Lily: Took you bitches long enough! I know
you missed me.

Lily: Oh! I have to tell you about what I saw
today. It has to do with a mime–

I lock my phone and put it in my pocket, knowing I'll end up standing here for the rest of the day reading about the rabbit hole Lily is about to go down. She's entertaining, that's for sure. A little out there for me, but entertaining, nonetheless.

I continue to take my time cleaning up the small drive up coffee stand because I know what's waiting for me when I get home. If I take too long, he might get bored and tired of waiting. Then he can go see whoever it is he goes to in the middle of the night.

The thought is sobering enough that I'm pissed off and annoyed. I'm not going to avoid my own house because of him. With that, I finish up a couple more things before locking up and driving home.

Wes's car is parked in his driveway, but instead of going over there, I walk into my house and immediately lock the door behind me.

Not even five minutes later, my phone goes off and somehow I know it's not from the group chat. I know it's him, but I refuse to look at it. Instead, I toss it onto the counter, face down and walk to my room.

I change out of my jeans and into some cotton shorts and a T-shirt when there's a pounding at my front door.

You've got to be kidding me.

Of course it's him.

"Go away," I tell him through the wood.

"You can't follow a simple instruction, can you?"

"I *can*. I just don't *want* to. Go away before I call the cops."

"You won't." His deep voice practically vibrates the wood separating us from how close he's clearly standing. The one thing keeping us apart right now suddenly doesn't feel protective enough for me. If he really wanted to, he could probably kick it in and not even break a sweat.

"Want to stick around and find out?" I threaten.

"Say the word then, Angel. Say the word, and I go away and this stops."

The word sticks in my throat. The one thing I know I can say to end this. The one thing I have yet to say.

There's a thunk on the other side, and I think it's his forehead hitting the door. "Say it." His tone sounds threatening, the growl in his voice goes straight between my thighs. He knows I won't. We both do.

It's all a part of the game, this back and forth we have.

"If you're not going to say it, then open this door before your punishment gets worse."

I steel my spine, yanking the door open. "You don't get to punish me like I'm some fucking child. What is *wrong* with yo–"

I'm cut off by Wes grabbing me, and tossing me over his shoulder, closing the door and walking us toward his house while I'm screaming at him to put me down, and smacking his back with my fists.

"Keep it up, Angel. Keep telling me how pissed off you are and how much you don't want me. We both know it's a lie, but I like hearing it because it'll only make it so much sweeter when your body won't stop coming for me."

I screech in protest as he carries me into his house, but the fact that his words made my pussy clench in anticipation is a bad sign. A *very* bad sign. I worry I'm only strong to a certain point, and after that I'm going to be so fucked.

CHAPTER 19

Wes

I BITE BACK my laughter as Bailey pounds at my back and kicks her feet. My arm is around the back of her knees, banding her legs so she can only kick her feet a little, and she's not able to hurt me. Though, she's certainly trying.

"You're really not helping your case, Angel." I grunt after she manages to punch a particularly sensitive spot on my back as I'm walking us through my front door.

"Put me down, you caveman," she screeches as I kick the door shut behind me.

"I'll put you down when I know you're not going to bolt out of here as soon as I do."

"You'd probably like chasing me down."

I shrug, jostling her more in the process. "Yeah, you might be right about that."

No point in lying at this point.

She lets out a loud groan of protest again. "What the fuck is wrong with you?"

I reach the top of my stairs and take her into my bedroom, tossing her onto my bed. Dropping down on top of her, I use my body to cage her in so she can't escape. It doesn't stop her from trying to squirm away, so I drop my hips onto hers. She squeaks and I smirk, my forearms resting on the bed next to her head, trapping her beneath me.

"A lot is probably wrong with me, but right now, this is about *you.*"

She swallows roughly. "What about me?"

"You're going to pay for everything you've done that I've told you not to do. I warned you what would happen. I told you to come here and not hide in your room, but what did you do?"

She sucks her bottom lip between her teeth, and I can tell she's trying not to smile.

I grip a fistful of her hair, tilting her head back with it. "*What did you do?*"

"I did it anyway," she breathes.

"Yeah, and what did I tell you would happen if you did that?"

She squirms again underneath me. I push down harder with my hips, pulling her hair back making her gasp.

"Tell me," I demand roughly.

"You'd punish me," she says reluctantly.

"Mhm, and how do you think I should do that this time?"

Bailey shrugs. "I don't know what kind of masochistic shit you like to do with your victims."

"If I'm a masochist then you're right there with me. I know how your pussy floods for me."

"You don't know anything," she retorts weakly.

"No? Sounds like I should check then."

I slide down her body, and she doesn't protest as I grip the hem of her shorts, and start to pull them down. My eyes look up to watch her reaction, waiting to see if she's going to stop me as I reveal more of her body. I move back, pulling the fabric off her legs, and pushing them open so I can see her bare in front of me, exactly how I expected her to be. Wet and ready. *For me.*

"Hm," I hum. "You going to try and deny what I can *clearly* see?"

"Depends on what you're going to do about it," she challenges, and I smirk. My dick is hard as stone behind my zipper, just like it has been since I tossed her over my shoulder.

Her fire only spurs me on even more. Instead of answering her with words, I toss her legs over my shoulders, and bury my face between them I lap up her arousal, groaning at the sweet taste of her.

She moans, arching her back, so I press her down with a firm hand on her stomach while I suck her clit into my mouth and she buries her hand in my hair, pulling roughly like I did to her. It only has me working harder to pull the first orgasm from her.

The first of many.

Because that's her punishment. She wants to deny how she wants me, to continue to play games with me and be a brat. I'm going to prove to her how badly she wants me. How her body craves me, and how I can make her feel good over and over again. Even when she doesn't think it can continue, I'll prove her wrong.

Her body is my playground.

I flick the sensitive bud with my tongue, and she seems to like that the most because her mewls of pleasure increase as she starts to writhe under me, and I keep holding her exactly where I want. Her cries get louder and her thighs tighten on the sides of my head.

It doesn't take long before she's yanking me harder against her, crying out with her release. I work her through the orgasm with my tongue, and when she loosens her grip, I know she's coming down.

Which means she's ready for another one.

Without giving her much of a reprieve, I keep my eyes on her while pushing a finger into her entrance.

"Wes," she cries, trying to push me away, but I don't let her. I move my thumb to her sensitive bud while thrusting my finger into her.

"Yeah, Angel?" I smirk.

"I can't, I'm too sensitive."

"Aw," I coo. "Too bad, you're going to."

I push another finger into her tight heat while she continues to protest. I wait to see if she'll say the one thing to get me to stop. There's one way to make this end and she knows exactly what that is.

She's been able to say it at any point, but she hasn't.

Just like now as I fuck her with my fingers, she cries out so many words. But none of them are *sunflower.*

It doesn't take long for me to pull another orgasm from her. This time, as her body convulses, I make sure to lap up her release. The sweet tang of her hitting my tongue makes me so desperate to get inside her that I can't help but thrust my hips against the bed.

As she comes down once again, I climb back up her body, trailing my wet fingers along her skin, up her stomach, pushing her shirt up along the way. I reach her chest as our faces are only a couple inches from each other and my hips are resting between her spread thighs.

I bring my hand up, lifting my fingers into my mouth and sucking the taste of her off them. Her mouth drops with a silent gasp as she watches the movement. When I remove them from between my lips, I hold them up to hers.

Without hesitating, she lets me push the digits into her mouth and sucks them. Immediately reminding me of the way it felt when she dropped to her knees in front of me in the shower.

"How do you taste?" I rasp.

"Not sure, all I taste is you." She runs her tongue along her bottom lip and it is so tempting. We haven't kissed, not even that first night, and the way I want to do it right now is so strong.

But not yet.

I bring our faces closer together, our breath mingling in the tiny open space between our lips.

"Then how do I taste?"

"Better than you should," she practically whispers.

My hips push forward at the softness of her voice because it's so different for Bailey. There's a hint of vulnerability in her eyes, and I know I almost have her where I want her.

That's why I slide my hand between us once again, while I drop my forehead to hers. "Maybe I'll let you taste more as long as you give me another one."

I graze her clit with the tip of my finger, and she arches up into me with a sharp cry. She shakes her head. "No, there's no way."

"Remember this the next time you want to be a brat."

She continues to protest all while chasing my hand with her hips. Her words are saying one thing, while her body says the opposite. She bites down on her bottom lip when I push a finger into her wetness once again and she's clenching around me as she finds yet another release she swears she couldn't handle.

Her chest rises and falls with heavy breaths. The air between us is thick with tension, and anticipation. And when her eyes open once again, I see it. Just for a moment. A glimpse of her softness.

Bailey Collee letting me in, if only just for a second.

"Are you okay?" I ask, the words catching me by surprise that I let them out.

They seem to do the same to her because her eyes widen slightly. I expect some smart ass response, but instead she just nods.

"Good," I grunt, standing up, and help pull her shorts back on.

She sits up on the edge of my bed; I lean forward, pressing my fists onto the mattress by her hips. "You did so well for me, keep it up and you can earn a reward next time."

There's a flash of surprise on her face, and even though I don't want this to end right now, I know it needs to.

If I'm not careful, I know Bailey could break down parts of myself that I didn't think existed. And that's not something I feel like I can handle.

This type of relationship, I can do. Sexual, controlled, boundaries.

Anything more is just not possible. Not with me.

CHAPTER 20

Bailey

I COULDN'T LEAVE Wes's house fast enough the other night. This seems to be our new routine and I'm not sure how I feel about it. We meet up, one of us comes, sometimes more than once. Then one of us leaves.

But we haven't kissed.

And we haven't had sex since that very first night when neither of us knew who the other one was.

It's one of the weirder situations I've found myself in. My mind is a mess of wanting to give into him at any point, and wanting to run far far away.

Sutton and Jameson are still on their honeymoon, and it's been a few days since I left Wes's house after his "punishment." I'd hardly say getting to have multiple orgasms is a bad thing, but I'm not about to tell him that.

I need to do something to distract myself that isn't working or fighting for my life in the group chat with Sutton and Lily. You'd think Sutton would want to be left alone on her honeymoon, but Lily is clearly missing us, or missing Amity. Or has an extremely bad case of senioritis.

One of the things I discovered when I moved here was that the local bar does line dancing. At first I wasn't sure about it. The thought of dancing in public was not appealing in the slightest. I would go, and watch once I dared step foot in the bar I met Wes in again.

I took Sutton there once, and it was certainly more fun to go with a friend. But I still have a good time alone. It's exactly what I need to get my mind off everything. Brynn has continued to reach out, but even after I spoke to Brent briefly, for some reason I can't bring myself to talk to my sister.

I know Brent wouldn't tell her we talked. If he did I know she would say something to me about it.

I feel bad not talking to her, but she's the one I want to protect the most, she always has been. As the two youngest in our family, there was a time when our older brothers weren't around anymore. And I did what I could to protect her, no matter what it took from me.

I just wanted one of us to turn out okay.

It seems like she has. She's successful, dating some hockey player on the same team as Brent. It doesn't matter that I'll never be okay, because she is. Which is why I can't bring myself to reply. I refuse to drag her down with me. It's best this way, even if she doesn't understand it.

And this is precisely why I need the distraction.

Summer is turning into fall, the warm nights being replaced with cooler temperatures once the sun sets so I pull on some jeans, a loose shirt, and my comfiest ankle boots. I pull my long hair up in a ponytail, taking one last look in the mirror and sigh.

I've never thought of myself as beautiful. There're so many others that are prettier than me. I'm tall, lanky, and the natural wave of my hair never cooperates. The bags under my eyes have been there for as long as I can remember. Scars have faded on my skin from the childhood I try to forget, but they will always remain. And there's nothing I can do about it. Sometimes I think about getting tattoos to cover them.

But I don't want to.

I hate the scars. I hate where they came from, and hate what they represent from my past, but they show I survived.

And that's what I try to remember.

THE BAR IS PACKED. I forgot it's a Saturday night, and it feels like every single person who lives in Amity is here making an appearance. The open floor is already in full swing with dancers, but I go to the bar first to get a drink.

The Jack and Diet Coke appears in front of me quickly, and I thank the bartender, making sure to tip well because I know how hard they work. I move to a spot out of the way to watch the dancers while I get at least one drink in me before I join.

I might be more comfortable dancing in public now, but I still need a little liquid courage to really let go.

After the first drink, the tension eases, and I'm loose enough to follow the steps without overthinking how ridiculous I might look.

It doesn't take long before I'm laughing with others as we move, and my mind is able to push everything else away. I'm not sure how long I dance until the music changes, signaling the end of the line dancing portion of the evening and the dance floor is open to everyone wanting to move to the upbeat music pumping through the speakers.

I go back to the bar for another drink, having danced the first one completely out of my system. Not that I should stay much longer, I don't have to wake up early tomorrow, but there's no point in staying out.

Unless I find a reason to. My eyes catch on an unfamiliar man on the other end of the bar. He's handsome, light brown hair falls over his forehead, obvious dimples on his cheeks. He looks clean cut and nice.

The complete opposite of Wes, and maybe that's the perfect distraction. To hook up with someone else. That's a guaranteed way to forget for a little while. Maybe then I won't be so tempted to fall into bed with my neighbor at the drop of a hat.

The man looks up, and notices me so I give him a soft smile. It's enough to have him approaching me.

"Hey," he greets, his voice is deep, but lacks the growl that sends a shot of electricity between my legs when a certain other man speaks to me.

"I don't recognize you." I tilt my head, trying to place him.

"You probably wouldn't, I'm not from here."

"Hm, I can tell." I let my eyes roam over his frame. He's about as tall as me and over dressed for this place, but I'm not going to fault him for that.

He chuckles, and again my body doesn't react the way it does for someone else. "I'm Dale."

"Bailey."

"That's pretty." He smiles, and I hide my grimace. I don't think my name is anything special, but sure if he wants to try and say that, I won't argue.

Not the way I'll argue with Wes over everything just to see what he'll do.

"So, what're you doing here since you clearly don't belong?" I ask, taking another sip from my drink.

"Just passing through." He shrugs.

I feel like there's more than that, Amity isn't exactly on the way to anywhere, but again, if that's what he wants to try to say, then I'm not about to argue.

"I saw you dancing a little bit ago, would you want to do a little more with me?" he questions. I want to tell him how lame of a line that is, but I can't bring myself to.

Instead, I agree and let him lead me back onto the dance floor while a song I don't particularly like plays. I try to lose myself in the feel of him behind me. Bodies moving against each other, just trying to see if I'll have any sort of reaction to him to spur me into going home with him.

I try, but nothing happens.

I'm about to give up, and tell him I'm going home for the night when another voice is behind me, this one deeper, rougher, and says one simple word, "Move."

I expect an argument, I expect *something*. But as I start to turn, a large strong hand is grabbing my hip, and pulling me back into a oversized hard body. One that *does* have me reacting.

He leans down to speak into my ear; I can smell the whiskey on his breath as he speaks and even *that* has me ready to mount him right here. Which is a problem.

"I'm going to pretend that you didn't want that asshole touching you," Wes says lowly.

I turn my head, bringing our mouths closer together, but not touching. "You can pretend all you want, but I was planning on going home with him."

I'm playing with fire, and I know it. But *fuck* I want it to burn me.

His hand tightens, and I let out a small squeak at the delicious pressure.

"Just when I thought you could be rewarded. You were right, you are no angel."

I shake my head. "And I never will be. Especially for you."

He spins me around suddenly, our chests colliding roughly and I huff at the contact. Wes bands his arm around my back so I can't go anywhere. Our bodies are completely pressed together, not moving in the middle of the dance floor. I'm sure we're being stared at, but I can't look away from his deep brown eyes.

"That's fine, I don't want you to be."

I swallow roughly, the words getting caught in my throat. "What *do* you want me to be?" I whisper so low I'm not even sure if he heard me.

He pulls me closer against him, I can feel the hard planes of his chest against mine. I rest my hands on his pec, feeling the steady rise and fall with each breath he takes while we continue to stare into each other's eyes.

Finally, he speaks and it's the last thing I expected him to say. "I just want you to be Bailey Collee."

I swear I misheard him, or something is in the air. A full moon. Something is wrong with him, with me. In no world did Wes Anderson just say those words to me.

Which can only mean one thing, and it's that he doesn't mean them. So I react like I always do with a scoff, and an eye roll as I try to push him away. "Yeah, right."

He doesn't let me go. Instead, he flexes his arms, holding me even tighter against him, unable to move or create any distance between us.

"You don't believe me?" he asks darkly.

"Considering we don't like each other, no I don't believe you."

"Who says I don't like you?"

I try to detect the snark in his voice, any indication he's fucking with me, but he's completely deadpan. All while keeping me completely pressed against him. I curl my fingers into him, gripping his shirt as I shake my head.

"You don't," I protest weakly.

His hand slides up to the back of my neck, gripping me roughly, immobilizing me even more.

"I don't usually make it a habit of doing the things we do with people I don't like."

"Really? I do it all the time," I retort sarcastically.

"Is that why you were going to go home with that idiot wearing a fucking button down in a shit hole like this?"

"Maybe." I narrowed my eyes at him. "Why does it matter to you?"

"Because I don't share. And the second you didn't say the safe word after we established it, you've been mine."

I scoff again. "I don't belong to anyone, especially not you."

"I'm going to prove to you how wrong you really are."

"Yeah? With another one of your little punishments? Do your

worst, but you can't stand here claiming you 'like me' when we've never even kissed."

"That what you need, Angel? You need to be wined and dined? Kissed at the end of the night? Move slowly while we dance around the things we both really want?" He chuckles, but it's lacking humor. "That's bullshit and we both know it."

"You don't know me."

I haven't even realized how close our faces have gotten until this moment, lips barely an inch apart. My heart feels like it's going to burst from my chest at the way he's looking at me. His words not even sinking in.

"If you want me to kiss you, then you'll have to wait because the first time isn't going to be in front of every eye in town. Especially because once I start, I know I'm not going to be able to stop."

And just like the time in the shower, he separates us, letting me go and leaving me confused, needy, and pissed off.

He doesn't even spare me a simple glance as he walks out of the bar. That's when I notice every single person has their attention on me and my face flames; I drop my head, not ready to be at the center of town gossip.

By the time I race out of the bar, Wes is nowhere to be found. I drop my head back letting the cool air hit my skin, trying to let it wash away all the feelings hitting me at once because there's no way any of that just happened.

Worst of all there's no way I actually wanted it to.

CHAPTER 21

Bailey

I'M GOING to regret this. I know I will.

I shouldn't do anything.

I should just go home, but instead I parked in my driveway and stormed over to Wes's door. His words have been playing on repeat in my mind the entire drive home. I don't believe him, I know there's no way he meant it.

But the way he looked at me as he said them has me questioning it.

Especially the last thing he said before leaving me cold, confused, and needier than I should be.

"If you want me to kiss you, then you'll have to wait because the first time isn't going to be in front of every eye in town. Especially because once I start, I know I'm not going to be able to stop."

I bang my fist on his front door, and it doesn't take long

before he's swinging it open, and leaning against the door frame, expectantly.

Suddenly, all my bravado has left the building with the way he's staring at me. I shake my head, turning to leave without either of us saying a word because this was clearly a mistake.

Wes doesn't let me leave, instead he grabs my hand and pulls me back into him. Without a single word, his hand grips my jaw, angling my head up, while his other hand tightens on my waist, and he's descending his mouth onto mine.

The moment his lips touch mine, everything else fades. I'm frozen, caught in some alternate reality where this is actually happening and I like it.

I *really* like it.

When his tongue peeks out, demanding entry, I open for him and that's when I know I've truly lost it. My hands find his shoulders, digging my fingers into his strong frame. He growls into my mouth, grabbing me even tighter while deepening the kiss. My hands move up to the back of his head, sinking into his hair while the last shred of my resistance fades into the air around us.

I hardly realize that we're still standing on his front porch, and that technically anyone could see us. But the only house across the street is still vacant since Sutton moved, and people don't typically come down this residential road.

Yet, neither of us move inside, even as Wes continues to devour my mouth in a way that has stars dancing behind my closed eyelids. Nothing else exists. All I can feel are his lips on mine, his hair slipping through my fingers, and the solid weight of his body pressed against me.

I don't know how long we stand here like this. I just know I don't want it to end. I want it to go further. I want to feel more of him. I want to lose myself in this moment and never have to face the reality lurking around the corner.

Wes separates us, and I hold back the whimper threatening to come out at the loss. For once, I don't even glare at him. I'm in too much shock and feel so completely overwhelmed by everything that just happened that I don't know what to do with my face, or monitor how I'm looking at him.

He moves a piece of hair that's fallen out of my ponytail out of my face, and I lean into his touch. His face is impossible to read, he's not smirking, no trace of disdain. He's just...looking.

"I thought you said you wouldn't be able to stop," I manage to squeak out.

This earns me a small upturn of his lips. "Remember that for next time. This was so you know I meant the other thing I said." I furrow my brow, but he's already walking away, backing through his door. "I have to tuck the kid into bed."

I open my mouth because he doesn't have a kid I know about, but he shuts the door, and I'm left once again turned on and confused. I can't even bring myself to be annoyed because the other two feelings are so strong.

I'm on autopilot as I walk back to my house, resisting the urge to ask what the fuck he meant, and what kid he's talking about. It's not until I'm up in my room, and glancing over to his room through the window that I see Bruno jumping on the edge of Wes's bed and I huff out a laugh.

That kid.

Wes comes into view, reaches behind his head and pulls off his shirt. I suck in a soft gasp at the sight of his muscular chest, the tattoos covering one arm, up onto his shoulder. He pushes his pants down, but leaves his boxers on, and I can see the bulge behind the fabric from the part of his body I would like to become even more acquainted with.

He knows I'm staring because he walks backwards toward his bed, and gives me a two finger salute right before he turns off the light.

Losing sight of him has me snapping back to reality. I turn around shaking my head and hoping by the time I wake up, I'll have my head back on straight.

I feel like I'm too far gone, and the only thing that can bring me back would be to create distance again. And while I may be strong, I know I'm not strong enough to do that.

Which means that I'm well and truly fucked.

* * *

My phone dings.

Lily: Bails!

Bailey: Please don't call me Bails.

Lily: Bailsey bug!

Bailey: That's not better.

Lily: Whatever I'm allowed to call you then! A little birdie has told me you were spotted getting really close with a certain neighbor.

Sutton: How close?!

Lily: Close enough that if clothes were off they would be inside each other.

Sutton: Uh…what?

Lily: You know what I mean.

Sutton: I don't know that I do actually…

Lily: Bailey, spill the tea!

Bailey: There's no tea to spill, your sources are mistaken.

Lily: My sources are never wrong.

Bailey: This time they are.

Lily: So you weren't dancing with Wes and practically humping him?

Bailey: Nope.

Sutton: *Side eye emoji*

Bailey: Don't look at me like that. Nothing happened.

Technically not a lie. Nothing happened at the bar, really.

Lily: Don't make me drive up there to get information out of you.

Bailey: We all know if you're coming here it would be to get something from Parker, not me.

Sutton: *Double side eye emojis*

Lily: Cold, Collee. You. Are. Cold.

Bailey: My sources tell me you are still talking to him.

Sutton: *Triple side eye emojis*

Lily: Who are your sources?!

Bailey: Not telling, and you aren't denying.

Lilly: How'd you manage to turn this around on me?

Bailey: It's a gift.

Sutton: You make me excited to come back home.

Lily: Rub it in, why don't you? I won't be back until Christmas.

Sutton: And we can't wait to see you then.

Bailey: I'm sure Parker is saying the same thing.

LILY HAS LEFT THE CHAT.

I put my phone face down on my bed with a chuckle at our group chat antics. I know I shouldn't goad her on especially since she somehow already heard about last night even though she's all the way in California.

It makes me wonder who the hell her sources are, and better yet, why they're snitching on me.

They didn't even see what happened after the bar.

I groan, trying to forget while I roll out of bed and bring myself downstairs to get some coffee. The morning sun is shining, but when I open the back door while my coffee brews, I feel how cool it is and I decide to take the hot drink out on my back patio.

I love mornings like this. Quiet, the slight chill in the coastal breeze hitting my skin while fall approaches, taking away the hot summer days. Closing my eyes I take a deep breath, filling my lungs with the air that feels so clean. It's the complete opposite of how I felt every day growing up.

There's a sense of peace that surrounds me when I just take a moment to appreciate where I am and that I never have to go back. My mind may always be partly stuck there, forever shaped by the trauma I endured. But physically I never have to go through that again.

The sound of a door sliding open catches my attention, and I hear Bruno stepping in the dew covered grass. I freeze, as if any little movement I make Wes will hear. My moment of peace is no longer because I don't want Wes to know I'm out here.

Last night comes back to me full force. Everything he said, the dancing, *the kiss.* I drop my head back against the chair and there's a soft thud that has me gasping, throwing my hand over my mouth to cover the small sound.

I think I'm safe when nothing happens, just the sound of Bruno walking around in the grass. Maybe Wes isn't out there with him.

I move my head forward again, about to bring my mug up to my lips for a sip when I see him standing at the fence; he's so tall he's able to easily rest his arms on top of it, looking at me. I jump, trying my hardest not to spill any of my coffee.

"What is wrong with you?" I snap.

"I'm just in my yard, is that a crime?"

I grind my teeth wanting to retort, but also not sure if I should goad him anymore because I know what will happen.

"I'm about to go to Jameson's before they come home tomorrow. Do you want to come with me?" Wes offers, and I can't hide the surprised look on my face.

"Why?" I can't help but ask.

He shrugs. "Up to you."

"That doesn't answer the question."

He's already walking away, and I have to admit I'm getting pretty tired of him doing that. Maybe that's why I storm inside, pull some clothes on, and end up agreeing to go with him.

CHAPTER 22

Wes

LAST NIGHT WAS the same as every other in regard to me not being able to sleep. What wasn't the same was that I could still feel Bailey's lips against mine. I had to consistently fight to not go over there. Instead, I stayed put and tried to will myself to sleep.

Of course it didn't happen, my leg pain flared as it does and as always, it brought me right back to that day. The explosions, the burning sensation, the screams, and the searing pain. At one point I put my noise canceling headphones on with music loud enough to try and drown out the noise in my head.

Nights like that would usually have me driving until the sun comes up. But I wasn't going anywhere–not with the slim chance Bailey might show up. However, lying in bed alone with nothing but my thoughts was brutal. The pain radiating through me dragged me to that dark place in my mind. The one where I wished my life was taken with theirs. Suddenly. Quickly. No longer having to deal with the pain I live with each and every day.

There's pressure on my uninjured leg, and I open my eyes to see Bruno resting his head on me, and I'm brought back to the present. Letting out a sigh I do everything I can to try and fall asleep once again.

When I crack my eyes open, I look around, and I think I actually managed a couple of hours eventually. My leg is stiff after not moving for a few hours, but thankfully, it's not as painful as it was last night. I limp slightly as Bruno and I go downstairs to let him out. I lean against the door frame enjoying the fresh air against the bare skin of my chest.

When I hear a noise from next door, I step over to the fence and see Bailey sitting curled up in one of her chairs, holding a mug between her hands. I just look at her, there's a furrow in her brow. Her long wavy hair is down, a little messy like she hasn't touched it since she rolled out of bed, and has a slight purse to her lips. She looks like she's thinking too hard with her eyebrows pinched together. The natural beauty she has that I don't even think she notices.

I've always noticed.

She might think I don't like her, but I don't really like anyone. I don't *dis*like her. We've had our disagreements over the years that we've lived next to each other, but she's always intrigued me.

Even that first night together I knew there was more to her than she seems to let on, and right now the way she's staring out into her yard has me wondering what that could be.

She raises her mug to her lips, but then sees me, and jumps.

Something comes over me—I don't know what—and has me inviting her to go with me to Jameson's. I don't think she'll agree, but as I walk outside, about to leave, she's waiting by my car. The sight of her ass leaning against the side shouldn't have me reacting in such a feral way, but it does. The way she was pressed against me just last night is at the forefront of my mind. Now her tall frame is right here with her arms crossed looking annoyed.

Bruno trots ahead of me, and bumps his head against her gently, allowing her to reach down and scratch his head.

"You joining us?" I ask, reaching around her to open the passenger door for Bruno to jump in.

"I thought about it, but I don't think there's room."

"There's plenty, you and Bruno can cuddle in the front seat. Or you can ride in my lap." I smirk.

Bailey scoffs, and rolls those pretty green eyes at me. I'm keeping track because at this point I'm going to have her ass so red from every single time she's done that to me. "That's dangerous, I'll leave you two to have your time together alone."

Standing up straight, I raise my eyebrow at her before signaling to Bruno to get into the small backseat. It's cramped and there isn't enough room for it to be a seat a person can actually fit into, but it's perfect for him and it frees up the front seat for my stubborn guest.

She grumbles something under her breath, but climbs in the car acting like I'm forcing her to come with me when she's the one that made the decision to join. Even though she doesn't want to admit it, I don't think she actually dislikes me all that much either.

*

ONCE WE GET to the barn and I start feeding the horses, I notice Bruno sticking by Bailey's side, which I find interesting. He's been friendly enough to Emily, but really the only other person he's been that comfortable with and attached to is me.

"What can I do?" Bailey asks.

"Entertain Bruno," I grunt, swinging another hay bale down to untwine.

"You wanted me to come with you to entertain your dog?"

I don't bother correcting her that he's technically not my dog because it seems like a pointless argument to have with her right now.

"You could entertain me, too," I joke.

"I think I'd rather entertain the dog."

"Come on. You're the one that said I don't know anything about you. So tell me something."

"You first."

I drop two flakes down into one of the stalls, moving onto the next one while I think about something I would be willing to share. "I'm from Arizona."

"Really? Why'd you move here?" She sounds surprised.

"Why did you?" I look at her from the hay loft, and she scrunches her face.

She doesn't say anything right away, and right when I think

we're just going to let the silence between us continue, she finally speaks again. "I'm from Ohio."

I try to hide my shocked expression that she even said anything.

"Where else have you lived?" she asks. The fact that she wants to know more about me enough to ask has a smile playing at my lips, but I hold back.

"Lots of places. You don't want the whole list. The Army moved me around quite a bit during the ten years I was in."

Would've moved me around more if I'd gotten to stay in like I planned.

"Which was your favorite?" she questions, and again I'm surprised she's asking more.

I think about it while feeding the last horse, then climbing down to the floor level. She's sitting in a chair petting Bruno as I answer.

"Japan."

"Why?"

"It's my turn to ask something."

"I didn't realize it had to be equal," she scoffs.

"Of course it does. Do you have any siblings?"

Bailey grumbles, "Yeah."

"How many?"

"My turn. Why was Japan your favorite? Let me guess, it had to do with women."

I tilt my head at her, narrowing my eyes. "Why do you think of me like that? Like I'm some sort of man whore."

"Aren't you? I'm sure you're out with women when you leave in the middle of the night."

I grunt, but don't tell her otherwise. There's no point if this is how she sees me for. Little does she know, the last woman I slept with was her. And before her, it had been years since I'd touched a woman.

"I liked the culture there. The sights, how different it is from the states. Being able to experience new things in such a different place without the imminent threat of danger was nice for a little while," I explain, and it clearly catches her off guard. "How many siblings do you have?"

"I had four."

I notice the way she says *had*, but I know she won't let me ask another question until she does. I grab a wheelbarrow and shovel to start mucking the horse stalls.

"What made you leave the Army?"

I freeze, staring at the sawdust covered ground and doing my best to control my breathing to not let the memories of the reason take over. To not let her know there is any real reason. But then she speaks up again.

"Is it because of what happened to your leg?"

I grunt out some variation of, "Yeah," before continuing to clean out the stall, refusing to turn around and face her until I'm sure my face won't give anything away.

"I had three brothers and one sister. One of my older brothers died of an overdose a couple years ago," she speaks softly, and while I'm able to hear her it gets me to turn around.

"I'm sorry to hear that."

She shrugs. "It's whatever. He made his choices, and my oldest brother Brent tried to help him for years. Brandon made his bed, and he ended up laying in it."

I don't tell her I know all too well what she means. Plenty of the guys I met during my time serving turned to destructive habits as a coping mechanism. Drugs, alcohol, self-harming behaviors. It's all too common for veterans. Especially those of us that get injured and are forced out against our will.

"I am a little surprised, though," she says, her tone lighter.

"About what?"

"That you don't know who my brother is. It seems like every-where I go my name is recognized thanks to him."

I turn toward her, leaning my elbow on the end of the picking tool while giving her a questioning look. "Is he famous or something?"

"You must not watch sports."

"Not really high on my list of hobbies. Sometimes I put golf on."

"Golf?" she sputters.

"Yeah, it's not too loud, kind of peaceful." I shrug, continuing to clean out the stalls. "What sport does your brother play that makes him so famous?"

"Hockey. My oldest brother, Brent, played for the Denver Dragons, but just retired," she explains softly.

"Hockey is cool, pretty violent though. Sounds like I don't want to piss him off."

She scoffs. "I wouldn't worry about that. I haven't seen him in years, and if you somehow did manage to piss him off, he's not one to fight. Even if he was, you could take him."

"That right?" I quirk an eyebrow.

"Uh yeah, have you looked in the mirror? You're a fucking tank."

"I take that as a compliment."

"Didn't intend for it to be, but whatever gets you off."

Her face flames as she looks away, realizing what she said and I hide my laughter, turning back toward the mess in the stall. When I'm not looking at her I'm able to share a little more. Especially since she shared something so vulnerable with me, which coming from Bailey is even more disconcerting.

"I wanted to have a career in the Army, it was the only plan for me. I was an Apache pilot, and there was an attack that took my future away." I can't look at her, just focusing on mucking the dirty ground and not allowing my mind to go back to the dark place it drifts to.

She doesn't speak right away, maybe she won't at all, and that's fine. I can do silence. I'm comfortable in the silence.

When she finally does, there's a sense of relief washing over me, and the feeling is both unexpected and frightening.

"Maybe it wasn't taking away your future, but putting you on the path you were really meant to be on instead."

CHAPTER 23

Bailey

I'VE NEVER BEEN as personable as Brynn. Never as in control as Brent, and never as fun as Bryson. And I've sure as fuck never been as careless as Brandon. I've always just been the one that everyone forgets about. The extra Collee who isn't anything special. The one who wanted to protect her sister from the horrors of the house they lived in, but could never protect herself.

Yet, for the first time in that barn with Wes while he was scooping horse shit from stalls and I pet his dog—because Bruno is his, I don't care what he says—I felt like someone who mattered. And that might be ridiculous, but Wes not knowing a single thing about my past or my family, especially Brent, made me feel like I could breathe for the first time.

To him I'm just me, and he asked me to come with him. He wanted to be around me, even in that moment. It all terrified me, and as soon as I realized what was happening I panicked. I had to get away, but of course he drove me so I found an excuse to go somewhere else.

I decided to feed the goats because the cows look like they

want to bulldoze me. Turns out the goats have the same plan because they keep ramming their horns into my legs as I try to feed them.

"I'm the one with your food, you know? Being mean to me is not the way to get it." I try to reason with the feral little things, but they don't seem to care.

I manage to get them their food, and as I walk back to the entrance of their pasture the giant man making me feel things I don't want to feel is standing there waiting for me.

"That was entertaining," he teases.

"Don't start with me," I mumble, keeping my head down as I walk past him through the gate, embarrassed because I can't believe I shared what I did with him.

I'm trying to remind myself that I don't like him, and despite what he may have said he also doesn't like me. That's something I'm sure of.

We end up finishing the tasks around the property mostly in silence. Which is because of me since I do everything I can to keep my distance. Though, he's never far and Bruno sticks by us both.

When we get back in the car to leave it feels even more crowded than it did on the way here. The tension between us is so thick, I swear even Bruno can feel it.

Once Wes parks in front of his house, and the loud engine cuts off, silence surrounds us. I can't get out of the car fast enough.

"Where are you running off to?" Wes asks. I pause but don't turn around to face him.

"I have stuff to do," I lie. I have no stuff. Not a single thing. I just can't be around him much longer for my own sanity.

"What do you have to do?" His tone is suspicious and it instantly makes me defensive.

"Stuff that doesn't concern you."

He's in front of me before I'm able to move; his hand is around the back of my neck holding me in place. "Want to try that again?" he practically growls.

I bite my bottom lip, stifling the urge to sass him even more. Stuck between wanting more of his punishments and finding out what a reward would feel like from him.

The fact that I'm even considering either of these options has me more concerned for the current state of my mental health.

"I just have stuff around the house to do," I finally say, all while trying not to melt against him completely.

He smirks, his grip tightening and I hold back my squeak. "I have stuff to do as well. Try not to be too distracted thinking about me."

"That won't be a problem," I retort without thinking.

Wes leans his face closer to mine. I'm convinced he's about to kiss me, our lips barely grazing and I'm dying to close the distance, but his hand on the back of my neck prevents me from moving.

"Yeah, I'm sure I'll see you later."

He leaves me standing there, yet again. I want to stomp my foot and demand he stop doing that because it's a routine I'm not fond of. But I know it'll only make whatever punishment I'm sure he already wants to give me worse.

I storm off into my house and I swear I hear the sound of his deep laughter as I shut the door.

I DON'T THINK my house has ever been so clean. I manage to busy myself with every little thing I usually avoid. I could've gone down to the coffee shop and busied myself there as well, but I focused on my house. It's spotless and I'm pretty sure my counter just sparkled like they do in cartoons.

Glancing out the window, I see that the sun has set and I'm a little surprised Wes hasn't bothered me. I check my phone for any messages and see the only thing I've missed is from Sutton.

Sutton: I'm making Jameson have a boy's night when we get back so we can have a girls night.

Bailey: Are you already sick of your husband? That's not a good sign.

Sutton: Ha ha very funny. No, but I'm still as independent as ever which means I need space sometimes too.

Sutton: Plus I'm pretty sure Parker has blown up his phone daily with how much he misses Jameson.

Bailey: Sounds like someone else we know…

Sutton: Those two are really meant to be.

Sutton: Just like these two grumps I happen to know…

Bailey: I'm not a grump!

Sutton: I never said you. *side eye emoji*

Bailey: You and that damn emoji I swear.

Sutton: Think of something fun for us to do, I'll be home soon!

There's a loud noise outside, then another. The banging noise catches me off guard until I realize it's fireworks. I rack my mind, trying to figure out if today is a holiday. It's not, so why would anyone be setting off fireworks right now?

After another several bangs there's yelling and it's a voice I recognize instantly. Racing outside, I see Wes storming into the street yelling out for whoever is setting off the explosives.

"What the fuck is wrong with you! Get out of here you fucking cowards!" he screams, stomping around, trying to find the source while continuing to scream out.

I run up to him, placing my hand on his chest. "It's probably a bunch of kids messing around, it's okay."

He won't even look at me. His eyes are wide, and he grabs my wrist as he continues his mission.

"Show your faces, don't just hide. Come out and fucking face me!"

"Hey, hey, let's go inside, they'll stop."

He's still not looking at me. It's like he's not here at all. He's somewhere else completely and blind to anything other than finding whoever set off the fireworks.

There isn't another one for a couple of minutes, and I'm able to get Wes back into his house. He lets go of my wrist he was holding onto to run his hands through his hair. Gripping the strands as he continues to pace around.

Bruno is on alert, watching out the window and when another one goes off Wes looks up. He starts to go toward the door again, but I step in front of it and block his way.

"Move."

"No, you don't need to go out there and scream at no one."

"You don't get it, they can't do that."

"They shouldn't do that, but you screaming isn't going to help anything."

He clenches his jaw, and another one goes off. This time he lets out a frustrated yell then goes to the couch, dropping down, burying his head in his hands. His leg is bouncing while he pulls at his hair.

I dare to step toward him, though I worry it's a mistake, but when he lets me sit next to him on the couch, I get bolder. I place a tentative hand on his leg, rubbing softly and he still doesn't move, but his leg stops bouncing.

Continuing the movements, I listen to his harsh breathing, but as minutes go by and no more fireworks occur, his body seems to slowly relax. His hand drops down to mine, gripping it tightly.

I stare at our hands while he almost crushes my bones, but I don't care. The longer we sit here in silence, the more I hear his breathing even out. I watch the tension leave his body and as his eyes swing over to mine, I see the anguish there. The battle he fights alone and doesn't let anyone see.

What I see is a reflection of what I feel within myself. Strong on the outside while the inside struggles to continue day to day. I see what we both refuse to admit. And the second his eyes drop down to my lips, just for a moment, I feel like I know exactly what he wants.

And it's something I'll give him because I'll take the distraction with open arms. It's something we both want. What we both need.

His mouth descends on mine and I'm willing to get lost in him, if only for this one night.

CHAPTER 24

Wes

I FUCKING HATE FIREWORKS. No matter what I do, they take me back to a time in my life where my life was constantly in danger. The loud noise brings me back to the moment we were attacked. Where everything around me was exploding. The shock, the panic, the helplessness. It threatens to consume me and all because some people like to see bright lights in the sky for a couple of seconds.

It's easier when I know to expect them. For the Fourth of July and New Years I go rent a place in the middle of nowhere, equipped with my noise canceling headphones, music, and some of my favorite movies.

But when some shithead kids decide to set them off on a random day in October, there's no way I could've prepared for that, and my fight or flight kicks in instantly. I hardly realize Bailey is outside talking to me, my focus solely on finding the source of the sound and destroying it.

I'm blind to everything else around me. Even her.

It isn't until we're inside, and I sit down that I realize she's with me. I do everything I can to get my heart rate back to normal and my mind out of the dark place it goes.

When I feel the warm pressure of her hand on my leg, moving gently as she squeezes, I grab it with my own and it helps.

I don't know why or how it helps, but it does.

I expect her to leave now that I'm not fully freaking out. She has no reason to stay.

What I don't expect is when I manage to look over at her she's not looking at me with pity or fear. She's just looking at me.

And the craziest part is I feel like she's actually seeing *me*.

My eyes drop down to her mouth, her lips slightly parted, enticing me to feel them again. I've wanted to every minute since we first kissed. I've wanted to even longer than that, but she's so closed off that me being in control in other sexual situations with us felt easier.

But right now, I don't care about any of that. Right now, I just want to feel her lips on mine. I want to lose myself in her, and to forget about the reasons why my head is so fucked beyond repair. I just want to *feel*.

Without thinking anymore I dip my head down, capturing her lips with mine. She melts into me so easily, and I want more. I *need* more. When she opens up for me, I know she's willing to give it, and I'm going to savor every single thing she offers.

My fingers tangle in her hair as I push my tongue into her mouth, and she moans, grabbing a fistful of my shirt and pulling me closer. I go easily, but push even further, laying her down on the couch while hovering over her body without breaking our kiss.

When she parts her legs and I'm able to settle my hips between them. I groan as she lets out a soft gasp into my mouth at the feeling of my weight pressing her down.

I told her before we kissed for the first time I didn't think I would be able to stop, but I somehow managed. This time there's no stopping. This time, she'll need to say the word if she wants this to stop because I'm so completely out of my mind there's no way I'm letting up.

In this moment, I'm a man possessed, desperate for the little bit of a distraction the woman underneath me is willing to give.

Our tongues tangle while my mouth dominates hers. The moment her hips tilt up, seeking more friction, I can't hold myself back from feeling her any longer. I hastily undo her pants with one hand, flicking the button open easily and shoving underneath her panties to find her completely soaked already.

"Angel, if you're going to stop me at any point tonight tell me now, because with your pussy this wet I need to do something about it." I pant against her lips.

"I'm not going to stop you," she breathes, and that's all I need to hear, plunging a finger into her and she cries out against my mouth.

"Fuck, you're going to choke my cock in this sweet little cunt."

Bailey whimpers, bucking her hips up as I take her lips once again, thrusting my finger methodically. She grabs for my back, nails digging into my skin through the fabric of my shirt.

The feel of her fingers digging into me throws every thought of taking any of this slow out the window. I should keep touching her until she comes at least twice before I even consider putting my dick inside her, but I can't wait.

Not tonight.

Not with the way she feels, and not with the way my mind is still trying to drown me. I refuse to let it.

Instead of even bothering to shed the rest of our clothes, I sit up, reluctantly removing my hand from her pants. Bailey is breathing heavily, lips red and kiss bitten which only makes my already rock solid cock even harder.

"Take them off," I demand, already unbuttoning my pants, and pushing them down just enough. She lifts her hips to push her own down, and mine are just barely over my ass before I'm on her again.

I push her legs up so I can pull her pants the rest of the way off before I drop my hips down between her thighs again. This time there's nothing in the way as my length rubs through her, getting covered in her slick arousal.

"Wes," Bailey moans my name gently, and I practically lose it. The sound is so perfect coming from her, I need to hear it again, and again.

"What do you need, Angel?"

"I don't, I just want to feel you. Please."

I thrust forward, rubbing against her sensitive clit and she moans, her arms wrapping around the back of my neck trying to pull my mouth down to hers again. As I position the tip to her entrance, I keep my lips just out of reach, barely grazing when I realize something.

"Fuck. Condom," I grind out, worried that if I break this bubble we're in my thoughts will completely consume me. That she'll run away and I don't even want to think about what the aftermath of all of this would look like.

She shakes her head vehemently, panting, "Fuck the condom. I'm on birth control, I haven't been with anyone in–"

I don't let her finish before I'm thrusting in roughly, dropping my forehead to hers with a groan while she cries out. "Me either," I tell her, not specifying that it's been three years for me.

Three years since I was last inside a woman. Three years since the night I was last inside her.

I don't even care that our shirts are still on or that I can't feel all of her. My pants aren't even all the way off, the only thing that matters is that I'm actually having sex with Bailey Collee again.

She feels even better than I remember. I grit my teeth as I try not to blow too soon while she squeezes me so tightly I can hardly see straight.

She moans my name again, and I can't help but turn feral at the sound. The feeling of her around me is all too much and also not quite enough. I pull back and then push forward roughly.

"I want you to remember this the next time you get an attitude with me." I thrust again. "Remember how badly you wanted this." *Thrust.* "Remember how good I make you feel." *Thrust.* "Remember all of this."

She wraps herself around me as I keep up my punishing pace. I drop to my elbows by her head, framing her face and burying my hands in her hair.

"Look at me, Angel," I demand, not thinking too much about it.

Sex doesn't require eye contact for me. In fact, I generally prefer if it doesn't have it. But right now I want her emerald eyes locked on mine. I want to watch her face while she comes for me. That way when she wants to deny me tomorrow, to try and act like this never happened, I can remind her of this moment. I can remind her how present she was with me. Right here, right now.

As soon as she looks at me, the side of my mouth pulls up. "There you are," I practically whisper.

I angle my hips, and Bailey cries out at the change in sensation, but keeps her eyes on mine.

And when she moans my name softly, I almost come undone. "Wes, I'm so close."

"I know, Angel. Come for me, show me how good I make you feel."

She tightens around me, her moans becoming louder as I hit the perfect spot for her. I'm fighting to hold back my own release because I need her to get there. I need it more than my next breath.

"Give it up, Angel," I growl against her lips right before kissing her roughly as the orgasm racks through her body.

She's shaking, squeezing and crying out into my mouth while I fuck her through the release. I'm not far behind, with the way that every inch of her is holding me I can't hold it back anymore.

My orgasm takes over, and for a moment I realize I probably should have pulled out, but it's too late for that. Plus the possessive side of me that only shows up for her takes over knowing my cum is inside her.

We're both breathing heavily as we come down from our releases. I gently move her hair off her sweat slicked forehead. I feel like I should say something, but the words just get caught in my throat.

Instead of attempting to speak, I kiss her. Softer than before, our mouths brushing gently against each other's. Just feeling, no end goal. No fight. No back and forth. Just here right now, together where nothing else matters except this.

It may not last forever, but for right now, I'm going to make this last as long as possible.

CHAPTER 25

Bailey

I CAN'T MOVE, and it's not just because of the man currently crushing me. My body is so worn out, even the thought of moving makes my muscles shake. I've never come that hard. Never experienced...whatever that was. Because that wasn't just sex. No, sex is two people getting off and moving on.

This was something else entirely.

Wes raises himself off me, and I watch as he pulls up his pants. I expect him to leave again, but he doesn't. This time, he scoops me up in his arms and I gasp as he cradles me to his chest.

He says nothing as he carries me upstairs. The thought that he's taking me to his bed has me panicking, but when we go into the bathroom I feel like I can breathe normally again.

For a moment, at least. Because after he sets me down on the counter and reaches behind his head to pull off his shirt, he turns his back to me and turns on the water in the shower, and my mouth goes dry.

The last time we were in the shower together I ended up on my knees with his dick in my mouth, coated in his release and left there.

Not that I minded, but right now that's not what I want.

I refuse to admit the small vulnerability I feel as his cum seeps out of me or that I'm sore from what just occurred. My mind replays how he demanded I look at him. I couldn't have looked away if I wanted to, and that one small thing was so much more than it should've been.

I'm watching my feet dangle over the tile floor, noting that it's identical to mine back home. Our floor plans are the same, just reversed so being here almost feels like I'm home. *Almost.*

Wes's hands slide up my still bare legs, up my hips to my waist, pushing my shirt up as he goes. I raise my arms, letting him take the fabric off, and watch as he drops it on the floor. He undoes my bra, sliding it off my arms so I'm bare in front of him.

Instead of letting me walk to the shower, he picks me up, and he's completely naked as well. I notice his dick is already hardening, and I don't know if I'll survive if he wants to fuck me again.

But once we're under the water, his eyes don't even drift down my body. He squirts some shampoo in his hand, and starts working it in my hair. His fingers methodically working the soap through my strands. I can't help the moan I let out at how good it feels.

He rinses my hair before doing the same with the conditioner. Once that's rinsed he takes extra care in washing my whole body. Even when he moves the washcloth between my legs, and I moan at the feeling, he ignores his erection to continue washing and rinsing my skin.

After he's finished, he keeps me warm in the spray while quickly washing himself. I realize now neither of us have said anything, but it's like we don't have to. It's not an awkward silence, there's just nothing that needs to be said in this moment. Especially because I don't know where his head is, and mine is so jumbled I know I would butcher any sentence I try to put together.

We get out of the shower and he wraps me in a towel before he does the same for himself. I want to make a sassy retort about it, but I'm so sated and afraid of ruining this simple, easy bubble we've found ourselves in.

But it has to end.

I don't spend the night with anyone. I really don't sleep somewhere that isn't my bed. The simple comfort that I struggle to fall asleep in anyway. Someone else's bed with another human? Not happening.

"Wait here," he grunts out, and I do, watching him leave the bathroom. I'm convinced he's not going to come back, which is fine by me. I pull on my shirt, foregoing my bra. I look around because there's no way I'm walking back over to my house without pants.

Wes comes back with said pants in his hand, and I give a small, grateful smile before pulling them on.

"Well, I should go," I tell him, realizing how awkward I sound. *Thanks for a solid dicking, gotta go.*

"I'm walking you home," he insists.

"It's next door, I think I'll survive."

"I'm walking you home," he says again, his tone more firm this time.

I snap my jaw shut so hard my teeth click, and I know there's no arguing with him about this. He steps into his room, pulling on some shorts and a shirt quickly.

The silence continues as we walk the twenty feet to my front door.

"All safe and sound," I joke.

Wes nods toward the door, and I furrow my brow. "You're not coming in."

"Yes I am, but I'm not staying."

I want to argue, but sigh when I realize there's no use.

He follows me inside, leads me up to my room with a hand on my back and the silence is back.

"Get ready for bed," he instructs gruffly, folding his arms across his chest.

It feels a lot like I'm being scrutinized while trying to get into pajamas. After I'm dressed, I turn back toward Wes and ask, "Happy?"

"Get into bed." He sounds so serious, almost like he's mad, but I know it's just him.

Again, I want to argue, though something stops me. I climb into bed, and Wes is right there. He does the last thing I ever expected he would be capable of. Especially after the night that started with him racing into the street screaming at people we couldn't find.

He tucks me into bed, leans over and presses a kiss to my forehead. "Goodnight. I'll make sure your door is locked."

And he's gone. I watch his back as he leaves, turning my light off and shutting my door on his way out. I expect to hear his car rev up so he can leave, but he doesn't. Instead the light in his bedroom turns on, and I look over, seeing his shadow for a few minutes before the light goes out.

I swear before I lose sight of him he stands there looking at me. Somehow, my eyelids feel heavy and I hardly notice when I finally fall asleep because I didn't need to toss and turn for it to happen.

I'll thank the orgasm, but refuse to give any credit to the man that made it happen. If I do that, things will have officially shifted, and I'm not going to admit that.

I can't. Things have to stay the same for my sanity to remain intact.

* * *

"What has two thumbs and is in complete denial over a guy?" Lily asks over FaceTime. Sutton and I are sitting on my couch and she demanded to be included in our girls night.

"Uh...you?" I offer.

"Nope, I actually started seeing someone if you both must know." She turns her head to the side with a smug grin.

"You did?" we both say at the same time, equally as shocked.

"Yup."

"What's his name? Who is he?" Sutton rapid fires her questions while I just sit back and enjoy that for the time being they aren't going to hound me about Wes.

"Name is Aaron, he's super nice and hot and most importantly, *not Parker.*"

"Mhm," Sutton says while I just shake my head.

"You guys should be happy for me, that's what friends do," Lily insists.

"We are, as long as you're happy," Sutton tells her.

"I am. He's graduating this year too, going to be an architect."

"And what about you? Have you decided what you're going to do after graduation?" I question.

"Well, way to bring down the room, Bails." She throws her hands up, exasperated.

"By asking what you're going to do?" I furrow my brow, confused how my question was a problem to her.

"Yes, that's the type of negativity that's not needed here. You can make it up to me by telling me about what has happened with Wes."

"Do you have cameras watching me or something?" I glance around my house because I'm starting to think her sources are herself and she has some spy equipment on me.

"That was a trap! Aha, so something *has* happened*!*"

Sutton leans to the side so she can give me a raised eyebrow look.

"I just wanted to have a nice calm girls night. I didn't think it would include getting the third degree from you two," I grumble.

"That's what a girls night *is*, silly." Lily chuckles. "We share all our secrets and give each other advice."

I huff out a breath, not really wanting to get into the Wes stuff when my mind still hasn't caught up on all of it. I don't think I could talk about it even if I tried right now.

"Sutton, anything to share or need advice on?" I ask.

She shakes her head. "Not really, everything is pretty good right now for me."

"Well *good* for *you*," Lily jokes sarcastically. "I shared about my new beau, so I guess that only leaves you, Bails."

"Still not my name," I grumble.

They both look at me, and I avoid their gazes as best I can, but the feeling of their eyes burning into me is bound to make me break. Instead of giving them the full story, I decide to give them just enough so they will leave me alone for now.

"I saw Wes at the bar when I went there for line dancing. We danced, came home. Nothing happened." The lie feels bitter on my tongue because *a lot* happened.

"Nothing happened? Not even a smooch?" Lily clearly doesn't believe me. She shouldn't.

"Not even a smooch." I don't know what pains me more, saying that word or lying about it happening.

"Well that's boring," she huffs.

"Guess I'm just a boring person." I shrug, hoping she'll let it go. When I look at Sutton, she's giving me a look that says she doesn't believe me, but Lily has already moved on and is talking about something she saw at school that I think included a chicken crossing the road. No, it's not even the punch line of a joke.

CHAPTER 26

Wes

I DON'T NEED to help out at Jameson's property now that he's back, but it's a part of my routine. He comes out while I'm finishing up with the horses, and I nod at him in greeting.

"How'd it go around here?" he asks.

"Good, no one gave me too much trouble." *No one here, anyway.*

"That's good, I know Juniper can be such a troublemaker," he jokes.

"Oh yeah, they all can be such a problem," I deadpan.

"Are you doing anything later? Dave and Parker are coming over because Sutton insists I have a 'guy's night.'"

"Uh, no I don't have plans, but you enjoy."

"Come on over, if you're free. I think the girls are going to

Bailey's house, so unless you want to hear them, you may be safer over here."

Part of me would love to hear them, just so I can know if Bailey says anything to her friends about what happened between us. If she lets anything slip out about how it felt for her. If it made her feel like everything has changed, like it has for me.

Though, I don't know what to do about it since I don't know where her head is. These feelings are entirely new territory for me. My initial instinct is to do what I always do. Avoid them completely.

Not avoid Bailey, because I've tried that before and we ended up here.

Avoiding feelings, that I'm practically a professional at.

"Maybe," I tell him.

"Just come by later if you decide to join." Jameson shrugs. I like that he's not too pushy. There's been plenty of times I've been here while he's working with the horses and he never pushes conversations, just lets me be if I want to be left alone.

As he walks away, I think of one thing that may affect my decision. "Can Bruno come?"

"Of course," he answers without even turning around.

I DECIDED to join Jameson's guy's night because the distraction sounds useful. Knowing Bailey is just next door and that I can't interrupt her time with her friends only cemented my decision.

As soon as I get to Jameson's house I see that his coworkers are already there. Being surrounded by guys I don't know very well makes me slightly uncomfortable, though I do everything I can to push past it.

The beer in my hand is helping just a little bit as I try to be somewhat social. Which for me is saying a couple words here and there in a conversation I really don't have much to contribute to.

Dave, Parker, and Jameson all work together so a lot of what they talk about has to do with firefighting which I know very little about. I did consider going into a first responder field after my life was derailed, but never followed through with any of the training.

"How was it holding down the fort here while Jameson was gone?" Parker asks me, and I shrug.

"Fine."

"Ma didn't bother you too much?" Jameson asks, and I shake my head.

"You missed a good call last night. Some shithead kids set off fireworks and one ended up in a tree," Dave says, changing the subject.

I try to cover my reaction at the mention of the fireworks. And what happened afterwards. I try not to think about how weak it made me look. What Bailey must have been thinking seeing me so out of control. I hate that I can't control my reactions to certain things.

"I think it was actually pretty close to your house, did you hear them?" Parker asks.

"Yeah, hard to miss. They were fucking loud," I grunt, taking a swig of my beer.

"How'd Bruno handle them?" Jameson asks, nodding his head to the dog curled up at my feet. He still hasn't warmed up to being in a space with these unfamiliar people, or the two other dogs quite yet.

"He hid," I answer, not wanting to talk about the way *I* handled them.

"I never understood the point of fireworks." Parker shakes his head. "They look cool I guess, but they are so dangerous. It's stupid."

"Not to mention dogs and veterans can struggle with the sounds," Dave says offhandedly, and my spine stiffens.

Luckily, no one asks me specifically about it. I catch Jameson looking at me, gauging the reaction I try to hide. Everyone moves on from the firework subject, and I try to stay engaged, but as the night goes on it gets harder and harder because all I'm doing is wondering about Bailey.

What's she doing with her friends? Are they having fun? What are they talking about? Will she be awake when I get back home? My mind is a constant rotation of *her*.

"Bet you can't wait for Lily to come back when she's done with school," Dave teases Parker.

The youngest guy scoffs, taking a big swig from his drink. "She's got some boyfriend I guess."

"How'd you find that out?" Jameson asks.

"She told me."

"She told you?" Jameson doesn't sound convinced and I feel like I'm missing something yet again. I know I'm an outsider, especially in their group, but this subject has me feeling like I'm missing crucial information.

"Yeah, she told me. Texted me to not talk to her because she's got a boyfriend and to leave her alone," Parker grumbles.

"Did you reach out to her first?" Dave raises his eyebrow.

"Does it matter?" Parker questions in a tone that tells me he most definitely did.

But I don't care about this juvenile drama. Right now all I want is to go back home, and be alone.

There's only one other person I would tolerate the presence of, but I have no idea if she feels the same.

◦

I DON'T SPEND TOO much time at Jameson's before making an excuse to go back home. Once I'm pulling into my driveway I see the other car still at Bailey's so any attempt at taking her goes out the window.

Even though I know it's going to be difficult to go to sleep, I'm going to try. My mind is tired from the socialization. Things like that take it out of me more than a workout does to my muscles. That, I can push through, being around people and needing to think about how to talk to them, hold a conversation, and be *personable*? That takes effort, and it's something I'd rather avoid if I can.

I look over into Bailey's room from my window, but it's dark, and I'm sure she's downstairs with Sutton.

Bruno jumps onto the bed, and makes himself comfortable at the end of it. He rests his head on his paws while I strip down to my boxers to climb under the covers and attempt to get some sleep.

As soon as my head hits the pillow I know it's going to be a futile attempt, but still I close my eyes and try to picture things that may help. Peaceful things.

Sunflowers.

I don't know why that's what comes to me, but it is. A field of sunflowers, and ahead of me is long dark blonde wavy hair bouncing as someone walks ahead of me. I start to walk closer, to see her. To confirm it's who I think it is.

The flowers surround us, blowing in the wind. As I get closer she turns to look over her shoulder and gives me the softest smile. I need to get to her, I want to feel her in my arms.

I speed up my steps, but before I'm able to reach her there's a familiar whirring sound of a helicopter. I look up and around trying to find the source of it. Bailey is still ahead of me, and she's getting further and further away.

The source of the noise makes itself known as the machine falls from the sky. I cry out for Bailey, but she's running right in the direction it's falling. I call out her name again, racing toward her but it's coming down so fast and I feel like I'm running through sludge.

The helicopter hits the ground in a fiery explosion and I scream out one more time, but this time it's real.

My throat is sore, I'm covered in sweat and breathing heavily as I look around the dark room.

It isn't real.

None of that was real.

But it's exactly what happens in my mind when I try to find peace within it to go to sleep.

Bruno's sitting up looking at me.

"It's okay," I tell him, trying to convince us both.

I scrub my hand down my face, and look over at Bailey's window though it's still dark. I'm not sure how late it is, and I don't care to look.

I know the chances of me falling asleep again are slim to none. That's why I resort to my oldest and best coping mechanism I've yet to find. Pulling my clothes on, I grab my keys and tell Bruno I'll be back.

When I get outside I see the Jeep that was at Bailey's house is gone and her whole house is dark like she's asleep. I debate for just a minute, then say fuck it. I need to check and make sure she's okay.

Rationally, I know my mind made up what I saw, but part of

it still feels real and that's the excuse I give myself as to why I bang on her front door harder than necessary. It takes her a moment to open it, and when she does, she looks pissed.

"What do you want?" She folds her arms across her chest. I can't help but notice she's changed into sleepwear and isn't wearing a bra.

"I just wanted to make sure you're okay," I grunt, not wanting to explain further than that.

Her eyes drop to my hand where my keys are. "Where are you going?"

"Where I always go in the middle of the night," I tell her, *really* not wanting to explain.

She raises an eyebrow, and tilts her head to the side. "And where is that?"

I debate just walking away, I don't need to tell her. Instead, I look down at my keys, shifting them between my fingers to hear the small chime. Then I do something I never thought I would.

"Want to come with me?"

CHAPTER 27

Bailey

"TO SEE whoever it is you meet up with for your midnight booty calls? I'll pass." I go to shut the door in his face, but he stops it with a strong hand.

"I thought we established there aren't any booty calls," he tells me darkly and I can see that comment irritated him. "Come with me and I'll show you."

I hesitate, looking down at what I'm wearing. My oversized T-shirt and boy shorts aren't exactly attire to leave the house in.

"Fine, let me change."

"Nope, no need." He grabs my hand and pulls me outside.

"Hold on, I at least need my keys." I try to pry my hand away from his, and he lets go reluctantly.

I grab my keys off the hook by the door, slip on some shoes before joining Wes on my porch again. I almost run upstairs to change, but for this one moment I'm going to trust him when he says I don't need to.

It's cold out tonight, and goosebumps cover my legs during the short walk to Wes's car. I climb inside, but he doesn't get in right away. I look around, seeing he's at the trunk grabbing something. Then my door is open and a thick piece of fabric is thrown onto my lap.

"Wha—" I ask, but he's shutting the door again. "Jerk," I mumble under my breath.

He climbs into the driver's seat and I have to appreciate this giant of a man in this sports car. It's different when the engine roars to life. Normally the loud sound irritates me, but as I'm sitting in the passenger seat there's something about it that feels... sensual.

The noise hardly registers, it's the way the seat vibrates with the power from the engine. I distract myself by looking at what Wes threw on me, and see that it's one of his hoodies. I drape it over myself to stay warm, but also to hide my legs and the way I'm pressing them together tightly.

He turns the heat on, but it doesn't kick on right away as he pulls out onto our street. Music starts to play from his phone, and he turns it up so loud we couldn't hear each other if we tried to have a conversation.

Which is fine by me, I don't need to have a conversation with him right now. I bring his hoodie up to my chin, and for once in my life, just go along for the ride.

I don't know where we're going or how long we'll be gone, but after several minutes I roll my head over to look at Wes. He has one arm on the steering wheel, the other resting on his thigh. His focus is purely on the road in front of us, but the hard lines that are normally on his face are softer. He's focused, but not intensely so.

He's always so serious, so intimidating when you first look at him, but right now part of that is gone. *He* looks softer, more at ease.

It's weird.

It makes me want to ruffle his feathers a bit. I'm caught between enjoying the peace we've found ourselves in for once, and annoying him so he threatens me with more punishments.

The longer we drive, the more the rumble from the engine causes my arousal to increase despite my efforts to tamp it down. I can't tell if it's from the vibration of the engine through the seat or the company that's causing my little problem. I've never felt turned on as easily as I am right now.

I haven't even been *touched* and I feel like this. Add in the fact that Wes and I slept together just yesterday. I've always enjoyed sex, it's a stress reliever, a way to get out of my head, a fun time. But I've never needed it like *this*. The fact that a car that's only irritated me up to this point, and the man driving being the cause of my raging hormones has me confused and concerned.

He reaches up to turn the music down. I watch the veins in his hand with the simple action, and have to squeeze my legs together even tighter. It makes me want to slap myself.

"You okay?" he asks gruffly.

"Yeah, why?"

"You just seem off." He still isn't looking at me. I narrow my eyes at him, not appreciating the fact that he's able to read me without even making eye contact.

"Well I was dragged out of my house in the middle of the night to apparently drive to nowhere," I deadpan.

"Driving nowhere is the best part."

"Is that really what you do? You don't go anywhere?"

He shrugs.

"Why? What's the point other than literally burning gas?"

He doesn't respond right away. I watch the way his hand tightens on the steering wheel and he clenches his jaw. "It keeps my mind occupied."

I think about that, how many times I wish my mind could be occupied and the ways I've tried to do that. Driving around has never been on that list because if I'm driving then I have a destination in mind.

Against my better judgment I ask, "Why do you need your mind occupied?"

He tightens his hand on the steering wheel again, his knuckles turn white. I'm worried my question overstepped whatever line in the sand we've drawn. Maybe it has, and he can take me home and forget about all of this.

Go back to how things were before. If that's even possible.

"Sometimes I struggle to sleep, too," I mumble softly.

"And why's that?" he asks, though I feel the same way he seems to about my question.

"I asked you first."

Silence surrounds us again, it seems to be a common theme when we're alone, which is happening a lot more often lately. He doesn't even move to turn up the music, and instead of answering my question he changes the subject.

"Would you want to drive?"

I rear back. "Your fancy shmancy car? So I can fuck something up on it and you blame me? No thanks."

"You wouldn't fuck something up on it."

I give him a disbelieving look, and he actually glances over at me, the smallest smile appearing on his mouth.

He ends up pulling over on the shoulder. "Come over here."

I look around, it's pitch black but we're very much out in the open. "Uh, no."

"I didn't ask, Angel. Come over here."

I look at him, then the steering wheel and the small space between them. "Wes, no."

"I'm not asking. Come over here, or I'll *put* you over here."

I bite my bottom lip and sigh. Unbuckling the seatbelt, I open the door because even if he thinks the two of us are about to fit in that seat together there's no chance my long ass legs are fitting over the middle console.

I stand outside the driver's side door, and wait. He opens it, and pats his lap, "Here's your seat."

"You're insane."

"Probably. But you're going to steer, and I'm going to work the pedals."

"You're *really* insane."

"Then join me in my insanity, Angel."

With a long drawn out breath I give in, climbing onto his lap. It's an extremely tight fit between his large body and the steering wheel. My head is grazing the top of the roof, and I don't know how he expects this to work. I swivel my hips, making him grunt which makes me smirk.

I turn my head to the side, and ask with a smug smile, "There a problem?"

He grabs my hip and has me move against him once again. I let out a squeak, feeling his hardening length under me. Which doesn't help the way I've already been feeling from the vibrations in this stupid car.

"There a problem?" he repeats my question back to me and I scowl even though he can't see me. "How about we get a little more insane?"

"Not sure how that's possible," I retort.

He hums, moving his hand from my hip toward the inside of my thigh, and I slap my hand over his. "What're you doing?"

"Are you going to stop me or are you going to let me continue?"

I open and shut my mouth wanting to say something about wanting to know *what exactly* he's wanting to continue. But when I don't say anything he slips his hand lower, up the inside of my thigh, under my shorts, grazing over the thin fabric covering my center. I can tell when he feels the dampness there because his chest rumbles in approval.

He runs the pad of his finger along my fabric covered seam and I drop my head back to his shoulder with a small moan.

"What'll it be, Angel?"

"Hm?" I hum, too busy getting lost in the sensations to think of any real response.

"Are you going to stop me, or let me continue?" he repeats, and I'm still too distracted by what his hand is doing, the simple act of rubbing me through my underwear.

He pauses and I want to scream, but he keeps a steady pressure with his hand pressed completely against me.

"Which will it be?" he demands, rougher this time. I squirm, trying to get him to move more, but he holds me firmly in place.

"Continue," I breathe out finally.

His hand finally moves again, this time he pulls my underwear to the side, and plunges a finger in. I buck against him, but the small space limits both our movements and I don't know if I'm going to be able to handle it like this.

"Wes," I moan breathily, reaching behind me to tangle my fingers in the hair on the back of his head.

"What is it, Angel?"

"I want more." I don't even think about what I'm saying. The words just fly out like I don't have control over them.

He lets out a soft chuckle, and then takes his hand away and I want to grab and force it back into me. But I'm not able to because he's pushing me forward so my chest collides with the steering wheel, and I hear clothes rustling.

"What're you doing?" I ask, panting while trying not to accidentally hit the horn.

He doesn't answer, instead I feel cool air on my backside as he pulls my shorts down over my ass. I squeal and try to get away, but there's no room for me to go anywhere. Wes pulls me back down, and I feel his bare cock against my ass. I have to bite my bottom lip to stifle my reaction. Though, I think trying to hide how I'm feeling is a moot point considering he just felt how wet I already am.

"Keep your hands at ten and two," he says casually, placing them there for me. I swing my head back to look at him, but he lets go of one of my hands to guide my face forward by my chin. "Always keep your eyes on the road."

"Wes, I'm not steering the car like this."

He shuffles underneath me, and I feel the tip of his dick press against my opening and my jaw drops in a gasp.

"No, you're not," he grinds out, pushing just barely so his tip is notched inside me. "You're going to drive the car while riding my cock just like this."

He pushes in a little more and I can't help but tighten around him.

"Don't bother acting like you don't love the way that sounds. I can feel how wet your pussy is for me."

"There's no way I'm going to be able to see straight," I moan.

"Well you better try, because you're the one in control. I just handle the speed." He pushes all the way in, burying himself completely. For some reason I feel like his words have double meaning, but I'm too distracted to read anything into it.

He adjusts his legs, presses the gas so the car engine revs. My hips move involuntarily, causing him to rub a particularly sensitive spot in my inner walls.

His foot moves over to the brake, and his hand to the gearshift. I'm white knuckling the steering wheel trying to not let my eyes cross from the pressure he's causing between my legs.

"Ready?" he asks.

"Not even a little bit."

Clearly my words don't hold enough weight because he's shifting the car and just trusting that as he hits the gas I'm going to be able to steer us back onto the road.

I'm caught between my need to fuck Wes and not kill us. I overcorrect the wheel as we pull out onto the street and luckily the road is completely deserted. Wes doesn't go slow, his foot stays on the gas driving just as fast as when he was the one steering.

This is completely insane.

Just when I feel like I'm able to block out the fact that I'm currently impaled on Wes's dick, he thrusts up and reminds me he's there. That causes me to turn the wheel too much and the car swerves.

"Don't do that, I have our lives in my hands," I say through heavy breaths.

"Don't do what? This?" He thrusts up again, and I cry out this time, doing everything I can to keep a strong grip on the wheel.

His foot presses harder on the gas; I watch the needle climb upward on the speedometer.

"How does it feel, Angel?" He groans, gripping my hips and guiding them forward and back.

"*So good*," I moan, starting to really struggle with keeping the car straight. "Wes, I don't know if I can keep this up."

"Yeah you can. Look at you driving my car while sitting on my cock, making you feel *so fucking good.*"

"*Please*," I plead, not even sure what I'm asking for. More, less, to not end up with this car wrapped around a pole or driving off a cliff.

"Look at you saying please," he coos. "Not being so much of a brat now, are you? Is this all it takes to get you to behave?"

I don't know what to say, all I can do is feel, and try to focus. I'm not doing a very good job because the car swerves again when Wes thrusts up and I feel the telltale signs of an orgasm.

"Please let me pull over," I beg, wanting to not risk our safety for the sake of release. Even though right now, as I squeeze and moan, I'm starting to care less and less about safety and am more focused on finding the peak of orgasm.

Instead of listening to me he speeds up even more. I cry out his name, feeling tears starting to form while I begin to shake. The threat of release so close.

"Hold it," he demands through gritted teeth.

I whimper, not sure if I can, but he lets the car slow down, and I turn the wheel to pull us off the road. As soon as he puts the car in park, I let out a loud moan of relief at the fact that we aren't about to die because I'm too blind from pleasure to control the car.

Wes lifts me off his lap, lightly tossing me over onto the passenger seat. My legs are draped over the middle console. I open my mouth to complain, but he's stepping out of the car. I stay frozen in the seat, watching him walk around the front with his pants barely hanging up on his hips.

He opens the passenger door, easily lifting me out, carrying me to the hood where he lays me down. The hot metal stings against my skin, but it hardly bothers me because Wes is immediately dropping down to his knees on the gravel, pulling my shorts off, and latching his mouth onto me.

I cry out, my back arching as he licks me, bringing me right back to the brink of the orgasm he stopped just a minute ago. My hands find the hair on the top of his head, yanking him harder against me.

He lets out a groan that sends a vibration through me. I moan his name loudly, not caring where we are or who could potentially be around. I don't care.

"That's it, Angel, come for me." I do what he says, detonating against his mouth.

I'm coming so violently I hardly notice him standing up, and slamming inside me once again, causing my release to explode even harder around him.

"Fuck yeah, that's what I wanted," he groans.

I grapple for him. Grabbing the back of his shirt, digging my nails into his skin as he fucks me brutally against the hood of his car. I swear it feels like my orgasm doesn't even end with the way he's hitting all the right spots.

Wes groans, dropping his lips onto mine, kissing me while he finds his own release. Even as we both come back down to Earth he doesn't stop kissing me. The worst part is, I don't want him to.

CHAPTER 28

Wes

I DRIVE US BACK HOME, and while there's a tiny part of me that wants to have Bailey in my bed for the rest of the night, I know I can't. Once our fun is over, we go our separate ways and that's just how it has to be. I don't sleep well, and even when I do the nightmares plague me. I know I can yell and thrash around and it wouldn't be safe for her. That's why I never share a bed with another person.

Add in the fact that I don't think she would even *want* to stay the night with me. What we just did is where our interactions end.

Even as I take my time driving through the winding roads, I notice the way she rests her head on the window and I swear I see her eyes close. I dare to reach my hand over and rest it on her thigh and she doesn't react right away.

I move my fingers lightly and she lets out the softest hum.

Surprisingly, her hand rests on top of mine and my shoulders drop for the first time in a very long time. There's a sense of peace and relaxation in the car that I don't want to end. But I know it has to as I pull into my driveway, and cut the engine.

Everything is quieter with the car off. It's like the calm world we found ourselves in has come to an end and we're back to reality.

Bailey doesn't move right away and I'm tempted to let her sleep in here. I'd sit here to make sure she's okay, but after a couple of seconds she raises her head, looks over at me, then realizes where we are.

"Guess you don't really go anywhere do you?" Her voice is groggy, and I swear I see the smallest smile grace her lips.

I shake my head.

"You just kidnap unsuspecting women to drive around?" she jokes.

"Something like that." I attempt to joke back, but my tone is more serious than I intend. "I'll walk you inside."

I get out of the car, my long strides get me to her side as she opens the door. I reach down, stretching my hand out toward her. I catch the way she looks up at me with a contemplative glare.

She slips her hand into mine hesitantly, and I help her stand up from the low vehicle. We're both so tall, it makes my car seem even shorter. I know she can do it, and maybe I just wanted another excuse to feel her skin against mine.

Especially since we've now fucked twice and both times has been so abrupt, and feral that we haven't gotten to shed all of our clothes.

Plus this time was a little public. Not that it would have stopped me from ripping every inch of fabric from her body.

I don't let go of her hand as we approach her door, and she doesn't move to let go either. She doesn't even question when I follow her inside and up to her room again. Even if we can't spend the night together I'm still going to do the same thing I did last time.

Make sure she's safe and comfortable in her bed, then leave.

Before she lays down, I step over to her dresser and pull out a new pair of underwear because even though she put her other pair on, I'm sure they aren't comfortable from the mix of our cum.

I do everything I can to tamp down the feelings bubbling up in my chest knowing I'm the reason she now has to change. Trying to will my dick to go down because she's tired and I don't need to push.

Bailey is sitting on the edge of her bed. I approach, hiding my wince as I kneel down onto the soft floor in front of her.

"Stand," I command softly, and to my surprise, she actually does it.

Gently, I pull down her shorts and underwear. The second I see the wetness I caused, I bite back a groan as she steps out of them. I toss the clothes over to her hamper in the corner, and guide her feet into the new pair.

I pull them up, grazing my fingers along her skin as I reach her hips once again. I keep my hands on her as I stand up, moving them up and over her hips then the dip of her waist as I rise to my full height. Our chests barely touch as she looks up at me, wide eyes, waiting.

"Get into bed," I tell her, and again she listens without a retort.

Her back is to me as she pulls back her covers and climbs into the large bed. I'm tempted to crawl into it with her. To see what it would feel like to pull her body against mine, feel the way her steady breathing evens out as she falls asleep. Maybe it would be enough to quiet the chaos just long enough for sleep to finally find me.

But the risk of my nightmares is too strong. I don't think I would hurt her, but I'm not exactly in control in those moments. I know I could, and that's not something I'm willing to risk.

Once I pull the blanket over her, I lean down pressing a kiss to her forehead. "Goodnight, Angel."

"Goodnight, Wes," she practically whispers.

I turn around and leave before I throw all caution to the wind and see what she'd do if I got into her bed with her.

When I get to my house after making sure Bailey's front door is locked, Bruno is laying on the couch with his head between his paws looking at me. He gives a single wag of his tail. And I feel like it's his way of reassuring me that everything is okay.

* * *

SINCE I'VE HARDLY GONE to the animal shelter while I've been busy helping at Jameson's property I decide to make an appearance, check in on the dogs, and see if there's been any interest in

Bruno. I worry about him getting too attached to my house and me if he's not going to stay.

I just know there's a better family out there for him. A family that doesn't wake him up in the middle of the night from nightmares. Someone that doesn't have to leave for hours on end just to drive around. He should have a family with kids to play with. Or someone at home to give him endless attention.

"Good morning, Wes," Gloria greets cheerfully as soon as I walk in.

I nod. "Morning. Any news on Bruno?"

"Why? Is there a problem with him?"

"No, he's fine, I just want to make sure he gets the best home."

"I know he will." She smiles widely. "Oh, that Lab from the last time you were here, Maverick? He did have a home. We were able to get ahold of them and reunite them."

"That's great," I surmise.

"It is. We do have some more dogs that I'm sure would love some extra attention."

"I have all day," I tell her honestly.

"Perfect."

I end up catching the eye of an extremely excitable Border Collie. He practically takes me for the walk along the path and doesn't even mind being put back in the sad kennel. There's another dog that reminds me of Bruno with the way she's laying on the dog cot. I look at her kennel tag and see her name is Sadie. She looks like some sort of Golden Retriever mix with more light golden fur.

I don't think twice about grabbing one of the thin leashes and opening up the door, offering a walk. She perks up a little, and walks toward me so I can pet her head then slip the lead around her before walking out.

She's a lot calmer than the Border Collie. It's nice to not feel like I'm being dragged around, and can enjoy the cool fall weather.

My phone goes off in my pocket, and I pull it out expecting to see something from Bailey, or worse, the group chat Jameson added me to with Dave and Parker.

I don't expect to see it's Chris once again, and the message catches me off guard a bit.

> Chris: Ever wish it was us that went down with the rest of them?

I stare at the screen, but Sadie doesn't try to pull me anywhere. I read the words over and over, unsure of what to say.

Honestly, yeah, I do. The amount of times I've wanted to scream about how I should've been one of the people to die is countless. Why was it them? They had families, people that loved and cared about them. I didn't and still don't have anyone, yet for some reason I got to walk away with a fucked up leg and endless nightmares.

But I feel like admitting that to Chris isn't the smartest decision. I don't know where this is coming from or why, but there must be a reason.

Wes: Why?

Chris: Because I do. A lot. I'm fucked up as it is. Should've taken me out of my misery before it had the chance to get this bad.

Again, I'm frozen just staring at the screen. He wasn't like this when we worked together; he had hopes and dreams and so much going for him. Even now, I thought he had a wife and child. He's always seemed happy other times I've talked to him, but this feels out of left field.

Wes: You talk to anyone? Like a therapist at the VA or anything?

Chris: I have. Doesn't seem like they give a fuck though since I can't get an appointment for awhile.

I can't say I disagree. I tried therapy briefly and that shit isn't for me. I'm fine and don't need someone trying to poke around in my head for shit neither of us can change.

Wes: I get that. Do you have anyone to talk to? Your wife?

Chris: Fucking left me about a year ago now, couldn't handle my "issues" she said.

I scrub my hand down my face with a subtle, "fuck."

Wes: I'm sorry. Do you need anything? What can I do?

Chris: Nah, I don't think there's anything anyone can do.

I don't know what to say to that. We may have walked in similar shoes with our experience from that horrible day, but I can't say I understand what he's feeling now since that's not something I've been through.

Wes: I'm here if you need me.

It's the only thing I can think of to say, but when he doesn't respond right away I tuck my phone back in my pocket. The nagging feeling in the back of my mind is telling me I should somehow do more. I just don't know what.

CHAPTER 29

Bailey

"SHUT UP, VERN!" Jerry Lee calls out as soon as I enter the grooming salon to bring Sutton the coffee she requested.

As soon as she sees me she lets out a loud groan, and reaches out for the cup. "Thank you so much. I owe you my life. Seriously."

I shake my head. "No you don't, but you are making me question if we should offer delivery."

"That's not a bad idea, actually." She raises her eyebrows over her cup and takes a healthy sip. "You need to get a dog for me to groom so we can make it even."

I chuckle. "I don't know about that."

"Why not? It's a built-in best friend. Bennet is always there for me and it's the best. He could use another friend, too."

"Duke not enough for him? And what about Bruno?"

"He wants even more friends, he told me."

"Did he? With his voice? That he definitely has?" I narrow my eyes even more at each question.

"Listen, you would understand if you had a dog."

I've never really considered getting a pet, but something about the way she's enticing me does make me consider it. I think about the way Bruno comes up to me and sits there. I think about how happy Jameson and Sutton seem when watching their dogs play.

"I'll think about it," I tell her honestly.

"Good. Oh, also I was going to ask you about Thanksgiving."

I look around trying to check for a calendar because I'm pretty sure I must be missing a chunk of time if we're talking about Thanksgiving. Last I checked it was the middle of October.

"Uh, what about Thanksgiving?" I ask.

"Do you have any plans for it? Going to see any family or anything?"

Immediately I shake my head, vehemently. "No, most definitely not."

"Would you want to come to our house? Last year we really didn't do anything because it wasn't long after...you know," she whispers, referencing the sudden passing of her father in law. "I want to make this year better, and hope to have a full table. I know Emily will love that."

"And by having a full table you mean you'll be inviting..." My voice trails off because she knows exactly who I'm talking about.

"You've been getting along with him lately, don't even try to hide it." She smirks.

"What? Do you have *sources* too?" I roll my eyes.

"Of course I do." She smiles. "Everyone in town knew my business when it came to Jameson last year, so it's only fair."

"That wasn't my fault," I mumble.

"So will you come?"

I groan. "Maybe. I don't really do groups of people. You're lucky I even went to your wedding."

"I know deep *deep* down you care for me."

"*Jizz! Bitch!*"

Sutton groans, and I bite back a laugh.

"Jerry Lee, Lily hasn't even been here."

"It's amazing how she's able to teach him those words so easily." I shake my head.

"I swear he just has to hear it one time and then chooses the worst things to repeat."

"*Hot guy, Jameson.*"

Sutton gives me a look like she's silently saying, "*see?*"

"Well, I'll leave you with your friend so I can get back to work that doesn't have a Jerry Lee."

"Want one?" she asks excitedly and I shake my head again.

"No, you can keep that one. I'd rather get a dog."

"And you should. Maybe Wes can go with you, doesn't he volunteer at the animal shelter?"

"Does he?" I question.

"Yeah, that's how he got Bruno. Does he still think he's not keeping that dog?"

"I think so." I shrug, and I don't miss the look she gives me that has my eyes rolling. "Goodbye."

I walk out with Sutton's laughter following me and get back to work where I'm not hounded about my neighbor. It's nice because Jenn clearly doesn't have the sources like Sutton supposedly does.

Which makes me pretty sure I know *who* her source is. Jameson's mom is a sweet woman, and since she knows all of us, I wouldn't be surprised if it was her.

•

AFTER CLOSING up for the day, a nap is calling my name. My body is exhausted, even though my night with Wes was a few days ago. The next day, I woke up sore, but not in an uncomfortable way. It was an *I want more* way.

After that night, I've busied myself with work, and he's been doing whatever it is he does so we haven't crossed paths. Every night I expect him to show up at my door, but he doesn't. I'm starting to become concerned with how badly I'm anticipating it...and maybe wanting it.

I guess it makes sense that Wes volunteers at the animal shelter. I know he helps Jameson, and doesn't have a job. Though, I also thought when he would leave at night he had a destination in mind. Someone to see, something to do, but it turns out that he just drives.

Of course with me, we ended up doing a bit more than just that. The adrenaline that ran through me was unlike anything I've ever felt before. The entire night seems like a dream, especially the part where he put me into bed again and kissed my forehead.

But we haven't seen each other since, so I can't help but think that's it. He's had his fun, and we can go back to ignoring each other. Maybe exchanging some remarks back and forth. Go back to pissing each other off and pretending like we don't know what the other one looks like naked.

But I don't think I want to go back to that.

I'm losing it.

Once I'm home I toss my keys on the counter and see my phone has an unread message from my sister. I sigh when I open it, knowing I'll probably end up leaving her on read again. Even seeing the entire thread that consists of years of unanswered texts has the guilt bubbling up.

> Brynn: I just wish you would talk to me. I miss you. We're still family.

I sigh, putting my phone face down on the counter and distract myself with getting some food because I've barely eaten all day. I don't feel like cooking, so I grab a bagel, put it in the toaster, and stare at my phone lying on the counter while I wait.

I could reply to her, just say something small. It wouldn't hurt, but then she may want more. She may want to see me. Then I would see Brent. And who knows, they may invite Bryson too. Then what? It's some big happy Collee family reunion? No way.

I think back to Sutton's invitation to Thanksgiving earlier. Brent always invites me to his house for the holidays in Denver. I've never gone, but he hasn't stopped inviting me. Every single year, even though I deny him every time, he still doesn't stop.

The ding of the toaster pulls my attention back to the bagel. After I take it out, smother it in cream cheese, and take a bite, I'm back to staring at my phone.

More like glaring at it, if I'm honest.

I don't look away from it. It's almost like I'm waiting for it to explode. Once I'm done with my food, I can't shake the thoughts of the texts from my sister.

When I pick up my phone, looking at the thread again my fingers hover over the keys, not sure what to say. If I should say anything.

Finally, I make up my mind. One text won't hurt. Maybe I'll feel better, and maybe it'll make her feel better as well.

Bailey: I miss you too.

I drop my phone down. It's not a lie, but it's also not something I've said in so long. I need a distraction. I almost want to message Wes, but that would require looking at my phone and I want to avoid that like the plague right now.

Glancing over at his house I see he's not home and let out a groan. I could take a page out of his book and go for a drive to nowhere, but that sounds a lot less appealing alone in the afternoon.

Instead, I opt to take a bath and try to distract my mind. I just hope it'll be able to shut off at least for a little. All I can hope for is the chance to relax.

Wes

KEEPING myself busy is not always easy, but I've managed to do it. Not because I'm avoiding Bailey, but because I feel like she wants to avoid me. I don't know where we stand and I don't want to ask.

I've been getting home late when her lights are already off. I haven't reached out because I don't want to push her after things started to escalate so quickly.

The one thing I have done every day is go back to the shelter. I like to see that some of the dogs are gone from the day before because they've been adopted. I check in on any interest in Bruno, and every day I get the same answer.

I've walked Sadie every day and a few others. I go to Jameson's to help. Sometimes I continue to drive around. Still, nothing feels fulfilling enough. Nothing like when I'm with *her*.

The texts from Chris continue to haunt me. He hasn't said anything else and I'm not sure if there's anything I can do. He may have just been having a bad day. Everyone has days where they're down and feeling shitty. Since I haven't heard from him again, I chalk it up to that. We used to be close, but now I don't really know him.

I'm leaving Jameson's and the weirdest thing happened when he saw me; he invited me to Thanksgiving.

"You do know that's a month away, right?" I ask, seriously concerned about his measure of time.

"Yeah, Sutton's trying to get ahead on planning."

I grunt my answer, "We'll see."

I haven't been to a real Thanksgiving since I was a kid when my parents were still alive. We would have makeshift holidays while I was in the Army. It consisted of a lot of food, and my battalion I saw every single day. That time of year was always hard on a lot of people because they missed their families, and wanted to be home.

There were a lot of phone and video calls. I had no one to call, so it didn't matter to me.

"I know Sutton is inviting Bailey," Jameson offers. I make a noise of acknowledgment, but don't really say anything before heading out.

The sound of her name has the need to see her again surging. It's been too long, I've given her space, but my patience has worn out.

When I get home, her car is parked in the driveway, but I need to let Bruno out. Sometimes he comes with me to Jameson's, but since I went to the shelter first he stayed home.

I stand in the open doorway, waiting for him to finish his business, when that familiar prickling sensation creeps up my spine—eyes on me. It's instinct now, second nature. I shift, standing taller, my posture ramrod straight as my gaze sweeps the area. I know someone's watching. I can feel it in my bones. So I search for the pair of eyes that haven't looked away.

I lock on Bailey's face looking over the top of the fence separating our yards. My body relaxes instantly at the sight, moving to lean against the doorframe once again. The setting sun creates an ethereal glow. I know she says she's not an angel, but right now, with the way the light is hitting her golden hair and making her mossy eyes shine, she looks angelic.

She looks perfect.

"What're you looking at, Angel?" I ask, in what I think is a playful tone, but I know comes across more deadpan.

"Just seeing who was out here making all the noise," she jokes. I crack a smile at the fact she's not rolling her eyes and storming away.

Though if she did then it would give me an excuse to go over there and get my hands on her again. Instead, I clench my fists to fight the urge.

"Must have been your other neighbor; we're quiet."

She looks behind her at the other side of the fence that she doesn't share with anyone. "No, I think it was you two."

I look over at Bruno and try to hide my smile. "Have you seen Sutton lately?"

"Uh yeah, why?"

"Just wondered if you got invited to the Thanksgiving thing," I grunt.

"Yeah, that isn't for a whole month? She did. Then she told me to get a dog."

"Why?"

"Said it might be good for me. I don't know. The bird that lives at the groomer was barking and screaming about jizz and Jameson." She freezes, and tries to backtrack. "That is not at all what it sounds like. He wasn't talking about that at the same time. Oh my God forget everything I just said."

I don't think I've ever heard Bailey talk so much or so quickly. Which is why I can't hold back my burst of laughter. I can't remember the last time I laughed. Fully laughed, but hearing her be nervous and stumble over her words is what does it.

"Shut up," she mumbles, tucking her head, though I can see how red her cheeks become.

"If you want a dog, Bruno is available." I nod toward the German Shepherd still sniffing around my yard.

"Something tells me he's spoken for already." She smirks.

"You could also go to the shelter. I could go with you if you wanted," I offer without thinking much of it.

"Why?" She furrows her brows.

"I know some of the dogs there. I could introduce you."

She scrunches her face. "Maybe."

"What're you doing tonight?" I ask, diverting the conversation.

Bailey smirks, leaning back with a grip on the top of the fence. "Wouldn't you like to know."

"I would, actually." I stand up straight and face her.

She hums. "I don't think I should tell you."

I step closer. "Why not?"

"It's none of your business."

I hum, getting even closer. "If you don't want to tell me, I'm sure I could get it out of you somehow."

I watch her throat bob with a swallow. "No you can't."

I raise my eyebrow. "Is that a challenge?"

Even though she's telling me one thing, the way her lips are quirked and her breathing speeds up she knows exactly what she's doing. We both do.

"You know," I start, "I've been thinking about how you haven't been properly fucked by me."

"That so?" she challenges.

"It is. The first night wasn't enough, we both know it. Every time since has been…frenzied. I haven't had the chance to really do what I want."

"Really? Fucking me while driving your car wasn't enough?"

I'm up against the fence, leaning down so our faces are only a couple of inches apart. Our chests would be touching if it weren't for the wood in the way. "Not even close."

"Then what're you going to do about that?"

I breathe out a small laugh. "Maybe you'll find out." I stand up straight, and start backing away from the fence. "But first you're going to come to the shelter with me tomorrow."

Her jaw drops, clearly caught off guard. When I brace for the argument I know is coming, she surprises me. Snapping it shut without a word.

"Enjoy your plans, Angel. I'll see you in the morning." I don't miss her dumbfounded look as I bring Bruno inside and turn off the porch light.

CHAPTER 31

Bailey

I HAVE NO PLANS. When would I have plans? *Why* would I have plans? I just wanted to see what he would do or say. Of course what he does is leave me questioning my sanity *once again*. The weirdest part of it all is I end up texting Jenn letting her know I may not make it in tomorrow. She and Ava are both working so they won't need me.

I may not have plans tonight, but I've gotten roped into going to the animal shelter with my neighbor in the morning. The man I'm still trying to convince myself I don't like, even though the lie is getting harder and harder to swallow.

The next morning, Wes is at my door right at 8:00 a.m. I'd like to say he's bright eyed and bushy tailed, but I don't think he has ever been that in his life. I look down and see two coffees in his hand and immediately recognize the cups as coming from Roasted Bean.

"You went to my shop to get me coffee?"

He shakes his head. "No, these both are for me."

"Makes sense." I shrug right before he hands one of the cups to me with a tiny smile.

"Ready?" he asks.

"Sure." I lock my front door and as we're walking to his car I say, "You know, I think you just want me to keep riding in your car so I'll stop complaining about it."

"Is it working?"

"No."

"Too bad."

I get into his car, buckling and then holding onto my coffee for dear life because if I don't, I worry I'll end up touching *him*. I can't help but think about the last time we were in this car together. Not only did we end up fucking, but I felt the warmth of his hand on my thigh, and I'm pretty sure we ended up holding hands.

The simple act feels more intimate than the sex ever did.

It's like kissing. How we danced around it for so long that when our lips finally met, nothing else compared. All the build-up, all the tension, and yet it was that one lingering kiss that unraveled me.

Everything between us seems anything but simple. The back and forth, the chemistry. It's all so complex and has my mind so jumbled all the time I can't even keep up.

Wes gets in the car, and I busy myself with drinking the coffee he brought so I don't have to say anything. It's not like he's a big talker anyway, which works out for me. I also can't think too much into how sweet it was that he brought me coffee, the exact order he knows I like. From my shop. Even though we could have easily swung by there, he chose to go get it himself.

The animal shelter isn't far, and Wes has his music playing while the roar of his engine—I've always found annoying—is almost soothing now. Or maybe it's the way the seat vibrates, and I squeeze my thighs together. He's conditioning me to like this stupid car, I know it.

We arrive and I managed to finish my coffee on the short drive because every time I wanted to say something, I took a sip instead. Wes continues to stay quiet as he gets out of the car, and meets me on my side, putting his hand out to help me out just like last time.

Just like the last time, I take it. Instead of keeping our fingers interlocked as we walk, he lets go. The disappointment I feel should be studied because I have no explanation for it.

When we walk inside, there's an older woman at the front desk and she smiles widely at the sight of us. I don't think I've ever seen such a positive greeting to Wes before. Or myself. I feel like I may have seen this woman around our small town before, but we've never officially met.

"Welcome back, Wes. You brought a friend." She smiles, addressing me. "I'm Gloria."

I take her outstretched hand in a firm handshake. "Bailey."

"So nice to meet you. Wes is one of our best volunteers. The dogs all love him."

"Bruno seems to be really happy living with him." I give a close lipped smile.

"I'm sure he does." She looks at him knowingly.

"Is Sadie still here?" he asks in that bored tone he's perfected that makes him seem even scarier than he looks.

"She is, and I'm sure she'll be happy to see you as well."

Wes nods and leads me through another door to a room lined with kennels. I see all the different types of dogs either laying or sitting down. Some look so sad, and some look excited with their tails wagging. One is even standing on his hind legs with his front paws hooked on the grated door.

I'm instantly aware why I don't come to a place like this because I feel so bad seeing their sweet faces looking at me. I may not be an animal person, but that's probably because I've never had one and never considered getting one either. Until now.

Wes stops in front of a kennel, taking a leash off the hook next to it, and I step closer to see the name tag that reads "Sadie."

"This is the famous Sadie?" I ask, seeing the medium sized dog with white golden fur. It's longer than Bruno's, but not as long as Sutton's dog Bennet's.

"Here she is," Wes agrees, opening the door and putting the leash around her head then handing me the looped end.

I take it, expecting her to try and pull me down the aisle to the door on the end I assume leads outside, but she doesn't. Even with the chaos around us, the cacophony of dogs barking and whining, she stands right next to me and looks up.

Wes walks ahead of us, and still she sticks by me as we head out the door to a lightly forested area. She doesn't try to pull me at all, just keeps up with the leisurely pace. I can't deny that being here with her, with both of them, does feel peaceful.

My mind doesn't feel like it's going a million miles a minute. I'm not fighting back memories trying to assault me. The cool breeze hits my face and the sense of calm surrounding me isn't something I'm used to.

Sadie seems to feel it too because her steps are even as her paws crunch on the fallen leaves. She looks ahead, enjoying not being in the stuffy kennel.

"When are you going to accept that you're keeping Bruno?" I ask suddenly without looking up at Wes.

"I'm not. I can't. He deserves more than I can give him," he insists and I furrow my brows, not sure why he thinks that.

"I think you're giving him exactly what he needs."

He shakes his head. "For now, but I'm not someone to plan a future with."

I nod, feeling like he's talking about us more than the dog, but that's fine. If that's his way of letting me know we will never have a relationship, he doesn't need to worry about that.

"Me either," I say honestly. Though, the more time I spend with Sadie walking next to me I think about what it would be like to have her at home, getting to do this every day. Someone to talk to who won't talk back and give an opinion I don't want. Someone who won't judge me.

A built-in-best friend that doesn't argue with me.

And she isn't a bird who can scream out embarrassing things, which is much more appealing.

"How were your plans last night?" he asks smugly. Probably because he saw my car parked in the driveway all night.

"They were great."

"Yeah? Want to tell me what they were now?"

"Not really."

He huffs out a laugh. "You can't help it can you?"

"Can't help what?"

"Being a brat."

"Obviously not."

He halts me with a hand on my arm, turning me toward him. Sadie stops walking as well, still sticking close to my side.

"You're testing me, aren't you?"

I shrug.

"Do you *want* to be punished?"

Another shrug.

"You been thinking about me since that night?"

Shrug.

"You've been desperate to see if I'll show up to your house? If I'll take you over my knee, and make your ass red before I make you ride my face so hard you soak my beard with how much you come for me?"

I gasp, leaning down to put my hands over Sadie's ears. "You can't talk that way in front of a child."

He smirks. "Tell me I'm wrong then. Tell me you don't want that."

"I can't."

"That's what I thought." He smiles smugly and then we continue walking again like nothing just happened. "Have you thought more about going to Jameson and Sutton's for Thanksgiving?"

My mind whirls with the stark subject change. I stutter trying to find my words once again because the spot between my thighs is throbbing from the visual he just painted. Somehow, now he's asking me about the holidays like it's no big deal.

"No, have you?"

"No. Don't you have parents or siblings to go see or something?" he asks and I can't help the grimace that appears on my face.

"Don't you?"

He looks down, kicking a dead leaf on the trail. "My parents aren't around anymore."

"I'm sorry," I sigh, the mood suddenly somber.

"It's fine, it's been a long time. Dad died when I was younger, and my mom passed while I was in the Army."

"That's awful, I'm very sorry," I tell him honestly.

"My dad is actually the reason I joined in the first place. He's the reason I wanted it to be my career."

I'm surprised Wes is saying as much as he is, but with the way he's opening up I'm not about to say anything to ruin it. It's the first real glimpse of him as a person, not my scary neighbor, not the obnoxious man with an even more obnoxious car. Not the man that likes to take total control in the bedroom and work my body in ways I never knew it could be worked.

This is just Wes.

"He died in battle, and I knew it would be a possibility for me. I accepted that, but for some reason getting injured and not being able to continue was the hand I was dealt. An Army career wasn't an option anymore."

He's mentioned that before and I didn't realize how this truly was a crucial part of his life. That without the Army he really didn't know who he was. And maybe I've been too harsh on him. Neither of us know what we're doing. Neither of us had the lives we thought we would.

Maybe it's that thought that gives me the strength to do something I never imagined I would do. Something I never even considered until this moment. Because maybe we both can learn to take chances on things that scare us.

We just have to take the leap.

I look down at Sadie, speaking to her, but I can sense the surprise from Wes when I say, "You ready to come home with me?"

CHAPTER 32

Wes

MY CAR IS REALLY NOT BUILT to have two people and a dog in it, but the fact that Bailey is smiling right now is enough to erase every complaint I may have. We've all fit in here with Bruno before, and he's bigger than Sadie.

Stopping by the pet store so Bailey can get the items she needs for Sadie, we end up stuck in the aisle with food and water dishes while she stares at them. Sadie just sits next to her new owner happily.

"Thinking too hard will cause your brain to explode," I tease.

She rears back, looking at me like I have two heads. "Did you just try to tell a joke?"

"Calling it what it is usually takes out the humor of it," I grumble.

"I just don't know which kind she will like the best." She sighs.

"Something tells me the food in the bowl is what she will care about most."

She nods. "I guess that's a good point."

She picks up a dark green ceramic bowl, holding it toward Sadie with a soft smile. "What do you think of this one?" she asks, tilting it slightly.

She sniffs it, and then sticks her tongue out panting.

"Does that mean she likes it?" Bailey asks me.

"I'm not a dog whisperer, but I think so."

She nods, and puts the bowl in the cart I'm pushing for her. We've already loaded up a large bag of food, a bed, some treats, and now a bowl. She puts another one in the cart, I assume for water and then we continue to the toy aisle.

Being here with her like this feels...normal. Unexpectedly so. And while I'd usually be searching for any excuse to leave, that urge isn't there. It's just easy being with her. No arguing. No tension. Not even anything sexual which is how I usually ground myself, how I stay in control. With her, right now, I don't need that. I don't *want* that. Just being here with her is enough.

We get to just be ourselves and it's simple. Easy.

After several minutes of Bailey giving Sadie toy options, she settles on a handful of toys stacked in the cart.

"I don't know how we're going to fit all of this in my car with the two of you," I tell her at the cash register. "I may have to make you guys walk home."

"This joking thing doesn't really suit you." She shakes her head, but I catch the smile she tries to hide.

"Better yet, Sadie can get a ride with me, and you can walk home."

"Now you've gone too far," she deadpans, but when she turns to pay I catch the smile that peeks out.

"I got it," I tell her, pulling out my wallet instinctively.

"Absolutely not." She puts her hand up, swiping her card. The second her palm is flat against my chest I see her sharp intake of breath while I try to control my own reaction.

"Have a great day," the cashier's voice breaks the strong tether of tension between Bailey and I.

We leave, and I manage to wrangle everything she just bought in the small trunk. If we knew this would be happening today, we probably would've taken her car, but I like being in such close proximity to her.

Once we get back, I pull into my driveway and immediately go around to the trunk to help unload everything she bought. I watch as she releases her seatbelt and tries to detangle Sadie and the leash from the backseat.

My arms are both full as I follow her to her front door.

"I guess you can just set that stuff over there," she instructs, removing the leash from Sadie's head so she can explore. "Thank you, but I could have gotten it."

"I know," I tell her, simply. "I'm going to check on Bruno; let me know if you need anything."

She nods, her hands slipping into her back pockets. This is the most awkward goodbye I think we've had. Do I kiss her? Hug her? Give her a high five?

I do none of the above, just giving her a single curt nod before walking out, feeling stupid and unsure. It shouldn't be this difficult. For some reason when I take control of the situation and when she's acting bratty it's so much easier to know what to do. It's natural. But in a simple, normal situation like this where all we're doing is saying goodbye, I'm lost.

Bruno looks up at me from his spot on the couch when I walk in. "There may be a new friend for you next door."

He wags his tail once, and I'd like to think he understands. Which is why I won't say that it's only temporary since he's bound to find his perfect family. I ask if he wants to go outside and he jumps off the couch, stretching his legs before following me to the back door. I can't help but keep my eyes on Bailey's place thinking about what she and Sadie might be doing.

I want to give them time to bond and get to know each other, but I also don't know if I'm going to be able to stay away. Not after the day we had. One of the most normal days I've had in I don't know how long. And all I want to do is end it buried inside the woman who lives next door.

I give her the day. It's all I'm able to manage because even after trying to do everything I can think of to wear myself out to attempt to sleep, I'm still restless as I lay in bed staring at her darkened window. I know she works early and I shouldn't disturb her.

But the longer I lay here and think about every single thing she's done to annoy me, test me, and be her bratty self, it gets harder and harder to justify *not* going over there. She practically begs me every time she tempts me with her smart tongue.

Bruno is snoring at the end of the bed, and I know I can get up without disturbing him. Sleep isn't going to find me anyway. Either I can go for a drive like I normally would, or I could do something different. I could take a risk.

Decision made. I swing my legs over the side of my bed and look over at her window one more time. I don't hesitate before pulling on a pair of sweatpants and don't even bother with a shirt. It's cold out, but I hardly feel it with the way my skin is burning at the thought of getting to touch her again.

This time, there's no holding back.

I knock on her door rapidly and debate just breaking it down to get inside, but I don't think Bailey would appreciate that. When it swings open I'm met with her wide eyes. "Wes?"

I hardly let her finish saying my name before my hand is gripping the back of her neck, and my lips are crashing down onto hers.

She doesn't hesitate, just opens for me, letting my tongue slide against hers, welcoming the kiss like she's been waiting for it. I groan, deep and guttural, as I push us inside, kicking the door shut behind me without breaking contact. Our mouths stay locked, desperate, hungry, like I need her to breathe.

We aren't moving fast enough through her house for my liking, but this time I'm not some reckless, possessed man acting on impulse. I'm in control. Fully. And I'm going to show her exactly what she needs. Remind her that what she craves is something only I can give.

She wants punishment?

Good.

Because I've spent the last three years waiting to deliver it.

How badly I've wanted her the entire time. How badly I've known she's wanted me. How we've both held back after our explosive first night together, even knowing how good it could be. It's finally time to show her everything.

My hands trail down her body, over the curve of her ass, then lower to the backs of her thighs. In one smooth motion I lift her into my arms. She comes willingly and I carry her up the stairs toward her bedroom. My leg protests with every step, but I barely feel it. All I can focus on is Bailey wrapped around me, her mouth on mine kissing me like she can't get close enough. Like she needs this just as badly as I do.

Once we're in her bedroom, I sit on the edge of the bed, keeping her in my lap while her tongue slides against mine. I could keep kissing her for hours, days, *years* and never get tired of it. When her hips start to move, slow and deliberate against me, I know she can feel the way my cock is thickening beneath her. Every grind sends a pulse of heat straight through me, and *fuck*, I want her to keep going. I want to feel her come undone right here in my lap. But not yet.

Not like this.

Not until I say so.

With a firm grip on her hair, I pull her head back, reluctantly separating our lips for the time being. She tries to close the inch I've just created between us, but I don't let her.

"So needy for someone who claims to hate me," I breathe.

"I don't *hate* you," she practically whispers.

"Maybe not now, not when you know I can give your desperate little pussy what it needs. Tell me, before I find out myself how wet you are."

She swivels her hips against me. "Hardly at all."

Her voice is breathy and gives away her lie. I chuckle. "You really do want to be punished, don't you?"

She squeaks in surprise, especially when I shift her in my lap maneuvering her until she's draped over my thighs. I band an arm around her lower back, holding her steady as my fingers trail up the back of her thigh, pushing her oversized T-shirt up over her ass covered in tight black underwear.

I hook a finger in the waistband and tug them down, slowly, savoring the reveal of her perfectly, round backside. My palm glides over the bare skin I'm already imagining turning red.

Then my hand moves lower, slipping between her thighs. And

the second my fingers meet the wet heat there, a groan tears from my chest. She's soaked. And all for me. It's the kind of feeling that makes me want to lose myself in her, to bury myself deep and never come back up.

But first, I'm going to make her desperate. I can wait. I can be patient.

My eyes catch on the small tattoo inked into the top of her right cheek, and I trace my finger over the two words.

Bite me.

A dark grin spreads across my face. "You know, I've wanted to, ever since I first saw this tattoo of yours," I murmur, and she knows *exactly* what I'm talking about.

She wiggles slightly, teasing. "Then what're you going to do about it?"

I answer with a sharp smack, landing my palm right over the dark ink. She yelps at the contact, but I don't miss the way she rocks her hips against my lap, confirming everything I need to know. She wants this. She *needs* this. And she wants it from *me*.

"Look at you, Angel." I groan, rubbing the sting I just left behind. "You're so fucking perfect."

I spank her again, and the sharp sound mixes with her low, needy moan. I do it again, and again until she's squirming, crying out, completely at my mercy.

"Had enough, baby?" I ask, kneading the heat blooming across her skin.

She shakes her head, breathless. "No. Give me more."

I smirk. Of course she wants more. And she's *mine* to give it to. I don't have time to freak out about the fleeting possessiveness in that thought, because she's already moaning again, and I'm already giving her exactly what she's begging for.

CHAPTER 33

Bailey

MY ASS IS ON FIRE, but I've never been this wet. Which I didn't think was possible after the car, but this? This is even more erotic. The way his hand smacks down on me, then kneads the sting away. The sharp pain giving way to pleasure. It sends a thrill through me I can't describe.

It should feel degrading being draped across his lap like this. I *shouldn't* want his hands on me in this way. But I do. *God, I do.* Which is why I asked for more.

And he gives me just that.

Several more slaps land on my ass, heat blooming under each one, and I can't help the way I grind myself against his leg like a cat in heat. But then I'm being lifted, flipped, and settled in his lap again. His mouth crashes into mine. The kiss is intense, just like they always are but this time there's more. It's just as rough, invading and all consuming, but there's an edge to it that was there when he took my mouth without a single word at my front door.

There's something unspoken between us. Something we don't know how to express, or say but we can show each other. At least like this.

Wes moves, laying me back on the bed, and he holds himself up over me. I expect him to kiss me again, but instead, he slides away with a smirk. I watch him, rising to my elbows, watching, curious, and breathless.

I take the time to appreciate his bare chest, the tattoos that cover his left arm up to his shoulder. The arms that are so big they might as well be the size of my head. My eyes roam down the rest of his chiseled body as his ab muscles tense and I want to be mad at how perfect he looks.

It's unfair how this man who's driven me absolutely insane for years has the audacity to look like *that*. But I meant what I said. I don't hate him. I couldn't.

My gaze drops lower, I can see his erection tenting his pants, and it makes my mouth water. I want to feel him, all of him, but I don't move. Because as much as I like to push him to see how close I can toe the line, right now I want to see what it's like when I don't.

He has some kind of hold over me. This time, I want to do exactly as he says. Especially when his voice drops and he growls, "Touch yourself."

"What?" I blink. Because with the way he was just touching me, it seems like I must have misheard him.

"Touch yourself, but don't come."

"That doesn't seem fair," I mutter before I can stop myself.

Immediately biting my bottom lip, regretting letting the words slip free.

"Oh, that's not fair, Angel?" he echoes, voice low and sharp. "You know what *isn't* fair?" I swallow roughly, worried about what he's going to say. "That I've had to live next to you for three damn years, knowing exactly what you feel like, what you *taste* like, and not being able to do a damn thing about it."

I suck in a sharp breath as he continues.

"Knowing you were probably in here touching that sweet cunt of yours, and I couldn't see it. Not once. That I haven't been with *anyone* for the last three years because the only woman I wanted lived next door and wanted nothing to do with me."

My jaw drops in a gasp at his confession. I never thought in a million years he hadn't been with *anyone* else since we were together all those years ago.

But neither have I.

"Tell me something, Angel. When you're in here all alone, can't sleep and your fingers slip into your underwear, who do you think about?"

I shrug, not wanting to answer.

"Tell me," he warns, "or I'll take you over my knee again."

The thought has me squirming, and not in a bad way.

"Would you think about that night?" he presses. "Would you think about me?"

I roll my lips in, still not wanting to answer. But then I nod.

"Say it."

"I'd think about your mouth on me," I admit.

"*Show* me."

I drift my hand up the inside of my thigh, resting my feet on the bed and spreading them. I hear his low growl when he sees me bare in front of him. I let out a small whimper the second my fingers graze my sensitive clit.

"What else did you think about?"

"How it felt to have you inside me."

"When you thought about that, did you push one of your fingers inside yourself, and realize it's not enough?"

I moan out a needy, "*Yes.*"

"Do it now," he demands, and I do. Pushing my middle finger in and moaning at the sensation. It's not enough. Not even close.

"Need another one, Angel?"

"Mhm."

"Then give yourself what you need."

I push another finger in along with the first, and thrust them gently, but I'm quickly frustrated at how it's not enough. I start to rub my palm against my clit while I try to get myself there with just my touch.

Wes watches me, his eyes honed on where my fingers are. I move my free hand up my stomach to my chest where I cup a breast, squeezing and plucking at my nipple while I try to pretend like my fingers are enough.

I moan his name in a small plea.

"What is it?" he asks tauntingly.

"I want you to touch me," I breathe.

"Mm not yet, but you can watch me."

I groan in frustration, watching as he pushes his sweatpants down, his cock bobbing free. He wraps his fist around it immediately, moving over it once, twice, and I swear I could come just from watching him.

"Did you see this in any of your fantasies?" he asks, voice low. "Or were you always too eager to have me touching you?"

"You were always...*shit,*" I cut myself off with the curse as I manage to touch a particularly sensitive spot that has my eyes crossing.

"I was always what?" he presses, voice rough. "Tell me what that mind of yours thought about while you were so desperate to feel me, but settled on touching yourself instead."

"You were always touching me," I manage to say, breath catching as I find a rhythm and pressure that's making me feel the telling signs of an orgasm starting.

"Was it my mouth? My fingers? My cock?"

"All of them," I admit. As I fall back into the fantasy remembering what it feels like when it's a reality.

"Take your shirt off. If you're going to play with your nipples, I want to see."

Without an ounce of hesitation, I rip the shirt over my head and toss it aside. I'm so turned on that I don't even have a second to spare to feel self conscious. Or think about the way I'm completely naked touching myself while Wes watches. Seeing how he's working his hand over his length, slow and deliberate, erases all hesitation I would have in this situation. His eyes burn into me, making me feel seen, but not only that. I feel beautiful and wanted. Wes *wants me.*

He wants every part of me he's seen physically and mentally. Instead of running away when I give him attitude, he wants more of it. He wants more of *me.*

Oh my God. I'm getting feelings for Wes.

"Stop," he commands, and I gasp, realizing how close I am to release.

But I don't stop. I don't move my hand away, and instead bite my bottom lip, and start to move slowly once again.

"Bailey," he growls.

"Yeah?" I ask, as I continue my movements.

"Stop."

"But it feels so good," I breathe, swiveling my hips, and moaning once again.

"I know it does, but you're not going to come yet."

"Maybe I am."

His voice dips, a low warning. "Bailey." A shiver runs down my spine, and the underlying threat only makes me continue my movements.

In a heartbeat, he's on me, pinning my hands above my head with one of his. I can feel his rock hard length pressed against me, and I hook my leg around him trying to pull him closer.

"Why do you always feel the need to test me?"

"If I say because it's fun will my punishment be worse?"

"I don't think punishments even work for you," he mutters with a laugh.

"Maybe you should try a different tactic."

"Oh yeah? Like what?"

I hum, dragging my foot slowly up the back of his calf. "Maybe you give me what we *both* want, and I'll behave."

"Somehow, I don't believe that."

"Why not?" I rub my leg against him again, wiggling my hips underneath him so I can feel more of his bare dick against me.

"Because I don't think you ever want to really be an angel. You're much happier being a fallen one...driving me insane."

"But you like it."

"I do."

His forehead drops down to mine.

"You like me," I state softly, it's not a question and it's barely above a whisper, but part of me needs to hear him say it.

"I do," he replies just as quietly.

I arch up to take his mouth with my own. He kisses me back fiercely, keeping my hands pinned while he rocks against me.

"Please fuck me," I beg. Words I never say. Asking for something I never would usually ask for, but my lost orgasm is controlling my mind and my body right now.

Wes smirks, and reaches down between us, guiding his erection through my wetness, up to my clit, down to my opening but not pushing in. I move my hips, straining to feel the way he's going to stretch me so perfectly, but he just does the move again.

I groan in protest, "*Please.*"

"One thing first." He pauses. "You like me, too."

He doesn't ask. He *knows*. He looks at me so intently, his brown eyes burning into mine just waiting for what I'm going to say. I could deny it, play it off like I usually do. Act like this is only physical. That I feel nothing for the man that is in fact making me feel *so much*.

"I do," I say so softly that I think there's no way he actually heard me.

Maybe he didn't because he doesn't acknowledge the words that I managed to say before he's thrusting inside me. The combination of pain and pleasure has me crying out while he stays still, fully seated and waiting for me to adjust to the feel of him.

"Is this what you wanted?" he asks smugly.

I swivel my hips and whimper at the feeling, but then manage to squeak out, "More."

With a small smirk he moves us quickly flipping us around so he's on his back and I'm straddling his hips. The new angle has him hitting deeper and my mouth drops open in a gasp as my eyes roll back.

"Ride me, Angel. Take what you're wanting."

And I do. Planting my hands on his hard chest, I pick up my hips and slam them back down against him. He groans, grabbing my waist, not guiding my movements, but just keeping them there while I move the way I need. Rubbing myself against him each time our bodies slap together.

"Do you know how fucking beautiful you are?" Wes moans, and it makes my movements stop.

I look down at him, trying to detect the lie, but it isn't there. His eyes are blazing with heat. He grabs my hips tighter, silently encouraging me to move again. I'm so lost in looking at him I open my mouth to say something, but nothing comes out.

He flexes his hips, pushing up into me and I cry out. It's enough to pull me out of my trance. His hands slide to my chest, cupping my breasts, squeezing and pushing them together. "What were you thinking?" he asks.

I drop my head back at all the sensations going on. "I was wondering if you're lying."

His arm bands behind my back as he sits up. Our chests colliding as he moves my legs so they wrap around him, relieving my knees.

"Have I ever lied to you?" The way he's holding me in place so I can't look away or move makes me feel exposed. Even more than the fact that we are naked and as close as two people can possibly be.

"Not that I know of," I whisper.

"I haven't. Not that first night, not in the three years since. And not now."

I swallow roughly at how deadly serious he is.

"I'm not going to start, either," he continues. "You're fucking beautiful, Bailey. We aren't talkative people, and I'm not good at compliments or feelings, but I've never felt like this before."

I gasp at what he's admitting. My heart rate kicks up and the urge to run overwhelms me. I don't know how to talk about this. I don't know what to say. The fact that Wes is saying *anything* has me completely dumbfounded.

He moves my hair from my face, and I have no words. I don't know what to say, so instead I kiss him. Hard. Deep. It takes the seriousness out of the moment and brings me back to more comfortable territory for me which is our out of control chemistry.

His tongue invades my mouth on a groan, and he fucks up into me, erasing all of the fear his words instilled. We move together like we were made to do just this, and when his hand slaps my sensitive ass once, again I moan and grind against him even harder.

I feel his smile against my mouth. "You fucking love that don't you, Angel?"

I nod against him, trying to chase the orgasm I feel building once again.

"What else do you like?"

"This," I moan, not wanting him to take away another release, knowing if he does I may actually lose my mind.

Of course I should know better because I'm tossed onto my back and quickly flipped onto my stomach. I gasp as he pulls my hips up, and presses into me again. I bury my face in the mattress, muffling all the noise I'm making. I swear I've never been as vocal as I am with him.

He pulls me up so my back is plastered to his front while he essentially uses me, moving me up and down on him as he thrusts into me. When his hand moves down my stomach to the area where we're connected, he rubs my clit and I drop my head back against his shoulder. My nails dig into his strong forearm around my stomach and then there's a sharp stinging where he was just rubbing as he slaps the sensitive nub.

I cry out, and his mouth grazes my ear. "How about that?"

I nod, and he does it again. And again. I'm barreling toward the orgasm that I've been denied too many times for my liking. He goes back to rubbing the area and fucking me at the perfect pace. I dig my nails into his skin as a silent threat because he better not stop.

"Please Wes, please," I plead, meeting his thrusts.

"Let go, Angel. Show me how tightly you can squeeze my cock."

His permission is all I need to get there, crying out as the release slams into me so hard, I swear I black out. I hardly register being pushed down onto the mattress while he pounds into me and groans when he finds his own release.

We're both breathing hard as we come down, and suddenly what we admitted to each other comes back and the fear crashes back into me. Wes lifts himself up, walking out of the room and I take an extra moment to make sure my muscles can actually move. As I sit there, he walks back in, kneeling between my thighs, and cleaning the area with one of my washcloths. He presses a gentle kiss to the inside of my thigh that has my breath catching.

Then, he grabs my discarded shirt from the floor, his voice low but firm. "Arms up."

I do, only because I'm feeling too vulnerable to be naked right now.

"Get into bed." His voice is back to that gruff demanding tone he generally has.

I'm so tired and sated to argue, even as the worries of what happens next linger just out of reach. I climb into bed, and watch him pull on his pants before approaching me again.

"Are you staying?" I manage to squeak out, not sure which answer I want more.

He freezes, clearly not expecting the question. "Do you want me to?"

I pull the blankets up to my chin because I don't know which answer he wants to hear, and I don't know which one I want to say.

"No, you need to be with Bruno," I manage to say, and he nods, though I don't miss the way his shoulders drop, either in relief or disappointment.

But he agrees, and does the same thing he's done each time he's left me in my bed before. Presses a kiss to my forehead, and whispers, "Goodnight, Angel."

CHAPTER 34

Wes

THINGS SHIFTED with Bailey after that night. Everything between us had been gradually changing between us. But that night was the turning point. Since then we've fallen into a kind of routine. Bruno and Sadie play and we end up in bed together, but never for the entire night.

Neither of us push to spend the night. It's like we both know that would officially change everything. And I'm still worried about what would happen if I were to share a bed with another person. Not only am I concerned about my ability to fall asleep, but what may happen once I do. If I hurt her I wouldn't be able to forgive myself.

Bailey never seems to mind because she likes her space. I think the semblance of distance makes her feel safe, which is fine by me because I never feel fully safe, even on my best days.

My time is mostly spent volunteering at the animal shelter, and I still don't have an update on Bruno. Bailey's been trying to convince me to make it official and adopt him, but something keeps holding me back. I don't know what it is, but I just can't take the final step past fostering him to making him mine.

I also continue helping Jameson at his property, and that's how I end up fully roped into Thanksgiving dinner at his house that Sutton has officially begun calling a "friendsgiving." The name alone made me not want to come.

Sutton also convinced Bailey to attend. While she put up an argument about us riding together, she finally gave in on one condition. We take her car so she's not squished with Bruno and Sadie.

To which I conceded on my own condition—that I drive.

"Fine," she huffs, tossing me her keys. She's wearing a dark red sweater dress that hangs above her knees. My mind immediately dove straight into thoughts of pushing it up and burying my face between her thighs, making *her* my meal for Thanksgiving instead of going to this dinner.

We get in the car and I have to adjust her seat all the way back because she may be tall, she's not as tall as me. The look she gives me is more of a glare while I adjust everything.

"Now I'm going to have to fix all of that back to how I like it," she grumbles.

I shrug.

"You could've just let me drive, it's not like it's far."

"I prefer to drive." *I prefer to be in control.* I don't tell her the full truth—that I don't like other people driving me at all because

I feel like they'll crash. It's not that I don't trust her specifically, I just don't trust *anyone*.

"Yeah, yeah," she grumbles.

"Watch the attitude or you know what will happen," I threaten and don't miss the shiver that runs down her spine. Yeah, I've always had a sense of what she likes but ever since whatever this is between us began, I've gotten to know her on a whole different level. What she craves, which lately has been anything to do with me. I've never experienced a connection like this before. It's addicting and comes with its own set of fears.

The last time I relied on something so heavily was my job, and that was ripped away from me. Even before that I rarely got close to anyone, never dated seriously or made any big commitments. The biggest and only one I ever made was to the Army.

"I think your threats have an opposite effect on me now," she taunts.

"Well, *I think* it just proves that you'll never learn."

"It's been thirty-one years for me; I'm already set in my ways."

"Good thing I like your ways." The words slip out without me thinking about it. This has been happening more and more with her. I'm so out of my mind when she's with me that my filter is nonexistent.

Just another thing that makes me worry about what's going on between us. I know she feels the same. It helps to not have the pressure knowing she's not going to hound me for a relationship that's sure to send me far away.

We get to the main house on Jameson's family property and Bailey tenses up next to me as I park. "I'll go in first, then you can come in a few minutes later."

I raise an eyebrow at her. "Why can't we walk in together?"

"Because that leads to questions that neither of us wants to answer."

"Or we're neighbors who carpooled," I tell her seriously and she seems to realize that is a completely valid explanation.

"Fine, but as far as everyone knows we still can't stand each other."

"Whatever you say, Angel."

We get out of the car and walk to the door, close but not touching. Even though I'm tempted knowing I shouldn't.

I knock on the door, and am greeted by Jameson, right before Sutton ducks under his arm and smiles. "Welcome!"

"Come on in." Jameson opens the door wider for us to enter.

The house smells delicious and it brings back distant memories of my childhood, the only time I ever had a real Thanksgiving. The myriad of scents wafting through the house makes my stomach growl.

"So nice of you to join us," Emily greets from the kitchen as we enter the large combined kitchen and dining area.

"Thank you for having me," I tell her honestly. She opens up the oven and I see the large pan with a turkey in it. "Do you need help?"

"If you wouldn't mind." She steps aside, giving me the oven mitts.

"Oh, you let someone *else* help you, but when I offer, you tell me to go away," Jameson says from across the room.

"That's different. You coddle me," Emily retorts.

"I care."

"I know you do." Emily lowers her voice so only I can hear. "Sometimes too much."

The smallest smile peeks out as I lean down to lift out the large cooked bird and place it on top of the stove. Emily checks the temperature before announcing it's done.

Another loud voice announces their presence, and I turn around seeing it's a little blonde woman that's here often. I think her name is Lily. When I look closer, I believe this is the same woman whose car Bailey asked me to look at before Jameson and Sutton's rehearsal.

"Gross. I didn't realize you let just *anyone* come," she says when she sees Jameson's coworker, Parker.

"Come give me a hug, Lil, I know how much you've missed me." Parker stretches out his arms toward her and she makes a face, displaying her extreme disgust at the idea.

"I have a boyfriend, don't touch me."

Parker narrows his eyes at her. "You're still dating that asshole?"

"He's nice, and doesn't fuck anything that walks so he's already leagues better than you."

"I don't fuck anything that walks," Parker grumbles.

"Who's ready to eat?" Jameson announces, putting an end to their bickering for now.

"What's their deal?" I whisper to Bailey as everyone gathers around the already set table.

"I don't know the whole story, but they used to date. She went to college and now has a boyfriend." She shrugs.

I hum, not wanting to get in the middle of any sort of these twenty somethings' drama, but the way I've seen them bicker leaves me curious. Especially considering I'm about to sit through a whole Thanksgiving dinner with them.

Sorry, *friendsgiving* dinner.

Bailey attempts to sit in a chair somewhere away from me, but I don't let her, making sure to grab the seat directly next to her. She stares daggers at me, but once we're sitting down I lean over to whisper in her ear. "Remember what happened when we were here for Jameson and Sutton's wedding. Keep it up if you want a repeat."

She sucks in a sharp breath and I sit up straight.

"Thank you all for coming," Emily says sweetly. "Thank you

Jameson and Sutton for organizing this and inviting you all here. You don't know what this means to me."

"To Mrs. Turner," Parker announces raising his glass, and the rest of us do the same in a cheers motion.

The table is full and as everyone starts to load up their plates, the noise level increases from the conversations. Looking around, I watch how Jameson and Sutton sit so close they're touching, and keep saying things to one another with smiles. Parker is sitting across from Lily who's sitting next to her mom. Some of Jameson's other coworkers are here, Dave and a woman I don't know. There's also another woman next to Lily's mom and they look so similar I'm assuming they're sisters or related somehow.

There's so many conversations going on at once, I couldn't keep up even if I wanted to. The noise is borderline too much for me, and I do my best to tune it all out, focusing on the food instead. I eat a little bit of everything, and it's delicious. But it's so loud I don't think Emily would hear me even if I said something to her about it.

I look around for Bruno and see him laying against a wall in the living room, he seems to look about the same as I feel. The other three dogs are around the table near their respective owners probably hoping for some food scraps to hit the floor.

I feel the pressure of a hand slide onto my thigh, and my eyes swing over to Bailey who has a concerned look on her face.

"Are you okay?" she asks gently.

Clearing my throat, I nod. "Fine."

I look away, and down to my plate that's now empty, but I

scrape my fork around like I'm collecting more food on it. I can feel Bailey's eyes on me like she doesn't believe me. Maybe that's why her hand remains on my thigh. Surprisingly, the heat of it is enough to help bring my heart rate down the smallest bit.

After dinner we all help clean up before dessert. I don't opt for any pie, but Emily gives me a playful glare and tells me that not having pie on Thanksgiving is a crime.

"You're offending the host." Bailey nudges me when she overhears the scolding I get.

"I'll make it up to her by helping with the dishes."

"If she lets you."

"She will, I'm clearly her favorite."

Bailey scoffs, shaking her head.

The rest of the evening goes by smoothly, other than the constant bickering between Lily and Parker, who single handedly became the entertainment. We don't need TV or music when those two are around because they're their own reality show.

I'm not going to pressure Bailey to leave before she's ready because I'm not going to rush her time with her friends. Though, as I watch her, she doesn't talk much either. Both of us remain mostly quiet, observing those around us more than participating in any conversations.

Which is why I'm not entirely surprised when shortly after dessert, when Emily did in fact shoot me down about helping her with the dishes, Bailey says she's ready to go.

We say goodbye to everyone; I notice she hangs back with Sutton and Lily for a few moments longer, and I head to the car with the dogs to wait for her.

Sadie lays down on the backseat while Bruno lays on the floor in the back. I glance back at them. "Good job, giving the lady the seat."

The passenger door opens and Bailey climbs in. We don't say anything as I drive us back to our neighborhood.

"Are you okay?" she asks after a couple silent minutes.

"Yeah."

"You sure? Because you seemed pretty tense."

I'm always tense. I almost say it, but decide against it at the last minute.

"I don't like crowds either." Bailey says quietly. "It reminds me of growing up in our tiny trailer with all seven of us. It was never quiet, and if it was, the silence just meant something even worse was coming."

I glance over at her, but see she's not looking at me, instead her gaze is fixed out the window.

"Sounds similar to a war zone," I grunt because I completely relate to what she's saying. It's never quiet, and if it is that's usually a bad sign.

That's why the sky was where I preferred to be. It wasn't as loud. Until it was.

"Yeah, I'd say my childhood was a bit of a war zone."

I'm not going to pry, the fact that she's sharing this much is surprising in itself. I just wait to see if she'll say anything else. She doesn't by the time I'm pulling up to our houses, and park in her driveway.

She looks over at me. "Thanks for driving, but I'll take my keys back now."

The heaviness from the moments before feels like it's pushed back, and that's fine by me. I hand her keys over, letting my hand rest on hers as I do it. She tries to hide her shocked gasp, but pulls her hand back quickly.

"Thanks again," she mumbles, getting out of the car and opening the back for the dogs.

I don't bother trying to come in. I know I could and she would let me, but I feel like if I did things would shift even more. I may even end up staying the night, or wanting to. And that's a step I don't know if either of us want to take right now.

Instead, I step up to her, tucking her hair behind her ear. "Goodnight," I say softly before pressing a featherlight kiss to her lips.

"Goodnight," she whispers against mine.

Even as I walk the short distance back to my house, I fight the urge to look back over my shoulder. I know if I get another glimpse, I'll end up going over there. That's why I don't even glance at her window before I climb into bed.

CHAPTER 35

Bailey

THE HOLIDAY SEASON is weird for me. I enjoy seeing the Christmas lights go up, the atmosphere of winter, and of course the festive drinks we get to create at the coffee shop.

The hard part for me comes at the mention of family. It's a free for all with everyone asking what your plans are, who you're going to see, etcetera.

Even worse is when my family ends up messaging me asking if I'm coming to visit them. Not my parents, they couldn't care less about me. They may as well be dead for all I know. It's not like they have anything worth giving to us that would warrant being notified about a will.

In fact, they'd probably be left in that trailer to rot until someone complained about the smell.

I finish up making the last peppermint mocha for the day and start to close up the shop while I try to avoid the unanswered text in my phone.

The one from Brent that asked if I'm coming to his house for Christmas. The fact that I didn't immediately say no is different for me. I usually make an excuse right away. But this year feels different.

After I make sure the small shop is cleaned, stocked and ready for tomorrow, I head home. Sadie greets me as soon as I'm through the door, which has been one of the best parts of my day. I used to like being alone, and I still do, but having her around is a different kind of company.

Then I realize she's the perfect excuse to tell Brent that I can't come. Although I know Sutton would be more than happy to watch her while I'm gone.

Still, it's an excuse I can use and actually mean this year. But for some reason there's a lingering feeling of disappointment at the thought. I don't know why, and maybe I should be worried about my current mental state because I must be losing it.

I pull out my phone to reply, and see there's yet another text from him, and one from Brynn as well.

> Brent: Are you coming here for Christmas?

> Brent: If you want to I'll get you a plane ticket.

> Brynn: I'd really like it if you could come visit for Christmas. It would be nice to see you.

I groan, staring at the screen. I reply to Brent first.

> Bailey: I can buy my own plane ticket.

I know he's always wanted to take care of all of us. He's a rich and famous athlete now, but I'm an adult and I don't need him taking care of me.

> Brent: But will you?

I hesitate again because I don't know if I will, and that's the whole problem.

Switching over to the other text thread with my sister, I debate what to say to her. I hate disappointing her all the time. It's not fair, and maybe I should go just this once. Maybe it would be okay.

> Bailey: It would be nice to see you, too. Is Bryson going?

Brynn responds right away, which isn't surprising.

> Brynn: No, I doubt it. But you should, and you could meet everyone.

Everyone has my heart rate kicking up in my chest because it's not just Brent and Brynn anymore. They have families of their own now and I'll just be by myself.

Christmas is in a week, so I know I need to make a decision sooner rather than later and plane tickets are going to be outrageously expensive.

The craziest part is how seriously I'm actually considering this.

> Bailey: I'll think about it.

> Brynn: That's Bailey talk for "no."

> Bailey: It's Bailey talk for "I'll think about it."

> Brynn: I hope you mean it this time.

Her comment hits me right in the chest, and before I can think about it too much I'm pulling up flights to Denver. They're insane, but I know if I try to use that as an excuse, Brent will just pay for it.

So I painfully buy the plane ticket and hope I'm not making a huge mistake in going to see my siblings.

A COUPLE of days later I'm dropping Sadie off at Sutton's house and feeling extremely conflicted. Especially when Sutton asks me how I'm feeling about the trip.

"Are you excited to see your siblings again?"

"I guess, sort of." I pet behind Sadie's ears, her favorite spot.

"You don't sound like it."

"Because I'm nervous. I haven't seen them in *years.*"

"You sure you don't want to bring Sadie with you? She might help."

"I thought about it, but a twenty hour drive sounds awful."

Sutton nods. "You're right, that does sound awful. That's about what I did when I moved here. Never again."

"Exactly. We'll see if I actually get on the plane in the morning." I make a sad attempt at a joke.

"Do you need a ride or anything else?"

"No, you're doing enough for me. I got it."

"Is Wes taking you?" She gives me a pointed look.

"What? No? Why would he do that?"

She shrugs, continuing to stare me down as though she's waiting for me to tell her more.

I groan. "There's nothing going on with him."

"I didn't say there was."

"Thought you had sources?"

"You're right, I do. So you might as well just tell me the truth about everything."

"There's nothing to tell, we've hooked up...a couple times."

"I knew it!" She points at me and I roll my eyes.

"Yeah, yeah, but it's nothing. He's just there, and you know, he's attractive enough." I shrug like it's not a big deal when lately it's been a bigger deal than I'm willing to admit.

In fact, it's felt like the biggest deal. Every time he looks at me, there's so much that passes between us with just a look. So many unspoken words, yet we both know exactly what the other is holding back.

It's terrifying, but I can't stop. We don't admit anything more, and we've never spent a full night together. We get lost in each other and then one of us leaves. I know the moment we do, then this thing between us officially shifts and the realness of the situation will get even scarier.

I know Wes has his own reasons for not wanting to spend the night together. He has trouble sleeping just like I do, and I can't help but wonder if he has nightmares, too. We both have histories we refuse to talk about and that's partly why we work so well. There's no pressure, no pushing. It's a mutual understanding and it's probably one of my favorite things about him.

"It always turns into something," she hedges.

"This isn't some romance book or movie. Two people can mess around and it not turn into anything more."

"Whatever you say," she singsongs.

"I think Lily is starting to rub off on you."

"Not quite. I don't have some crazy rubber duck bondage story to tell."

"What?" I splutter.

She waves me off. "Don't ask. Seriously, don't."

I double check that she has everything she needs for Sadie while I'm gone, still feeling guilty leaving her behind. She's still getting used to me and my house and now she's in another new place. I kneel down, rubbing her ears as I talk to her.

"I hope you have fun. I'm not abandoning you here, I promise. You're still safe with me and I'll be back soon."

She sticks her tongue out, panting which makes it look like she's smiling as her tail wags. I wish it helped ease the guilt I feel, but it doesn't and I'm about to cancel this whole trip.

"Don't worry about her. She's going to have so much fun with Bennet and Duke," Sutton tries reassuring me. Even though I know she's right, it still doesn't completely erase how I feel.

"Go have fun. Enjoy seeing your family." Sutton leads me out of the house and back to my car.

I try to drag my feet a little bit more, but she doesn't let me. Even as I'm backing out of her driveway, I feel like I should go back and get Sadie, cancel my ticket, and hide in my house through the entire holiday season. At this point, I don't think Sutton would even let me because she just stands there with her arms crossed as she continues to watch me drive away.

For some reason, once I get home every single emotion I've held back breaks through. My forehead drops onto my steering wheel as everything bubbles to the surface, and I feel like I can't breathe. Tears I can't control are streaming down my face while I gasp for breath and dig my nails into my thighs.

I can't do this. I can't see my family. They don't want to see me. I'm just going to ruin them like I ruin everything. I can't go there, they don't really want me there. It's better for me to stay home. I go to pick up my phone, but my hands are shaking so bad I fumble with it, and it falls somewhere on the floor which only makes everything worse.

I bang my hands against the steering wheel, letting out a scream, hoping it will take away everything I'm feeling, but it doesn't.

The tears fall harder, and I'm just trying to catch my breath but it feels like that will never happen. Maybe I'm having a heart attack, because this isn't like anything I've experienced before. I hardly even register the door opening, even when someone's hands are on my legs, swinging them out. There's a voice but I can't understand him. I can't understand anything right now. I'm too lost in my own mind and I don't think I'm going to get it back.

CHAPTER 36

Wes

I NOTICED BAILEY COME HOME, but what I didn't notice was her getting out of her car. After several minutes, I get concerned and go outside. What I see makes my stomach drop. I act without much thought after the scream she lets out. I race over to her, pull open the door, and check to make sure she's not hurt.

Physically she seems okay, but there's clearly something wrong. I don't even try to ask because I know I'm not going to get any information out of her right now with the way she's gasping for breath and has no reaction to me.

That's okay, she doesn't need to talk to me. All I want right now is to help her.

Before taking her into my arms, I grab her keys out of the ignition, and then scoop her up. She goes willingly, burying her face into my shoulder. I feel her tears and it makes me hold her tighter as I bring her inside her house. She's shaking, gasping, and crying. My stomach knots and anger peaks as I want to destroy whoever or whatever caused this because the woman in my arms is not the strong, attitude filled Bailey that I know.

Something caused this, and I want to know what it was.

Once we get inside, I sit on the couch, draping Bailey's legs over mine and just hold her. She sobs into my shoulder while I rub her back as she lets everything out. I don't try to talk, just waiting for her to be ready.

I don't know how long we sit like this, but I finally feel Bailey's breathing start to even out and her tears slow down. She lifts her head to look at me, her eyes and nose are red, and she seems to just be becoming aware that I'm here with her.

"What's going on?" I ask, moving the hair that's stuck to her wet face.

She opens her mouth, but no words come out. Her eyes starting to well up with tears again.

"Don't tell me right now, come on." I lift her, and carry her upstairs to her room.

"I'm really not in the mood for sex right now," she grumbles roughly against my chest where her face is buried.

"Me either," I tell her honestly before moving into the bathroom and depositing her onto the counter. "Wait here."

After I make sure she's not going to collapse and fall, I step toward her bathtub to start the water. I let the cold water run until it feels like a comfortable temperature, then step back over to Bailey, standing between her legs, her eyes remain locked on the floor.

"Do you want help?" I ask as gently as possible, knowing the question may piss her off or cause her tears to start once again.

It does neither of those things, and instead she raises her arms up above her head, but she's still not looking at me. I accept her silent request, lifting her shirt up and off, then unclasping her bra and dropping them on the floor. She lowers her arms, gripping the edge of the counter.

"Can you stand?" I ask, ready to hold her up if I need to.

Without answering, she slides off to stand in front of me. There's no space between our bodies and this moment that would usually be fueled by sexual tension feels anything but. Even when I'm pushing down her pants and underwear. Kneeling on the hard floor, my previous injury screams out, I breathe through it because I want to help her.

She steps out of the rest of her clothes, and I go check the bath to make sure it's good for her. She steps up behind me as I run my hand through the water, and doesn't say anything before stepping in. I help her keep her balance as she lowers herself down. Once inside, lets out a sigh, laying back and closing her eyes.

I wait for a minute to make sure she's okay before picking up her discarded clothes and getting new ones. I also grab the thickest towel I can find and go downstairs to put it in the dryer while I grab her a cup full of ice water.

When I get back upstairs with the hot towel and cold water I see her hugging her knees against her chest with her chin resting on top of them. She turns her head to look at me, then notices what I have in my hands.

"You don't have to get out yet, I just wanted to be ready when you are."

"I can get out," her voice cracks.

"You don't have to," I try again, but she's already starting to stand up. I hold the towel out for her, and wrap it around her body once she's standing.

Her mouth opens in shock when she realizes it's warm, and I just shrug. I turn around to grab the T-shirt I brought for her, just holding it until she's ready.

"What're you doing?" she whispers, pulling the towel around herself tighter.

"Helping."

"Why?"

"Because I want to."

She's looking at me with a skeptical range of emotions on her face but I just stand there ready to help with her shirt. She hesitates for a few more seconds before agreeing and letting me pull the shirt over her head, helping slip her arms through the designated holes and dropping the towel.

Again, I kneel on the ground even though my leg is killing me. She holds onto my shoulder stepping into the small underwear shorts I've seen her wear. When I stand up I get a good look at her face. She looks tired, eyes still red rimmed and I want to know what caused this breakdown.

"I'm going to lay down," she murmurs, walking toward her room, as I follow.

She climbs in, laying on the edge, but I'm not leaving.

"Scoot over," I instruct.

She looks up at me surprised. I kick off my shoes before climbing onto the bed, scooting her over myself.

Without another word I wrap my arms around her, pulling her into me. She stiffens, and I expect a fight, but after several seconds she melts into me with a sigh. And we stay just like this.

Finally, I manage to ask, "What happened?"

She stiffens again, but I don't loosen my grip around her. She remains silent for a while, and I think she's not going to say anything, but finally she does and I feel my own shoulders drop in relief that she's talking.

"I'm leaving to see my brother and sister tomorrow."

"And that gave you a panic attack?"

"I haven't seen them in over ten years."

I pull her into me a little more, hoping it's providing the comfort I want it to. I've never needed to be the comfort for someone before and I'm not sure I'm doing this right. That's why I don't try to fill the silence, I just wait for her to continue.

"I'm flying to Denver in the morning, but I shouldn't go."

"Why not?"

She's quiet again, but doesn't try to leave my arms either.

"Because we had a shitty childhood. Really shitty. We're all better apart and I don't want to be the reason their lives fall apart again."

That comment makes me tense. "Why the fuck would you think that?"

"I just do," she says softly.

I sigh, not grasping her thought process, but I also don't know the extent of what they all went through as children either.

Before I can think too much about it, I offer up the first thing that pops into my mind. "I'll come with you."

"What?" She sits up quickly, looking at me.

"I'll join you, and if and when you want to leave, we will."

She shakes her head. "No, you don't have to do that."

I put my hand on the one she has resting on my chest. "I know I don't have to. I want to."

"No way, plane tickets are way too expensive."

"I'll pay for it."

"You don't know anyone there."

"I know you."

"You hate being around people."

"So do you."

"They're my family."

"You just had a panic attack about that."

Her mouth snaps shut and she shakes her head. "You're not coming with me."

"Yes, I am," I insist, pulling my phone out of my pocket. "What time is your flight?"

CHAPTER 37

Bailey

EVEN AS I watched Wes buy his plane ticket online yesterday, I didn't think he was serious about coming with me. He must be completely out of his mind. When he left, saying he was taking Bruno to stay with Jameson and Sutton, I tried to convince him once again that he didn't need to come with me.

"We're overloading their house with dogs. You're not coming."

"They like it."

That's all he said before heading out. I convinced myself throughout the night he wouldn't be back. That I'll leave tomorrow—alone—as planned.

The next morning, I grab my backpack and suitcase ready to head out when I see Wes leaning against my car with his own duffel laying on the ground by his feet. "Ready?"

"Are you serious?" I ask in disbelief.

"I told you I'm coming. I don't know why you think I would lie to you."

"Because this is insane," I huff, walking to the trunk, opening it and before I can lift my suitcase in, Wes is behind me, speaking against my ear. His breath hitting my skin sends a shiver down my spine.

"Like I've said before, join me in my insanity then, Angel."

I gasp remembering *exactly* when he said that before. This situation is a bit different than last time, but still when he picks up my suitcase, loading it into my trunk, and then his own, it hits me. It really sinks in that he's serious.

He stretches his hand out for my keys, and I hesitate.

"Do you really not want me to come with you?"

I bite my bottom lip thinking about it. It's crazy, I know it is. But at the same time, having someone with me that I know does bring a sense of comfort. Having *Wes* with me brings comfort. I'm about to see my siblings that I haven't seen in a long time. Plus their families who I've never met. It's a lot of people, and I'll be the odd one out.

Knowing I'll have Wes with me does make me feel a little better. Especially with how he helped calm me down yesterday. I don't know how he knew what to do, or that he was capable of being so sweet.

It really hits me that everything I've been holding back, the feelings I've been attempting to suppress about Wes, are about to consume me. That thought alone could send me into another spiral, but I refuse to let it.

Instead, shaking my head as I hold his steady gaze, I hand my keys over and allow him to drive us to the airport. Hoping like hell I don't regret letting him come with me.

●

SOMEHOW I MANAGE to keep myself together throughout the drive to the airport. I can't read Wes because he's always so stoic, but once we're seated on the plane I can sense how tense he is. I place my hand on his thigh as the plane is taking off.

"Are you okay?"

"Yeah," he grunts unconvincingly.

"Are you afraid of flying?" I don't expect that from him, but I guess I really don't know that much about Wes when I think about it.

The look he gives me is almost smug. "No, I'm not afraid of flying. I was an Apache pilot in the Army."

My jaw drops because I don't know how I missed that piece of information before. But he doesn't talk about his past, just like me. I do know both his parents passed away and that the Army was his life, but that's the extent of my knowledge of his past.

Though, all that really matters is the present anyway. I know he's more caring than he wants people to believe. That his heart is so much bigger than he lets on and he probably doesn't even realize it. He's thoughtful, considerate, and not the obnoxious asshole I convinced myself he was for years.

Yes, he drives a loud car, but I also know he's proud of that car and that it's one of the only big purchases he's made for himself. His car and his house. Other than that, he doesn't care about material things.

Which I guess is why my heart has become much more involved than it should have. Even with my limited knowledge of his past, I've managed to fall for the man sitting next to me, and yet he can never know it. Because if I were to tell him, I would surely lose him. And much to my dismay, I'd rather have him in the capacity I do now than not at all.

"If you're not scared then why are you so tense?" I ask, rubbing my hand up his corded forearm.

"Same reason I always have to drive. I don't like not being in control," he grinds out. I nod in understanding. He does need control in all aspects of his life it seems, and this is no different.

I don't complain, though. The bedroom—where he gets to have all the control—is where I reap the benefits. It's where I also *give* him that control. I just make him work for it, but that's half the fun.

"You just need to be distracted," I suggest.

He looks over at me with a raised eyebrow. "Are you offering the mile high club to me, Angel?"

I chuckle, shaking my head. "No, getting arrested is not on my list of to dos."

"We wouldn't get arrested."

"Yeah, I'm thinking we would. The only way to have privacy

on this plane is the bathroom and I don't think my six foot ass and your six foot five ass are fitting in there together."

"I'm six foot six, but thank you for that."

"You really need that extra inch?"

He smirks. "No, I don't think I need any extra inches, do you?"

I bite the corner of my lip to stifle my smile, enjoying the banter. Especially enjoying the fact that he's managed to become less tense. I feel an even bigger sense of accomplishment at that.

Throughout the rest of the plane ride, I do my best to distract Wes. I prepare him for what he's about to walk into after I realize I didn't tell him about Brent's unique relationship. It also proves that he didn't research my brother since it's one of the first things that comes up.

"Okay, you should know that my brother Brent is in a relationship with this woman named Chandler," I begin. Wes nods along while I think about how to phrase the next part. "She's also in a relationship with two other guys. I don't remember their names, but they all live together. And have a daughter named Evie. Oh, and they're also expecting another."

"Like a polyamorous relationship?" he asks, voice completely even.

"Yeah, I guess so."

"Okay. What else?"

I'm taken aback. "You don't have any more questions? You

don't think it's weird? Sure you don't want the pilot to turn the plane around?"

He shakes his head. "Not at all. Whatever makes people happy is their business. How is it fair for me to judge anyone's happiness?"

I'm pleasantly surprised that he's not weirded out by that piece of my family, so I continue.

"My sister, Brynn, is married to one of Brent's previous teammates. I don't know his name either. She's nice, but can be talkative which is the complete opposite of Brent and me."

"You don't say?"

"Was that sarcasm?" I gasp.

"I don't know why you're always so surprised when I joke around with you."

"Because you're *you*, maybe?"

"What does that mean?"

"You look like you torture people in your free time," I deadpan.

He furrows his brows at me, clearly not liking that comment.

"Oh, you're the only one allowed to joke around now?"

The side of his lips kick up in a smirk. "My jokes are just better."

"Whatever." I shove his shoulder lightly as he chuckles.

It's nice that the lighthearted energy between us remains throughout the rest of the flight. We don't stop talking, and the little bit of self preservation I tried to keep going into this trip evaporates because Wes has infiltrated my heart in a way there's no coming back from.

I just hope this trip won't ruin that.

CHAPTER 38

Bailey

AFTER LANDING IN DENVER, we get the rental car, and I already know Wes is going to drive. I don't even bother arguing when he passes his license to the worker. I do try to argue about paying for it, but he just pushes my card away silently.

It's freezing here, the snow lining the sides of the road looks a few days old. I grew up in the cold and snow, but living in a coastal town like Amity where it stays mostly temperate throughout the year leaves me shocked at the freezing temperatures.

"Do we need to get you a thicker coat?" Wes asks as we get into the car, and I attempt to hide my shiver.

"No, I'm fine," I insist.

He shrugs, and I glare at him from the side, knowing if he catches me he'll likely threaten me with another punishment. One that I would happily take right here in this car. Anything to delay getting to my brother's house would be a welcome distraction.

We drive through the unfamiliar roads following the GPS on Wes's phone until we reach a large two story house and my jaw drops. I know my brother makes a lot of money, but for some reason I didn't expect *this* level of wealth. Even for a professional hockey player.

Wes parks, turning the car off then shifting toward me. "You okay?"

I nod. "Yeah, I'll be fine."

"I'll be here if you need."

I look at him wide eyed. "You're not coming inside?"

He looks confused.

"You said you'll be here, like in the car."

He lets out a huff. "And you say I'm not good at joking."

Without thinking, I lean over the console and press a kiss to his lips. It's brief, just a peck really, but the action surprises me more than anything. I didn't think twice about it, I just wanted to. I wanted the small comfort he brings me. I want him to know how grateful I am that he came. I just wanted to kiss him without it leading to more.

Because I'm falling for Wes.

Or maybe I've already fallen.

"Ready?" he asks, pulling me from my thoughts before I have a chance to fall into another spiral before we even go inside.

I nod, opening the door and the cool air whips me in the face. Wes grabs our bags from the trunk and I swing my backpack over my shoulder. We step up to the front door, and I force myself to knock before I end up running in the other direction. Wringing my hands together nervously, I wait to see who's going to answer. To see who the first person I come face-to-face will be.

I just hope that whoever it is won't have me running in the other direction. My heart rate kicks up as I hear the lock, and even more when the door actually starts to open.

My breath hitches as I come face-to-face with my brother, who I haven't seen in years. He looks almost exactly the same as I remember him. Tall, about the same height as Wes. His blond hair, a shade lighter than mine, but our green eyes match almost exactly.

"Hi Bailey," he says, his voice somehow seems deeper.

"Hi Brent." My own voice cracks saying his name, and I fight the urge to hug him. Which is unusual because we've never been a physically affectionate family, but something about this moment makes me want to anyway.

I hear another familiar voice right before she appears and I don't have the chance to blink before Brynn is pushing our brother out of the way. She doesn't bother even trying to hold back her tears, and doesn't hesitate to throw her arms around me in a hug.

I hardly get a chance to look at her, but she looks different than the last time I saw her. She's older, more mature. Her blonde hair is lighter than both Brent's and mine.

"Hi Brynn," I say softly. For some reason that only makes her cry harder. Now we're standing right outside Brent's front door in the freezing cold with my sister hanging onto me like a koala has me questioning my decision even more.

"I'm Brent." I hear my brother introduce himself and realize they don't know anything about Wes, or that he was even joining me.

I manage to pry myself away from Brynn, and seeing her tear stained face makes me feel even more guilty for how distant I've been from their lives.

"Wes." I hear the man with me introduce before shaking hands with Brent, and it pulls me back to reality for a minute.

"Sorry. This is Wes my, um." I look up at him hoping he'll help with what he is to me. Friends? *Are we even friends?* Boyfriend doesn't sound right, that sounds too official for us.

Brynn looks from me to the large man, lifting her eyebrow just waiting for me to finish my sentence that I really don't know how to complete.

"We're together," Wes assists.

"We'll get more into that." Brynn gives me a suspicious look, then pulls me inside the house.

"We didn't know you were bringing someone with you so I only have one of the guest rooms ready," Brent tells me.

"You don't have at least seven in this big ass house?" I scoff.

"It's okay," Wes says and I swing my gaze over to him. "We can share a room."

I narrow my eyes at that because we've never stayed the night together. I feel like it happening for the first time at my brother's house is even more awkward.

"I bet you will." Brynn winks at me.

"Auntie Brynn! Back!" A small voice calls out from another room and is followed by stomping footsteps. A little girl with curly brown hair, blue eyes, and a wide smile appears. Her smile seems to dim the slightest bit as she swings her gaze between me and Wes before tilting her head. "Who you?"

"Evie, I told you Auntie would be right back," another voice calls out, this one sounding out of breath. As she comes around the corner, I see the heavily pregnant woman I recognize from the pictures Brent sent of her with baby Evie.

"Sorry, I figured you'd want to get settled before meeting us." Chandler smiles softly, picking up her daughter. Brent is quick to offer to take the child from her arms.

"It's okay. I'm Bailey. And this is Wes. It's nice to meet you."

She smiles. "Chandler. It's so nice to finally meet you. I've heard a lot about you."

She's extremely beautiful with her long brown hair and soft eyes.

"Let's let them set their stuff down before Dumont, McQuaid, and Wheeler get in here and overwhelm them," Brent announces. I don't bother telling him it's too late because even hearing the unfamiliar names has my nerves ratcheting up once again.

Wes places a hand on the small of my back and the tiny action calms me more than I'm willing to admit.

They lead us down a hall on one side of the massive house and when we approach a bedroom, I gasp. It's the size of the entire second story of my house. A king size bed sits in the middle of the room with a simple TV on the wall. There's an en suite bathroom off to the side, and I don't have to look to see it's fancier than what I have at home.

"Hope this works for you," Brent grunts, stuffing his hands in his pockets as Wes steps inside and sets our suitcases down.

"Thank you," Wes tells him.

"Yeah, I guess this will do." I shrug teasingly. I catch the playful glare Wes shoots my way.

"I'm glad you decided to come," Brent says quietly.

"Me too."

I just hope that doesn't change.

Brent leaves, closing the door behind him with a click. Everything seems to hit me all at once as I stand in the unfamiliar room alone with Wes. I'm in Denver, in Brent's house that he shares with his family. Brynn's here. I just saw them for the first time in over ten years. We're about to spend the holidays together.

Wes is here with me. *Wes,* who insisted on coming with me, and hasn't shied away from a single thing since we got here. Wes, who helped me through my panic attack yesterday instead of running away screaming.

"Are you okay?" Wes asks, and I feel as though he can see the panic starting to bubble up once again.

When I don't answer right away, he steps up to me, cupping my face and forcing my gaze up to him. "What do you need?"

I try to shake my head, but it's subtle with the way he's holding me. "I just need a minute, if that's okay."

"Yeah. I'm going to take a shower."

"Okay," I whisper and his eyes search mine. Before he lets go he leans down and presses his mouth to mine, just like I did to him in the car.

His isn't as quick as mine was. He lingers there as our lips touch gently, and I feel myself melting against him. Especially when his tongue brushes against my bottom lip, and I open for him. This kiss is intense but not in the way it usually is. We aren't trying to rip each other's clothes off or fighting for dominance.

Right now, we're just kissing to feel. To be there for each other. To silently say all the things we can't voice.

When he pulls back, I think this is the first time I've seen his eyes so soft when he's looking at me. "Let me know if you need anything."

I nod and sway as he lets me go before walking into the bathroom and shutting the door.

My shoulders drop as the feelings return full force. I turn toward the bed as it's practically calling my name. I step toward it and as soon as I'm close enough to fall face first into the soft comforter, I do just that.

I let out a long breath, listening to the shower turn on in the other room, and think about Wes in there. Which inevitably leads to me thinking about what he looks like as he strips out of his clothes and steps under the water.

Turning my head to the side, I just listen to the sound of water hitting the tile thinking about what he could be doing in there. Then I think about what we could be doing in there together. I get up, not thinking about where we are because I just want the distraction. The kind that only he can give me.

I remove my clothes and leave them on the floor on my way to the bathroom, opening the door slowly so I can watch him for a couple moments before he sees me. Of course, it's Wes and he's hyper aware of everything that as soon as his body is in view through the glass shower he's already looking at me.

"I thought you wanted some time." He wipes the water from his face. I watch his arm flex at the movement, which only spurs me on to walk forward. The spot between my thighs is throbbing, needing the man currently looking at me with so much heat I think we both might spontaneously combust.

Opening the door to the shower, I tell him softly, "I had enough."

The steam surrounds me as I close the door behind me, keeping my eyes locked on his as I close the distance between us. I can't even appreciate how fancy this bathroom is because all I see is him.

"And what do you want now?" He doesn't move, just waits to see what I'm going to do or say.

I let my eyes roam over him, lingering on his chest where I bring my fingertips up to a scar there. I want to ask what it's from, but I don't want to ruin this moment. I move to another mark, then another. I trace the muscles on his chest while taking in the small scars decorating his skin. They remind me of the big one on the back of his leg, and about how I'm curious where it came from but I won't dare ask.

Instead, I move my hand lower to his thickened cock and wrap my hand around him tightly. He grunts, but doesn't try to stop me, just keeping his gaze trained on me. Not at my hand, not my body. He's looking at *me*.

I stroke him once, twice to see if he's going to try and regain control. I expect him to yank my hand away and slam me against the wall. But he doesn't. He just keeps his eyes locked on mine as I move my fist over him at a leisurely pace.

"How does that feel?" I ask, just barely above a whisper.

"Everything you do feels good, Angel. You make everything feel good."

I bring my bottom lip between my teeth, and think about what he's saying. I refuse to read too much into it, but it's hard not to when I'm feeling so vulnerable. It's like being here has my chest open leaving my heart completely exposed for him to do whatever he wants with it. He could take it and protect it. Or destroy it, like no one ever has.

Either way, it's not up to me anymore. It's up to him.

"Make me feel good," I tell him. I just want a few minutes to get lost in him.

When I expect him to be rough and put me in my place like he usually does, that's not what happens. He slides down onto the ground, turning and pushing my back against the tile wall. I yelp at how cold it is, but I quickly forget as soon as he tosses my leg over his shoulder and starts devouring me like I'm the only thing he needs in this world.

CHAPTER 39

Wes

I CAN TELL Bailey needs this. She needs this just as badly as I do. I'm doing my best to not show how uncomfortable I am being here because I want to do this. I know how hard this is for her, and I want to be here for her if she needs me. Just like the plane ride, I tried to hide how uncomfortable I was. I'm not afraid of flying. I just don't like *other* people flying for me.

But she knew what I needed. She got me talking and surprisingly, it made me feel better. She makes everything feel better for me lately. Now it's my turn to do the same for her.

Not that it's a hardship to be down here with my face buried in her delicious pussy. My leg hates the position, but I can handle the discomfort while knowing I'm making Bailey feel good. Giving her what she needs trumps anything I could be feeling right now.

That's how I know I've fallen so far for this woman, there's no going back. But she might not feel the same. These feelings are so unfamiliar, so overwhelming, I can't bring myself to say them out loud. But I feel something, and I have for so long. And they're only getting stronger.

Especially right now as my tongue is buried in her. She's got her hands fisted in my hair, roughly trying to keep me exactly where she wants me. I groan against her, and I know she loves the vibration it sends through her body.

"You're going to soak my face, Angel, and after that I'm going to fuck you nice and hard just like you need."

She moans, and I know she likes the sound of it. Especially because she starts rubbing herself even harder against my mouth. But I know she needs more. That's why I push a finger in, curling it to find that spot she likes. It barely takes any time at all with my tongue flicking her clit and my finger fucking her before she's detonating.

She throws her hand over her mouth to muffle her screams. I'm annoyed at the move, but the tiny rational part of my brain that is still functioning knows she did the right thing.

As soon as she's come down from her release, I stand up, keeping one hand on the thigh I just lowered from my shoulder. I guide it around my hip instead. I know she's ready, I've known for a while so I don't waste another second. I angle myself at her entrance and push in.

She gasps at the sudden pressure, and I drop my forehead to hers. "I know, baby, you're doing so well. You always do so well for me."

She melts at the praise, and I keep that in mind. She's always fighting back. She loves to be challenged and to give as good as she takes. But right now, she just wants to feel good, and I can give her that, happily.

I push in to the hilt, burying myself in her warmth with a groan. I capture her mouth with my own to stifle both our cries while I fuck her steadily. We lose each other in the sensations as our mouths dance together and our hips collide in a desperate rhythm.

The hot water hits my back, and I don't even think about where we are or what we're doing. Because nothing else matters except the two of us right now.

"I need another one from you, Angel. Give it to me so I can fill up your pretty pussy with my cum."

That does her in. Suddenly, she's clenching around me, already reaching the peak once again. "Atta girl," I growl against her mouth, fucking her harder through her orgasm. It doesn't take long before my own takes over as I push in as deep as I can, making sure to fill her just like I said I would.

The water starts to cool, so after I clean her up, we get out and I make sure to wrap her in one of the large towels. She looks around the bathroom like she's actually seeing it for the first time.

"Damn, I never thought of Brent having a place this nice," she mumbles.

I don't know how to respond to that and she seems like she's talking to herself more than me anyway.

After we get dressed again, I check in on what she wants to do.

"Are you wanting to see everyone, or stay up here for a little longer?"

Bailey sighs. "I want to stay up here, but I know we should see everyone. You don't have to go if you don't want to."

I step closer to her. "I'll be wherever you are."

Her breath catches, but she nods. "Okay, let's go down there then."

I stick close to Bailey's side as we make our way downstairs and there's now several more people in the large living room than there was before.

"There you are. I was convinced you were going to hide the rest of the day," Bailey's sister, Brynn, teases and I bite back a smile. Even though they haven't seen each other in so long, she clearly still knows her.

"I thought about it," Bailey grumbles as we reach the bottom of the stairs.

"This is my husband, Colton. If he gives you shit, feel free to smack him upside the head," Brynn says to us both.

"I'm perfectly nice," Colton retorts, stretching his hand out toward us both. I take it firmly. He's a big guy. All of the men here are, which isn't surprising since they're all hockey players. Normally, I stick out in any place I go since I'm usually the biggest in the room, but here I feel like I fit in a little more. This has a different sense of calm wash over me.

"Oh, so it's opposite day?" Brynn looks at her husband with

narrowed eyes. The move reminds me so much of Bailey. I want to laugh and call her out, but this isn't the time.

Colton wraps his arm around Brynn's shoulders and pulls her into him with a forced smile. "These Collee girls are something else, aren't they?" he teases.

I look at Bailey, who's surveying the other people in the room. "Yes, they really are."

"Come on. You can meet everyone." Brynn breaks away from Colton's hold, grabbing Bailey's hand and pulling her further into the living room.

I follow slowly and Colton sticks next to me. "Brynn is so happy Bailey decided to come. She's missed her a lot."

I just nod, knowing how hard this was for Bailey. I hope seeing how happy her siblings are to see her will make it all worth it.

"This is Chandler's second partner, Vince," I hear Brynn introduce, motioning to the guy lounging on the couch with Evie sitting on his lap. He gives a small wave. "And this is partner number three, Matt."

"Wait, why am I number three?" the guy, Matt, huffs.

"Because you pissed me off earlier," Brynn deadpans.

"How? You weren't even here before I went to practice."

"I don't always need a reason."

"What do you mean? Of course you need a reason—"

"Watch it, McQuaid," Colton snaps, stepping up behind Brynn.

"I didn't even do anything." Matt throws his arms up and drops them back down.

"Just let it go," Chandler says, placating him with a light tap to his chest walking by on her way to check on her daughter as she laughs with Vince.

I can tell this is all too much for Bailey. She's quiet, just watching it happen. It's a lot for me too, but my entire focus is on her and what she needs. I can't even think about myself at this moment. That's how I end up stepping closer to her, not touching because I don't think she wants that. But just close enough that she knows I'm here.

"So, how did you two meet?" Brent asks. It takes me a second to realize he's talking to us, and looking directly at me.

I freeze because they don't need to know the real story, but we didn't exactly come up with a fake one either.

"We're neighbors," Bailey answers and I nod in agreement.

"How long have you been together?" Brynn chimes in.

This time, the question has us both freezing.

"Come on. You guys don't need to bombard them right away," Chandler speaks up, and I decide she's the most rational one here.

"Sit down. Why are you just standing around?" Brynn asks and that's when I realize we're the only two still standing.

There's plenty of seating options, but everything feels so awkward. How close does Bailey want me? Where does she want to be? I'm used to my very simple, straightforward life and being here is anything but.

Bailey settles on a small couch section, and when she gives me a look—silently telling me doesn't want me far—I sit next to her. It takes a minute before the conversations start up around us again in a way that feels natural. I can tell how close this group is with each other. They all so easily give each other shit, and take it in stride. I see how the guy's are with Evie and it's evident they all love her like their own.

"Who's ready for some dinner?" Chandler asks, pushing herself up off the couch, but Brent guides her back down.

"You stay, we got this."

"Got what? Ordering pizza?"

"Precisely." He smiles at her and she shakes her head.

"Pizza sounds great to me," Bailey announces, and I'm quick to agree.

"So, Wes, what do you do?" Colton asks.

I clear my throat, and can tell Bailey gets nervous that I'm about to talk about myself.

"I'm a Veteran and just do some volunteer work right now," I answered simply.

"Oh shit, you are? What branch? What did you do?" Colton rapid fires questions.

"Army. I was an Apache pilot."

"That's so fucking cool. Are you trained in combat and shit?"

"Colton!" Brynn exclaims, throwing her hand over his mouth. "I'm sorry, I've been trying to teach him how to talk to people, but he never learns."

"That's okay." I try to keep my voice light, attempting not to think too much about the negative from that time. "Yes I am."

Colton pulls Brynn's hand from his mouth. "How long do you think it would take you to take us all out?"

"A group of hockey players?" I look at the four other men and smirk. "Seven seconds."

He laughs and they all join in with him while I chuckle with my half joke. It feels nice to not be completely serious. It feels good to just let go for a minute.

The rest of the night goes by easily. There's a lightness around us and as the sun goes down, the large Christmas tree set up in front of the floor to ceiling windows looking out to the Denver mountain landscape lights up. Even as we all eat pizza and sit around telling stories that aren't too deep, I learn a little more about all these new people.

I mostly learned how close this group is. Not just because all the guys have played on the same hockey team for years, either, but because they've created their own family. Their own *chosen* family. That's something I never really even considered as a possibility. Seeing them and seeing how happy they all are makes me feel like maybe living how I have—closed off to everyone—wasn't my only option.

Especially with Bailey sitting next to me. She's scooted closer without either of us noticing. I've gotten more comfortable and more relaxed, draping my arm around the back of the couch around her.

It's simple. Easy. Even with the chaos, it is oddly peaceful.

When it gets late, and the exhaustion hits, we don't even think twice about going upstairs to go to bed together. For the first time. Even though I'm nervous, I refuse to show it. I don't know if I'll be able to sleep, or what I may do when I inevitably have nightmares. Any small hesitation I have about the situation flies out the window as soon as Bailey speaks.

"If you're uncomfortable I can go sleep on the couch or something," she offers, not looking at me as she changes.

"Fuck no," I snap immediately. "If I had a problem, then I would be the one sleeping on the couch. But I don't."

She looks at me skeptically.

"Get into bed, Angel," I commanded, pulling my shirt off with one hand behind my neck.

She settles into the large bed and after I push my pants off, I climb in on the other side, keeping my distance from her.

Neither of us says anything, even as I turn off the light. She shuffles around in the blankets, and I lay facing the ceiling like I do every single night.

"Wes?" Bailey whispers into the darkness.

"Yeah?"

"Are you going to kiss me goodnight?"

I take that as the permission it is to roll over and move closer to her. Leaning over her, I hold myself up with my hands resting on either side of her head. Dipping my head down, I whisper right before my lips touch hers, "Goodnight, Bailey."

CHAPTER 40

Bailey

I WAS nervous about falling asleep so close to Wes. I didn't know if I was going to struggle to fall asleep like I normally would, or if he would. But I feel like everything hits me all at once and exhaustion takes over. The weirdest part is that after he kissed the breath out of me, he pulled me into his body and I drifted off easily.

When I open my eyes the next morning I realize it's Christmas morning and instead of the usual thought of dread consuming me, I feel...*comfortable*. I'm surrounded by warmth. It's not just a normal warmth it's like a space heater. And I quickly realize why.

I'm completely pressed against Wes with my arm draped across his stomach. I'm afraid to move because I don't want to startle him. As carefully as I can, I look up to his face, where I'm met with his already open eyes.

"Did you sleep at all?" I ask, trying to move away, but he stops me with his arm tucked under me that I didn't even notice.

"Yeah, I just woke up." His voice is rough, giving away that he's not lying. "I actually think it was my best night's sleep in a long time."

"Me too," I murmur softly.

"Are you ready for day two with everyone?"

I sigh. "I guess so."

"Everyone seems nice."

"Yeah. How're you holding up?"

"I'm fine."

I twist my lips to the side because "fine" isn't a great answer, but I can tell that's all he's going to give me.

"I didn't get you a gift, though," I admit.

"Well now you've crossed the line."

I bark out a laugh, and he joins me with his low rumble. "Come on, let's find you some coffee."

⁎

AFTER WE GET DRESSED and go downstairs, Chandler is already sitting on the floor with Evie who's currently working on unwrapping a present. Matt and Vince are sitting close by on the couch, watching the scene in front of them.

Chandler notices us, and smiles. "Good morning. We were going to wait, but I told her she could open one present."

"It's okay. You don't need to wait for us," I tell her.

"I'll grab you some coffee," Wes says, as I take a seat in a chair close to where Evie and Chandler are sitting.

"Brent is in there making some. He can help you, that machine is complicated." Chandler gives me a look like she's silently wishing him luck.

"Hopefully he can teach me." Wes heads toward the kitchen, and Matt immediately speaks up.

"Hopefully he doesn't give your boyfriend a hard time like he did to Brynn."

"You gave Colton a harder time than he did," Vince scoffs.

"That had nothing to do with Brynn, I just hated the guy."

"And now look at you two. You all love each other *so* much." Chandler rolls her eyes for only me to see and I let out a small smile.

"Seems like I've missed out on a lot," I admit, especially looking at Evie as she shakes around the box with the new toy she just opened.

"You're here now, and that's all that matters." Chandler smiles.

I try to return it, but I'm hit with the guilt of not being around as much as I should be, purely based on an irrational fear. Wes returns with a mug full of steaming liquid at the same time Brent returns with an iced drink for Chandler.

"You two can get your own," Brent tells the other two men who grumble.

"You're a brave soul, putting up with three guys all the time," I tease, taking a sip of the drink that I'm surprised to find is perfect.

"That's what I'm told." She chuckles.

The front door opens, and Brynn announces herself as she and Colton enter with several bags full of presents. "You all can stop crying. We're here now. Sorry we're late."

"No one is crying," Brent deadpans and Brynn glares at him.

"You have no sense of humor. Did I get all the joking genes?" Brynn looks at me and I shrug.

"That's a yes," she groans. "I also got the good shopping genes, so everyone move aside."

They bring the bags into the living room and I watch as Evie lights up at the sight of all the presents. Even though the tree is filled even more than when we saw it last night because Santa must have made a delivery.

Brynn pulls out a box, and hands it to me. "Merry Christmas, sis."

She turns away to unpack the other gifts, and I hold back my tears looking at the perfectly wrapped box with a bow on top. I don't move to open it; I just stare at the shiny paper and rub the ribbon between my index finger and thumb.

"Oh Brent, don't forget about all those presents you have for

Bailey in the closet you think no one knows about," Brynn announces as she's handing a box to our brother.

"What?" I look at them and see the shit eating grin on Brynn's face as she reveals the secret.

"I was going to get them," he grumbles.

"You don't need to do that. I didn't get anything for you guys," I tell them honestly, feeling worse because I wasn't even sure I would come.

The guilt hits me again. Instead of having my freak out yesterday, I should've gone last minute shopping. Then again, I don't know what I could have even gotten because they are essentially strangers to me now.

"It's okay, you came. That's the best present." Brynn smiles widely and I can see the tears she's trying to hold back.

"Open more please!" Evie calls out, and the room fills with chuckles.

We all watch Evie open her presents, getting excited every time a new toy is revealed. When she opens some clothes, she just ends up throwing them to the side and tries to find something more exciting. Watching her has me smiling without even noticing. I'm not a fan of kids, but she's so cute and entertaining.

After Evie is done with her presents and is thoroughly entertained playing with her new toys, Brynn tells everyone to open the presents she brought. I hesitate to open mine because of my guilt, but Brynn gives me a small nod of encouragement.

I carefully pull back the paper, not ripping into it like crazy.

There's a plain white box that I open to reveal a shirt and it says, "Auntie." I chuckle, mostly because I would never wear something like this.

"Really?" Chandler sounds like she's crying. I see she's holding up the shirt and looking at the back.

I pick the one I have up as well and see it says, "Baby Wheeler…x 2."

My eyes shoot up to my sister and I see her already crying. "You're pregnant? With twins?"

"I am," she sobs. "I told him I wanted one and of course he didn't listen."

"Fuck yeah." Vince high fives Colton and I don't miss the way Brent glares at the two of them. He's always been overprotective, and that clearly hasn't changed one bit.

Still, he gives Brynn a half hug while she remains sitting. "Congrats, shorty."

She scoffs at the nickname and I let out a small laugh because it's been so long since I've heard him call her that. Us Collee's are tall, and my brothers all range from six foot four to six foot six. I'm six foot, but Brynn is the shortest of all at five foot nine and I was always jealous that she wasn't a giant like me. Though, I wasn't jealous of the shit our brothers would give her for it when they were being playful.

"Are you going to congratulate me too, bro?" Colton stretches his arms out like he's offering a hug.

Brent looks at him deadpan. "No."

"You love me, don't even pretend," Colton ribs him.

"I tolerate you. Don't push it."

"Bailey, remind me to tell you later about the fight these two got into a couple years back." Brynn practically bounces in her seat.

That piques my interest because I can't see Brent getting into a fight, especially with his teammate. He and our brother Brandon used to get into arguments, but when Brandon would attempt to turn it physical, Brent always had the advantage of being sober, and didn't really need to fight him to end it.

But this fight with Brynn's husband? That sounds like something I want to know.

"We don't need to relive that." Brent shakes his head.

Brynn just looks at me and winks. It's like we have a secret and it makes me feel closer to her. It helps the tightness in my chest loosen a bit. Maybe everything with us can be okay.

CHAPTER 41

Wes

WATCHING Bailey let her guard down around her family is the greatest thing I've ever seen. Slowly but surely throughout the day, she seems to get lighter and lighter. I just watch, not involving myself too much because I don't have anything to add to the conversations. I'm just here for Bailey. Watching her be like this with her family after she was so worried makes me feel so much better about coming.

I think of the alternative where I would've been alone in my house with Bruno, not doing anything. Maybe I could've gone to the animal shelter. Those dogs still need attention, even on the holidays. Once we're back, I'll make sure to bring treats to spoil them.

Even though I'm not used to being around so many people at one time, I manage to feel good around this group. Brent and Bailey are similar in how quiet they are, always observing everyone. Brynn is a lot more outspoken than they are and so is her husband. Though I can see how the rest of the guys didn't get along with him.

The day is mostly peaceful, and it's the best Christmas I've had since I was a kid. I try to fight off the memories of my own family, of what it was like when my parents were still around. Of the happy house we had, and then what it was like after my dad died. My mom still tried, she really did, but it was never the same. Then I was grown and out of the house and before I knew it, she was gone, too.

It's just been me ever since. So being here with this large family is foreign, but not entirely awful like I would've thought it would be.

I think I've got Bailey to thank for that. I know she was scared to see her family after so long. I know there are things I don't know about their history, but from what I've seen none of that even matters.

"She seems like she's doing well," Brent says quietly while everyone else is talking.

"She is." I nod.

"Thanks for being there for her, I know she's a stubborn one."

I huff a small laugh. "Yeah she is."

"Wait. Did you say the bird talks?" Chandler tries to clarify after Bailey tells them about life in Amity.

"Yeah. Jerry Lee, he says some wild shit." She looks wide eyed at Evie who's still preoccupied with her toys, but corrects herself. "Stuff. Anyway, he's wild and Lily has started teaching him more things she probably shouldn't."

"Lily sounds like my kind of girl." Brynn smiles. "Brent, you should get a bird."

"Absolutely not. We're about to have two little girls around here. *You* get a bird."

"No can do, big bro. I'm about to have two little somethings running around of my own. Well, I guess mine won't be running for a while." Brynn smiles down at her still mostly flat stomach, and pats it lightly.

I've never wanted kids. But the way her husband places his hand over hers, the love in their eyes as they talk about the future has the piece of stone in my chest where a heart used to be crumbling as it starts to feel things.

"I got a dog," Bailey blurts.

"Aw, I would love a dog." Brynn looks like she may start crying again. "What kind?"

"She's a Golden mix and her name is Sadie." Bailey smiles talking about her new friend and I can't help but smile with her.

"Next time, you should bring her." Brynn's face dims slightly, "I mean, if you plan to come back again."

Bailey's shoulders drop, and I can feel her guilt from here. "I will. I promise."

"I don't know about the rest of you, but I want some pie," Matt announces, breaking the simmering tension.

"What pie?" Brent questions.

"The one Chandler made last night when she couldn't sleep because the future hockey player she's growing wouldn't stop kicking," Matt explains.

Brent looks at Chandler. "You could've asked for help."

"Sleeping? I don't think there's anything you could have done to help." Chandler chuckles.

"Don't start being gross." Brynn grimaces.

"How is that being gross?" Brent asks.

"It was only a matter of time." Brynn glares at her brother who just shakes his head.

Matt ends up bringing out the pie. There's a small altercation about him not serving everyone. Afterwards, they all end up migrating to the kitchen while Bailey and I hang back for a couple extra minutes.

"I got you a present too, but I wanted to give it to you in private," I tell her.

"If it's some sort of sex toy, you should wait until we're back home."

"It's not." I shake my head. "I'm not some deviant, you know?"

Bailey gives me a look that reads like, "*are you sure?*"

I stand up, yanking her with me so our chests collapse. "Don't be a brat. I'm no stranger to pulling you into a bathroom or closet to punish you."

Her breath catches, and I almost think she's going to tempt me even more when her name is called from the kitchen.

"Guess you'll have to hold out on that punishment until later." She winks, walking ahead of me into the kitchen.

I rub my chest, watching her go and thinking about how wild it is, how far we've come from where we were just a few months ago. About how I should be afraid of how close we've gotten. And yet, all I can think about is how I don't want it to end.

WHEN I OFFERED to come here with Bailey, I didn't expect it to be so easy. I figured there would be family drama to sort out, and while I'm sure she does have some things to talk to her siblings about, it's been simple and fun. Which is something I never expected.

Christmas began with presents and ended with all of us sitting in the outdoor covered patio. There's a small fire going for warmth, but we still need blankets. Which is how Bailey and I got cuddled together under a large blanket surrounded by these people who were just strangers to me yesterday.

"You guys should stay until after New Years," Brynn suggests during a lull in conversation.

Bailey shakes her head, her hair grazing me with the movement. "No, we have to get back before then. I don't want Jameson and Sutton stuck with the dogs for that long."

"Come on, please?" Brynn purses her bottom lip in a pout.

"If they can't stay, they can't stay," Brent says, pointedly.

"Sorry, forgot Captain Buzzkill was still here."

I lean down to whisper to Bailey, "If you want to stay, we can always ask."

She turns her head toward me. "I'm sure you want to get back, too."

"Get back to what? You're here."

She sucks in a gasp as her eyes go wide, and I pull her against me even tighter.

"Well you guys think about that, but I'm exhausted." Brynn starts to stand up, stretching her arms up, and Colton follows.

"Yeah, I'm pretty tired too," Bailey agrees.

I fold the blanket we were using before setting it on the bench seat we were just on as Brynn pulls her sister in for a long hug. I take my time, letting them have their moment before we turn in for the night.

Bailey decides to take a shower. While I'm tempted to join her, I also want to get the present I got for her out of my bag and try to make it special.

I'm not a romantic guy, and never have been. I don't even know if I'm doing it right, or if she will even like this. I spend the several minutes she's in the bathroom arguing with myself that this is a bad idea, and to just return it. Or throw it away. She never has to know, I'm sure she forgot about me saying I had something for her.

Or I can say I actually forgot it.

It was something I ordered last week, and even at the time I wasn't sure if I would end up giving it to her. That uncertain feeling is only amplified knowing she's just in the other room and bound to come back in here any minute.

I'm holding the black box that holds the necklace inside of it as I bounce it between my hands, continuing to debate even as I hear the shower turn off. My time is running out to make a decision, but as I'm walking toward my duffel to put it away and forget the whole thing the bathroom door swings open.

Bailey is wearing a T-shirt like she always does when she goes to sleep, but I notice this time it's not one of hers. It's mine.

Mine.

I look down at the box, and it solidifies my decision to give it to her. Even if it backfires, if she hates it or freaks out. I have to throw caution to the wind for once, and just do it.

Her hair is damp, falling around her shoulders as she narrows her eyes at me, probably seeing my internal battle even as I try to mask it. Her eyes drop to my hands. "What's that?"

I look at the box, stepping closer to her. "It's your Christmas present."

"I really wish you wouldn't have gotten me anything. I already feel bad enough that I didn't bring presents for anyone else."

"You don't need to get me anything," I insist, leading her to the bed and sitting next to her on the foot of it.

Handing over the box as soon as her fingers graze mine, I know there's no going back. She hesitates opening it, and I just watch, waiting to see how she's going to react.

I'm watching her face as she lifts the lid to reveal the thin chain necklace with a circle in the middle that has beads on it that represent a message in morse code. The gold represents the dashes, and the black represents the dots.

The colors of a sunflower.

-- .. -. .
Mine.

I gauge her reaction, waiting to see if this was a bad idea, or too far. Her mouth is open slightly, but she hasn't looked at me yet. Her fingers trace the tiny beads along the circle, and she finally speaks. "This is beautiful."

"Remind you of anything?"

She nods, turning toward me. "I don't want to say what because you told me if I say it, this stops."

The side of my lips quirk in a small smile. She doesn't want to say the safe word because she doesn't want this to stop. That thought alone makes me happier than it probably should.

"It's a message in morse code."

"What is it?

"It says 'mine.'"

She lunges at me, wrapping her arms around my neck, crashing her mouth onto mine. I wrap my arms around her back, pulling her to straddle my lap. I groan against her mouth, pushing my tongue in roughly, wanting to taste her, feel her. Love her.

I freeze for a second at the realization, but quickly pull her tighter against me and kiss her even harder. She moans, rubbing herself against me. I'm already hard for her and I know she can feel it.

When she whispers two words against my mouth, I lose all sense of myself because I've already lost myself to her, but her whispered words make it official.

"I'm yours."

CHAPTER 42

Bailey

I'VE BEEN GOING BACK and forth about staying through New Years. But after talking to Sutton, who said Sadie and Bruno are having the time of their lives and that she really doesn't mind, I decide to stay.

I try to tell Wes he can go back early if he doesn't want to stay, but he insists that he wants to be where I am. The shift between us is evident and it only seems to solidify each day that we're here. I always thought I'd get tired of someone being around me all the time if we were together. I've yet to become sick of Wes, even after spending so much time together and sleeping in the same bed.

Who would've thought?

Everything's been fun and easy going, just spending time with everyone, but I know I need to talk to Brent and Brynn. I need to apologize for the distance I put between us and work on trying to rebuild our family. We're all we have and I don't want to lose them. I want to know my future nieces and nephews. I want to continue to know my siblings. Bryson is another story, but maybe one day he'll come around too.

We've been here for a few days now, and I sneak down-stairs for some water after thinking everyone is in bed, but find my brother sitting in a recliner in front of the fire. For some reason it makes him look more mature. I've always looked at Brent like he was so much older than he is. Probably because he's basically had a parental role in my life since I was born. Even right now, he seems much older than thirty-six.

After I get my glass of water, I sit on the couch next to him. Neither of us say anything, and I'm sure he's waiting for me to speak first. That's something about my brother; he'll sit in silence as long as it takes to get the other person to speak.

Sounds like someone else I know, which is an odd realization to have. I shake away the comparisons of Brent and Wes because that's just weird.

"I'm really glad you're doing so well," I tell him honestly.

"You too." He turns to look at me. "Though I wish you would've visited a little sooner."

I groan, rolling my head back against the couch. "Look. I'm sorry I had my own shit I needed to work out. I didn't need you guys being dragged down. I needed to distance myself."

He nods. "I know, but you didn't think some of that could've been done while still seeing us every once in a while?"

"I get it," I grit my teeth.

"I'm just saying. We all have shit, Bailey."

"I told you, I get it. But tell me, what do you think happened when you left, Brent? Did you think everything was fine?"

"No, I thought Bryson would step up and help since we all knew Brandon wouldn't. I did everything I could. I sent money. I came home to help when I was able. I just wanted the best for you guys. I always have."

"I know you did, and I don't blame you for leaving, we all wanted to. But Brynn and I were the youngest and I wanted to protect her. You, Brandon and Bryson eventually left and it was just us. Who do you think took the brunt of everything once you three left?"

"I should've done more." He clenches his jaw.

I shake my head. "You did what you could. You can't go back. None of us can and we've all made our choices."

"Look where that's gotten us."

"Yeah, look, it's gotten you a family you clearly love more than anything. It's gotten Brynn the same. You both have what we never did."

"It also left Brandon dead and Bryson partying his way through the country. And what about you?"

I sigh. *What about me?*

"It has me owning a business and living my life."

"Are you happy?"

There was a time I don't think I was. And some days I'm not.

Life will always come with struggles. It can never be perfect, but I think about my life lately. My friends, actually having them. *Wes.*

"Yes, I'm happy."

"Then why do you think we wouldn't want to see you? Why do you think that would make our lives worse?"

I sigh, suddenly unsure how to answer because for the first time, the rationale I've told myself for years doesn't make sense. Having Brent ask for some reason brings it into perspective and I can't explain it.

"I don't know."

He grunts in that way he always does. He doesn't want to be a know it all, but I know what he's not saying.

"Talk to Brynn. All she's wanted is for us to all get along again. She's just wanted to have you back in our lives."

I sigh, knowing he's right. Brynn has made that known, and I'm the asshole who's ignored her.

"I will," I finally agree.

"Good."

The next day, I let Wes know I'm going to have lunch with Brynn, alone. Brent and I cleared some of the air last night, and I want to do the same with my sister so we can start to move forward without the past lingering over all of us like a dark cloud.

Brynn has been the publicist for a famous pop star, Spencer Sparks, for years. After she started settling down and started her family, she hasn't been in the public eye as much, so it sounds like Brynn's job hasn't been too hard. Apparently she and Spencer are also really good friends, so that also helps her get extended time off.

The guys had to leave for an away game yesterday, but apparently come back tomorrow. I remember Brent's hockey schedule was always crazy when we were younger, but the professional level is insanity.

Brynn was more than happy to meet with me, especially since Colton's gone. She said normally she would spend the day with Chandler helping with Evie, but now that Brent is home after his retirement, she said it's "lame to not have her girl time."

We meet at a small brunch place she recommended and I get us a table while I wait. She walks in, noticing me almost immediately. Her face breaks into a huge smile as she walks over, and I stand so we can wrap each other in a hug because I know she wants that. Honestly, so do I.

After we sit down, the waitress comes over and I just order a water, but when Brynn orders a "virgin mimosa" I give her a questioning look.

"You could just say orange juice, you know?"

"Bailey," she shakes her head, "Just let me have this."

I chuckle, agreeing with her antics.

Our cold drinks are delivered and as she takes a sip of the orange juice I ask, "How's the *virgin mimosa?*"

"Perfectly mixed." She sets it down as a serious look settles on her face. "I'm really glad you came to see us, and I hope you'll be around more. I would really like for you to be in these two's lives." She rubs her stomach and I smile softly thinking about my future nieces or nephews.

"Do you have any guess on what they're going to be?"

"I think one boy, one girl. Colton thinks two boys."

"When do you find out?"

"In a couple of weeks we can get a blood test to find out, but we may wait until a little later. Mostly because I know the waiting is killing Colton."

I chuckle, thinking about how I would be the same way if I was in her position, but also have the sobering realization that I won't be. And it's for the best. While I may be able to get past my fears when it comes to being back in their lives, I know, without a shadow of a doubt, I wouldn't want to subject a child in the mess that is mine.

The closest I'll have to a child is Sadie, and that's more than okay with me.

"I can't wait to meet them. I'm sorry I haven't been around. I realize now it may have been for a stupid reason."

"Whatever it is, I'm sure it's not stupid," she insists. "I know you all tried to protect me because I'm the youngest. I'm grateful for it, but I still saw everything. It messed all of us up in our own ways, but none of us resent each other because of it. At least, I don't resent any of you."

I swallow roughly. "What about Brandon?"

She sighs. "I don't resent him. I had a lot of guilt about his death, but I've had to realize that he made his own decisions. He chose to turn to drugs. Even when Brent offered to help him get sober, time and again, he decided not to accept it. There's only so much we can do, Bailey."

I nod, agreeing. "I know, I had guilt about it too. I didn't want the same thing to happen to any of you. I didn't want to be the reason anything changed in the lives you've built."

Brynn shakes her head, adamantly. "That would've never happened. The only way you could change it is for the good, I hope you know that."

I give her a close lipped smile. "I do now."

"Good, because I may technically be a Wheeler now, but I'll always be a Collee at heart."

I smile at that. "And I'll just always be a Collee."

"Really? You don't think you'll ever be Mrs. Wes...what's his last name?"

"Anderson." I chuckle. "But no, I don't know." Instinctively I reach up to touch the necklace he gave me, remembering what it stands for. What he claimed. What we said without fully saying it.

Mine.

I'm yours.

"Sure ya won't. Trust me, sis, it's a lot easier when you just give into your feelings."

I don't tell her that she's probably right. Instead, I divert with something she mentioned previously. "Speaking of, are you going to tell me about the fight Brent and Colton got into?"

She gets excited at the thought. "Oh, yeah it was a good one. I wasn't there as Colton and I were going through a bit of a separation. One day at practice he told Brent something about wanting to be in bed with me and he *lost it.*"

I sputter out a laugh, imagining the scene. The thought of Brent fighting like that is surprising, but knowing what was said to cause it makes a lot more sense.

"They've mostly gotten along since then," she explains. "Now that Brent is retired and not his captain anymore, I think they'll become besties."

"Really?" I don't hide my surprise.

"No. Definitely not, but it would be funny."

I agree with her because the visual I have of Brent being "besties" with anyone is pretty funny. He may be cool with his teammates and even in a different type of relationship, but I know that's purely because of how he feels about Chandler, not Matt and Vince. He's head over heels for that woman, and it's clear as day.

It's the same with how Colton is with Brynn. Again, I think of the necklace around my neck, and maybe it's even how Wes is with me.

CHAPTER 43

Bailey

IT'S weird not having the constant feeling of guilt hanging over me. After I talked to Brent and Brynn I feel lighter, happier even. The thought of coming back to see them again doesn't fill me with anxiety, and the thought of going home makes me a little sad.

Of course I miss Amity. My house, Sadie, and even Sutton. The one thing I don't miss is that when we get home, Wes and I will go back to our own houses. I'm used to sharing a bed with him and having him around. I'm used to how things can be with *us*.

I hope that when we go back home it can continue like this, and doesn't have to go back to how things were. We're leaving the day after New Years, and I'm both looking forward to it and dreading it at the same time.

Vince, Matt, and Colton are back from their away game, and have a home one on New Years that we're all planning on attending. I'm not particularly looking forward to it. I went to enough when I was younger, but I'm trying to participate with my siblings.

We're making plans for New Years Eve, even though I insisted we don't have to do anything besides enjoy the last couple of days before Wes and I leave.

"I'm fine not doing anything, but we have to get fireworks," Matt explains.

"No," I almost shout. "No. Wes doesn't do well with fireworks."

Wes tenses next to me, and I turn to look at him, wondering why. He won't look at me, just faces forward, jaw clenched and body stiff.

"Fine, no fireworks. But I'm at least getting sparklers. Evie will like them."

I tune out the rest of the conversation, suddenly focused on how Wes is frozen next to me. He looks almost angry.

"Hey, what's wrong?" I whisper, but he ignores me.

He stands up stiffly and announces he's turning in for the night. I continue to look at him as he walks away. I decide to follow him because I want to know what just happened.

When I get to the bedroom, he's storming around as I shut the door behind me.

"What's wrong?" I demand with my hands on my hips. The way he's throwing around his clothes into his duffel bag already has me pissed off and ready for a fight. Especially because I don't know what happened.

"Why'd you say that to them?"

"Say what? That you don't like fireworks? You don't?"

"You said I don't do well with them, like I'm some fucking child that can't handle them. I'm not a child, Bailey." His tone is harsh and leaves me feeling both angry at the way he's talking to me and nervous about how mad *he* is.

"You're mad because I care about your wellbeing?" I scoff.

"No, I'm mad that you think I'm *weak*. That you announced it to everyone. It wasn't your place to say anything."

"Okay, fine. I should've let you tell them, but I was just trying to look out for you. I've seen how you are with fireworks. I didn't want that to happen again."

"Yeah, you saw me *weak*."

Shaking my head, I step toward him. "That wasn't you being weak, that was you having a natural reaction."

"A natural reaction," he scoffs. "That's not natural for anyone and you fucking know it."

I reach up to put my hands on his chest, I don't want to fight, but I feel like he's blowing this way out of proportion.

"Sunflower." My hands freeze at the single word he utters.

Our safe word. The word we established means this stops.

My hands drop slowly to my side, and I take a step back, away from him even though my entire body is screaming at me not to. Especially when he closes his bag and swings it over his shoulder.

"I'm heading home."

"What? Right now?"

"Yes." His voice is cold. Detached, empty and devoid of emotion.

"Don't go right now. If you still want to in the morning then—"

"I'm leaving," he states firmly. "Enjoy your time with your family."

"Wes, please." I try to get him to stop, still not moving from the spot I'm rooted to. I'm in disbelief over how he's handling this. "Why can't you just talk to me about this?"

"You don't understand. You don't get to tell other people about me and my shit. I'm leaving."

I feel the tears welling up in my eyes, but I refuse to let them fall. I can feel him pulling away more and more. I want to ask if I'll see him once we're back home, but I don't think I can handle his answer if it's no.

Reaching behind my neck I unclasp the necklace. "Might as well take this with you, it only makes sense to wear it if I'm yours."

My throat constricts as he looks at the necklace, then back at me, but doesn't move to take it. "Goodbye, Bailey."

He walks out, and my chest caves at the sight. The worst part is not knowing where we'll stand when I get back. I'd just gotten used to the idea of what we could be—what we've been—and now I have no idea what I'll be walking back into.

I drop down to the ground and the tears finally fall, splattering directly on the necklace still cupped in my hand. That goodbye felt a lot more final than any of our previous ones. Suddenly the lightness I've been feeling is gone as everything comes crashing down around me. I started the day feeling light as a feather and now it's ending like I'm being crushed.

Wes is gone. I couldn't sleep last night, but I did hope he would come back at some point. I thought maybe he would take a drive like he does, and come back and feel better.

But he didn't.

The sun rose, shining brightly off the snow, and I was still alone in bed.

When I go downstairs, Chandler is feeding Evie her breakfast. She gives me a smile that quickly fades when she takes in my appearance. I'm sure I have bags under my red rimmed eyes. I don't even try to hide my current state of misery.

"What's wrong?"

"Wes went back home. We got into a fight."

"I'm sorry, are you okay?"

"I don't know," I tell her honestly. "I don't even really under-stand what happened, but he didn't want to talk about it either."

"Men are complicated creatures, trust me," she grumbles. "I'm sure he just needed some space, but if you want to head home as well, I don't think anyone will blame you. We've just been so happy you came to visit."

I think about what she's saying, but shake my head. "No. I'm not going to run back home just because he's being a jerk. If he wants his space, he can have it."

Chandler nods solemnly, and Evie has the perfect timing of happily announcing she's done with her meal. Clearly, she doesn't feel the air of sadness currently surrounding me and that's good. I can hold it together for two more days.

Maybe when I get back home and Wes has had his space every-thing will be fine. That's the hope I have to hold onto so I don't completely break down.

I pretend like I'm okay for the rest of the trip, but on New Year's Eve I notice that no one sets a single firework off. For some reason that alone hits me harder than it should. Mostly because I know no one thinks Wes is weak for not wanting fireworks. Even though he left, they still chose not to have them, and I feel like that just shows how caring my entire family is. If only he saw it that way instead of whatever way he took it.

By the time I get back to my room, I can't hold back my tears any more. The harder I try, the harder they fall, until my whole body is racked with sobs. I gasp, trying to breathe through the despair racing through me. The worst part of it all is that the one person that could help me through this is the reason for my tears in the first place.

CHAPTER 44

Wes

MY HOUSE IS dark and quiet when I get home. I got on the first flight out of Denver and came right back here. I thought it would help me feel like I could breathe, but the entire plane ride I was tense without a single distraction. I tried putting my headphones on and using loud music to drown out the thoughts threatening to consume me, but it didn't work.

All I wanted was Bailey next to me, her soft hand on my arm, talking to me about anything and everything. Drawing my mind away from the fact that I'm not the one driving the plane. Without her here, all I have is myself and my thoughts. Which means that every time I try closing my eyes all I see is the explosions around me. All I hear is the sound of them with the calls of my fellow soldiers. All I feel is the pain in my leg from the brutal injury and the metal sticking from it.

I thought I would feel better once I was back home, but it's worse. Bruno is still with Jameson and Sutton. I'll go get him in the morning and then I'll probably have to tell Gloria I can't keep him anymore. I shouldn't have let him get so comfortable, but I've been selfish.

I've been selfish with everyone. With him, with Bailey, and this is why I keep to myself. I let her in and she reminded me why I can't do that. I don't need everyone to know fireworks set me off. It just reminded me of how she sees me, and how anyone sees me once they learn anything about me.

Weak.

I'm fucking *weak*.

I may not look like it. To everyone else I look big, intimidating, but inside all I am is fucking weak.

Because my mind won't stop, I resort to the single and only coping mechanism I know that works. I get in my car and drive. I know this is going to be a long one because I don't see myself sleeping for a while.

I drive until the sun is rising on the horizon, and then I go to Jameson's in an attempt to distract myself by working around the farm. Nothing is helping, driving at least occupies my mind enough that the flashbacks don't play as rampantly. I don't feel better, but I'm as close to numb as I possibly can be.

I'm running on autopilot, keeping busy with whatever tasks I can find around the barn when Jameson appears in the entryway.

"Hey, I thought you weren't coming back until after the new year?" he asks.

"Came back early," I grunt, moving the last bale of hay. My hands are burning from the twine digging into my skin and my muscles ache from the heavy lifting, but it still doesn't feel like enough.

"I can see that. Was there a problem?"

"Just needed to be back."

I can tell he doesn't believe me and he shouldn't, but I'm not saying anything else about it. The last thing I need is more people finding out the truth about me. The one Bailey already knows, and had to announce to her family. The thought has me pissed off all over again.

"Bruno will be happy to see you, I'm sure."

"Mhm."

I'm sure Jameson can tell he's not getting more out of me as I continue with the manual labor. I hear the steady sounds of paws hitting the ground before I see the four dogs appearing in the barn followed closely by Sutton.

"Hey Wes, I didn't expect you to be here."

"Yup." I can feel the tenseness in the air, I just don't know if it's all coming from me. It probably is, but who gives a fuck. "I'll just take Bruno off your hands and head out."

"Sure. He had fun and can come back over any time." Sutton smiles softly.

"Do you want to keep him?" I can't help but ask.

"No, that dog is yours through and through."

Yeah, except he's not.

"See ya," I tell them because I don't know what else to say. The moment is awkward and I don't foresee it getting any better.

"Okay, bye," Sutton says softly. I can hear the concern in her voice, but I don't want it. All I want is for people to leave me the fuck alone.

I don't want people looking at me with pity, thinking I'm weak, concerned about my wellbeing. I suddenly miss the days where I never really talked to anyone. I did what I wanted without the concern of others.

It helps me remember why I don't let people into my life because this is what happens and I'm over it.

Bruno hops in my car, and I don't even say anything to him, but I think he can tell something is wrong. He drops his head and even though there's a hint of guilt as I drive toward the animal shelter, the numbness takes over.

It would be selfish to keep him. He can't live like this and he doesn't deserve it, either. He doesn't need someone who can't give him enough. I can never give anyone enough of myself because there's nothing to give.

Once we get there, I'm greeted by Gloria whose smile drops when she sees Bruno next to me.

"Is something wrong?" she asks, concerned.

"No, I just don't think I can foster him anymore."

"Oh," she sighs. "Well, I really thought this would end a little differently and it would be easier to tell you."

"What are you talking about?"

"You weren't fostering him. I had you fill out the adoption paperwork. I was sure you'd decide to keep him."

"You what?" I snap, harsher than I probably should.

"I saw you and him together and I was so sure you'd decide you wanted to keep him."

"Well that wasn't your decision to make, was it?"

Her voice is dejected as she continues. "No, it wasn't. I really am sorry. If you really don't want to keep him, we can go through the surrender process."

I grip his leash tighter, the leather biting into my skin. "No."

Even though I feel completely lost, there's no way I could live with myself if I left him in there once again. To let him think he was rejected from another home just because I'm the problem.

And I *am* the problem. I'm going to be selfish, and when we get back in the car I sigh heavily. "Sorry, you're stuck with me, and what a shitty life that is."

I don't even want to be in my own life, and now I'm subjecting someone else to it.

Fucking selfish.

Fucking weak.

Bailey's been back, but I haven't seen her. I haven't seen anyone. I'm avoiding everyone because I don't want to see the looks on their faces or hear what they have to say. I haven't even looked at my phone in several days.

When I finally do, I see several missed calls from Chris. Which is extremely unusual and even though I would rather not talk to anyone, I manage to call him back, a sinking feeling taking root in my gut. Especially after our last conversation where he was clearly struggling.

A woman answers the phone. "Hello?" Her voice cracks and my stomach drops.

"Hi. I have a few missed calls from Chris, is he around?"

The woman sniffles. "It was from me. I saw he talked to you before...." Her voice trails off and the pit in my stomach only grows. This isn't the first phone call like this I've gotten, and I feel like I know exactly what's coming. She doesn't even need to say it, but she speaks through her sobs. "I found him two days ago."

I can hear what she's not saying. She found him. *Dead.*

She continues on, as though she's reliving the moment and I don't say anything. "He wasn't answering me and when I came to check on him he was already gone."

"I'm sorry for your loss." My voice is steady, but sounds so far away to my own ears.

Her sobs take over and I'm unable to understand anything else she says. I don't do well with crying, but even more so I don't know what I'm feeling. It's like my mind has shut off completely.

Detached itself. My body, my mind, and my emotions, they're all separated.

"I'm sorry." She sniffles. "His funeral is next weekend if you're able to come."

Again, my voice doesn't sound like my own. "Maybe."

She makes a noise of understanding before we hang up. As soon as we do, the heaviness hits me. The thoughts I try to keep at bay. The guilt of survival is back in full force. Chris had people in his life that loved and cared about him. He had more than I do and still he chose to end it all. He's not the first of my friends to do so. In fact, we were a couple of the only people from our team still living. Now he's gone too.

What's stopping me from doing the same? I shouldn't be alive anyway.

CHAPTER 45

Bailey

SOMETIMES WHEN I let Sadie out in the backyard, I can hear Bruno out in Wes's and that's the only way I know he's still around. That and seeing his car in his driveway, occasionally. But he hasn't reached out. Neither have I.

Sadie will walk up to the fence and sniff, sometimes letting out a little cry when she realizes Bruno is over there. I can't help but feel so bad for her. I want her to be able to play with her friend. I want to talk to Wes. But it's clear he doesn't want the same and I'm not going to push it.

His car is gone more than it's there anyway, and I don't know what he's out doing. He might be driving around like he does. Or maybe he's at Jameson's, or the animal shelter. Maybe he's found another hobby to fill his time.

Maybe he's found someone else to fill his time.

I haven't put the necklace back on since the day he walked away and left, but I look at it every day. It's on my bathroom counter, taunting me, tempting me to reach out to him, but I refuse. I'm not going to fight for someone who doesn't want me. I almost let him in. I gave him more of myself than I should have and now I have to live next door and it's worse than it was before.

It used to be a mutual dislike, even if he won't admit that. We had arguments and disagreements, but it was just who we were. Then everything went and changed, altering my entire reality and in the blink of an eye, it was gone. Now I'm here, not knowing where we stand.

I lead Sadie inside, and she trots happily in front of me. I wish I could be as happy as she is every day. She always looks like she's smiling, wagging her tail. Sutton gave her a bath for me and when I picked her up I needed to go check inventory since the girls told me we were running low on some items. I brought Sadie with and everyone loved it.

I just wish I could be like that. I feel like I'm living on autopilot, waiting for something to happen that isn't going to. I don't even know what I'm waiting for, just something.

After a week of this, Sutton calls me for her coffee delivery. I bring it to her and as soon as I'm through the door I'm greeted as always, but not by a person.

"Hi bitch," Jerry Lee barks. I think back to Brynn telling Brent to get a bird, and it makes me crack a small smile for the first time in over a week.

"Jerry Lee, how many times do I have to tell you, you can't greet people like that." Sutton sounds exasperated with the bird.

I reach out, handing her the coffee she asked for, and she takes it thankfully. My smile must drop because Sutton suddenly looks serious.

"How have you been doing?" she asks.

I drop my eyes to my shoes. "Fine," I mumble.

"Have you seen him?"

I shake my head, still not looking up at her.

"Have you reached out at all?"

I do the same thing again and hear her sigh.

"Has he been by your place?" I risk looking up to see her reaction.

She hesitates before slowly shaking her head and I deflate. I don't know if I hoped he had and that he looked like he's doing well, or that he looked as miserable as I feel. But the not knowing is worse.

"He still has Bruno." I shrug. "I assume he would need to bring him in here to see you soon, right?"

"Right." Sutton smiles. It seems forced, like she's just placating me.

My shoulders deflate again. "I don't know, Sutton. It was like a flip switched. Everything was fine. Great even. Then before I knew what was happening he just—" I shake my head at the memory of the moment he said *sunflower*. The word we agreed ended everything, and the one thing I never expected him to say.

I also never expected to fall in love with him either, but here we are.

"Obviously none of us know everything he went through when he was in the military, but do you know if he's ever gotten help or seen anyone about it?"

I shake my head. "I don't know."

"I have a feeling whatever happened doesn't actually have much to do with you and has more to do with him. Even if he doesn't realize it."

I narrowed my eyes at her. "Were you a therapist in a past life?"

Sutton chuckles. "Definitely not."

"Well, in your non-expert opinion, what should I do?"

"What do you want to do?"

I bite my bottom lip, thinking about that. I don't know what I want to do. All I know is that I want things to go back to how they were. I want to go back to when everything was happier. Maybe we were a ticking time bomb, but at least while it was ticking I was happy. Even if the explosion ends it all, I want to know I did everything I could to try and defuse it.

"I want to talk to him," I say softly.

"Then you should. I bet he wants to talk to you too, but you both are just too stubborn to do anything about it."

I glare at her. "Really? I'm stubborn? I remember you didn't want to date either, Mrs. Married-to-the-man-you-insisted-you-couldn't-be-friends-with."

"Hey, this isn't about me."

"Fine, we can make it about Lily. Now *she's* stubborn. I mean do we really think she's serious about this new boyfriend of hers when she's so clearly hung up on Parker."

"Now, I *know* you aren't okay." Sutton folds her arms across her chest.

"Why?"

"Because you're talking a bunch, clearly as a diversion." She glares at me. "Because you're stubborn."

I groan, rolling my eyes. "Fine, you're welcome for your coffee."

"Thank you." She takes a sip, and when she lowers the cup from her mouth she looks at me softly. "Just talk to him. You'll be mad if you don't try. And it's clear you're both hurting."

I deflate again. "I'll try."

"It'll be okay," Sutton tries to comfort.

Right on time, Jerry Lee inserts himself into the conversation, "*Shut up, Vern! Jizz!*"

"Way to ruin a moment, Jerry Lee." Sutton shakes her head, and I leave before I'm subjected to any more of the bird's—or my friend's—wisdom.

The rest of my work day goes by as normal, but I'm distracted thinking about Wes and the best way to try and talk to him. The fact that he hasn't been going to Jameson's is concerning. I wonder if he's been going to the animal shelter. After I close, I head over there to check.

I walk in, and am immediately greeted by Gloria, the friendly woman from before. "Hi Bailey, it's nice to see you again. How's Sadie?"

"Oh, she's great. I'm so glad I found her. I'm actually here to ask if you've seen Wes lately?"

Her face drops, smile dimming. "I actually haven't. Not since I told him I gave him adoption paperwork for Bruno instead of foster paperwork. He may be a bit upset about that."

"Wait, what?" I sputter.

"Oh, did he not tell you? He came in here about a week ago saying he couldn't foster Bruno anymore, and I had to break the news to him that he never actually was." She shrugs. "I saw how he was with that dog and I really assumed he would come around to keeping him."

"Me too," I admit softly. Then, I think about how many times I've heard him in the backyard since then. "He didn't leave him here, did he?"

"No, he didn't. But he didn't seem happy about it. He hasn't been back since."

I sigh, thanking her for her time before leaving. Knowing he hasn't been to Jameson's or the shelter has me even more concerned about where he's been going, and what he has or hasn't been doing.

I psych up myself the entire ride home. I'm going over to his house to talk to him. I'm going to do it. But when I get there his car is gone and I deflate, slumping back in my seat. I need to talk to him. And I will. As soon as I see him come home, I'm going to storm over there and demand he speak to me.

That's what I tell myself, until I'm laying in bed and finally hear his car rumble down the street. I jump out of bed, trying to get a glimpse of him walking inside, but he must've moved quickly because by the time I get to the window his door is already shutting.

I watch his bedroom window, the same window the blinds are drawn over, exactly as they have been ever since I got back. The light never even turns on, and as I sit on my bed hugging my knees to my chest, I watch and wait for any sign of him.

But it never comes.

When I leave for work the next morning, Wes's car is still parked in his driveway. When I come home it's still there. I sit in my car debating on going over there, but I'm back to not knowing what to say. Everything I prepared last night is now gone so instead of storming over to his house, I go inside.

I let Sadie outside, and look over at the house that's almost identical to mine, waiting to see any sign of him or his dog, but there's nothing. My concern only grows, which is probably why I end up sitting outside for a lot longer than I intend, just waiting. Eventually, I convince myself that maybe he's just sleeping or taking Bruno on a walk. The chill from the air starts to seep into my bones, so Sadie and I go inside.

Another day passes without any sign of Wes and my worry is back tenfold. I didn't hear his car leave last night, which I was weirdly anticipating. As I come home from work again, seeing his car unmoved, something feels wrong. I try to shake it off, but when I let Sadie outside and look over to his house, I can't get the worry to dissipate.

The backdoor looks like it's open, and that's what does it for me. Something is wrong. I race inside, Sadie following me closely. "I'll be back," I tell her as I'm rushing out the front door and over to Wes's house.

I try to open his front door, only to find that it's locked. I glance around at our empty street, making sure no one is watching me as I go around the side of the house, through the gate into the backyard.

When I step through the open sliding glass door, the house is cold and dark. My heart races, afraid of what I'm walking into. Gently, I call out his name, not wanting to scare or sneak up on him.

He doesn't answer, and I walk deeper inside, and my heart completely bottoms out at what I see. Wes is here, sitting on the floor, surrounded by empty bottles of alcohol while Bruno lays by him, concerned.

"Wes?" I call softly, tears already welling in my eyes.

He looks up at me, completely broken and I shatter along with him.

CHAPTER 46

Wes

MY ENTIRE ADULT life has been a constant spiral of shit upon shit and then more shit. I had a brief glimpse of happiness when I was with Bailey, but she's gone. I know she won't come back, and I don't even know if I want her to. I'm not worthy enough to have someone as perfect as her in my life. She deserves better. She deserves someone who can bring her joy instead of bringing her down into the depths of hell I'm currently living amidst.

After the phone call with Chris's ex-wife, I feel like I lost sight of anything good in my life. My worthless, meaningless life. The flashbacks have been almost constant and I don't know when the last time I slept without the assistance of alcohol was. I tried to pretend to be okay, but I'm not.

I've never been okay.

I never will be.

It was a normal day. Inspections were normal, we woke up and ate breakfast and fucked around like we normally did before we were supposed to head out for the day.

As soon as the first explosion sounded, everything changed forever. I knew people were caught in it, and I wanted to help. The pain in my leg from the impact of flying metal seared into me, stopping me from being able to help. I just wanted to help save my friends—my brothers—even if it killed me.

But all I could do was lay there waiting to die. When the darkness took over, I thought maybe I had.

Until I woke up in the hospital, knowing my life changed forever. Not only did I lose friends, I lost the one thing that made me who I was. My job was my identity and that was gone along with the lives of others.

I finish another bottle, slamming it down, and see Bruno laying on the floor next to me, concerned wide eyes pinned on me. This is what I didn't want for him. He could've had a better life. I look toward the open back door for him. I'm facing it because I want to see any threat that could come in. Not that I could do anything about it.

Not that I would even want to.

Someone else could end my misery. Remove me from this Earth and take away the pain I've carried with me for so long, and I would be relieved. I could do it myself, I could do what others I know have done. Make it quick and painless. End it all. End the suffering and the madness.

I just want it to stop.

The memories, the sounds, the thoughts, the feelings.

Life.

I try to reach for another bottle, but it feels out of reach. Everything is fuzzy, and I don't know if it's from the amount of alcohol in my system or the lack of sleep. Or maybe, this is what dying slowly feels like.

There's a noise in the backyard, and I think maybe it's someone coming to end it for me. *Just end it.*

I faintly recognize my name being called out by a familiar voice, but I can't look up to see. I don't want to because maybe this isn't someone coming to end it for me. Now my mind is just playing tricks on me.

The voice almost sounded like Bailey, but there's no way she'd come here. She's done with me. I pushed her away because I couldn't take it anymore. She saw how damaged I truly am and she doesn't want that in her life. It's a special kind of torture that she lives right next door to me, but that's why I just stay in here, drinking myself into oblivion so she doesn't have to see me.

"Wes?" She sounds closer, like she's inside. I don't believe she's actually here. My mind just wants to fuck with me more. It wants to punish me for pushing her away, for continuing to live.

I hear her soft sob, and I finally find the strength to lift my head enough to see if she's really here. And she is. She's standing in front of me, eyes wide and looking at me with so much pain, but I hardly feel anything, everything in me is so numb.

She rushes over and drops to her knees in front of me, but I don't move. I can't. I just watch her. She looks around at all the bottles around me, and back to Bruno, who still hasn't left my side. I see the tears streaming down her cheeks and how glassy her eyes are when they finally look at me once again.

"What happened?" she sobs and it's when I faintly feel wetness on my own cheeks; I think it's coming from my eyes but it's hard to tell right now when everything feels so numb.

I shake my head, but the movement makes my stomach turn and my head dizzy. When I speak it's rough and raspy, burning my throat I've only been using to guzzle down the biting alcohol. "Sunflower."

She moves closer to me, kneeling between my spread legs. "I'm not leaving."

I clench my fists. "There's just no point anymore."

Bailey's tears fall harder. "No point to what? Wes, please what's going on?"

"Anything."

She gasps. "No." Her voice takes a serious turn. "No. I know you're not saying what I think you are."

"Everyone else I know is gone. They all had more of a reason to live and still didn't."

"Listen to me." She grabs my face, forcing me to look at her while the tears continue to fall for both of us. "You're not leaving me. If you go, then I go, because in no world can I live without you. We are both fucked up and damaged beyond repair, but together we're different. There's no point in living in a world that doesn't have you in it."

I can't do this, I can't let her ruin her life. I can't drag her down with me. But I want to be selfish and keep her. The same way I've been selfish and kept Bruno here with me to watch me completely fall apart.

I wrap my arms around Bailey, pulling her against me and burying my face in her shoulder as I let the tears flow without holding back. I breathe her in, feeling her against me. I let her be the reason every thought gets silenced in my mind while we just sit here, letting it all out.

The words start flowing from my mouth without thinking about it. I don't care if it scares her, or what she thinks. I continue to hold her tightly against me, refusing to let her go. "I should've been able to save them. I watched them die and couldn't do anything about it. I wanted to join them. Everyone is dead, why am I the only one still alive? It's not fair."

She comforts me by not saying anything, just holding onto me and letting me get it all out. The tears, the thoughts, all of it.

We stay like this for so long I lose track of time and it's dark outside when I finally lift my head from her shoulder. Her eyes are red, and I bring her forehead down to mine. We're both breathing heavily. "I shouldn't have left like that," I confess.

She moves her head against mine. "I shouldn't have said anything. It wasn't my place."

"It was, though. You cared about me."

Her hand reaches up to rub her thumb along my cheek. "I still care, Wes. I'll always care."

I pull her closer, our lips almost touching. "You lied. You

really are an angel." I kiss her before she can say anything. The second her lips are on mine the world seems to right itself again. There're so many things that need to be worked out. I know this doesn't solve everything, but right now at this moment, I feel like it's okay. At least while her mouth is on mine.

She melts against me, kissing me back, and even when I thought she might pull away, she doesn't. I refuse to let her go.

"Lay with me," I say against her mouth. I just want to feel her next to me again. I want to feel her steady breathing. Even when sleep doesn't easily find me, having her here makes it easier to keep the thoughts at bay. Right now that's all I want.

I may not know what tomorrow is going to look like. I may not know what the future holds for either of us. But right now, all I want is to have her here next to me because she brings me peace.

Bailey stands up, stretching her hand out, and I almost laugh. If I gave her my full weight, she would come barreling back down on top of me. I work to try and stand up myself, pushing off the ground, even though it takes a couple tries before I get to my feet. Once I do, I sway, the world is spinning around me and I close my eyes, fighting the feeling off. I feel Bailey's arm wrap around my back, her palm on my stomach as she helps steady me.

We stay like this as we walk up to my room. I think Bruno is following us, but I'm so focused on putting one foot in front of the other as we walk up the stairs so I don't topple down and take Bailey with me that I don't look back to check.

Once we're in my room, she helps me lay down on the soft surface I haven't been on in days. I've been alternating between the floor and the couch when I pass out because even the thought of walking up the stairs was repulsive.

She doesn't get into bed with me right away and I reach for her, but she's already too far.

"I'm just going to shut the backdoor."

"I got it," I grunt, swinging my legs off the bed, but I'm pushed back gently.

"You stay right here, I'll be back I promise."

I don't like that she's leaving me here like this, I feel like she's not going to come back. She just said that stuff downstairs in the moment. My eyelids get heavy, but I fight it off because if she's not coming back then I'm grabbing another bottle.

She walks back in and I try to speak, but it doesn't work. Not even as she's climbing into the bed with me. My limbs feel heavy, but I manage to pull her against me before I give up the fight to let my eyes fall shut.

CHAPTER 47

Bailey

I DON'T KNOW what I expected to see when I walked into Wes's house. But it wasn't what I found. I never thought I would see the man, larger than life, quiet, and reserved, the one I've fallen completely in love with, so broken.

He's holding me like his life depends on it, and maybe it does. Clearly, he needs more help than I'm going to be able to give him. I just hope that he'll be open to asking for it. He's been closed off for so long, refusing to acknowledge the demons he obviously carries around. I hope he's ready to heal.

I struggle to fall asleep, just in case Wes ends up waking up, but his body clearly needs the rest and he doesn't stir all night. Maybe that's why after several hours, I'm able to let sleep pull me under as well.

When I wake up, I'm still plastered against Wes while he's on his back with one arm across his face, covering his eyes. At first I think he's still sleeping until he shifts. I sit up and he removes his arm so I can see the bags under his red eyes. The defeated look on his face has me feeling dejected.

"Thank you." His voice is rough and it sounds painful for him to get the words out.

"I'm going to get some water," I say, knowing if I mention it's for him he will refuse it.

When I return with the two glasses he's sitting on the side of the bed. His shirt is laying on the floor and he's holding his head in his hands. I set the glasses on the nightstand next to him, and kneel on the floor.

"I was going to get in the shower, but this is as far as I got," he admits. I can tell it's tough for him to say, but it already feels like progress.

"Do you want help?" I offer.

"No, I just need a minute."

I sigh. Placing a hand on his knee. "Wes, it's okay to admit you need help sometimes."

He puts his own hand over mine. "I know, but I don't want you thinking I'm any weaker than you already do."

I force myself between his legs, reaching up to hold his cheeks, his beard scratches my palms as I make him look at me. "I don't think you're weak. I never have, and never could. I want to help you. *Please* let me help you."

He clenches his jaw, and I know it's hard for him to accept help, let alone ask for it. When he nods I know that's all I'm going to get. But it feels like the first step in the right direction.

I help him get into the shower, and stay close by but don't get in with him. My body is screaming to be close to him, but I don't want to fall into old habits of having sex to avoid everything else. This is too important to distract ourselves with orgasms just because it's easy. We know we can do that. He can get the control he thinks he needs from me and my body, but what he actually *needs* is control over his life again.

I do what he did for me when I needed him. I get clothes for him to change into when he gets out of the shower and he doesn't even fight me on it. I can see cleaning up helped him a little bit, though. He doesn't look as tired, though I'm sure his hangover is awful.

After he's dressed again, he sits on the edge of his bed, and says something I never thought I would hear him say.

"I want to tell you about what happened, the reason I'm...like this."

I nod, sitting next to him. "I want to hear about it, but I would never push you."

Wes puts his hand on my thigh, just resting it there while he seems to gather his thoughts. I wait for whatever he's going to tell me. Getting some of it out seems like another good step, even though I think we both know he needs a therapist. But if he wants to tell me, I'm here.

"I should've told you sooner. We were deployed, I'm not supposed to talk about where, but just know it wasn't a fun place. We were doing our normal inspections on the helicopters before taking off when we were attacked." He pauses, staring off at the floor as he continues. "There were explosions all around us as the missiles fell from the sky. We took cover, but I tried to help some of the injured guys. I couldn't get to them in time, though."

I squeeze his hand resting on my thigh, silently letting him know that I'm here, and that he's safe to keep going with me.

"I caught some shrapnel in my leg. That's what the scar there is from. I couldn't do anything to help, and I don't remember much else because I passed out from the pain, or blood loss. I'm not totally sure, I just know I woke up in the hospital. That's where I learned just how many of my men died that day. Those of us that survived weren't the same."

He still isn't looking at me, just at the floor like he's lost in his mind as he retells the worst day he's gone through.

"Even the guys that survived are gone now. My copilot, Chris, just…" He trails off and this must have been what made him completely spiral.

"It's okay, you don't have to say it."

His shoulders drop in relief.

"Thank you for telling me," I say softly. "I just want you to know that I'm glad you're here."

Now he looks at me, complete and total vulnerability in his eyes. "I'm here because of you. You're my reason. My everything. My angel."

I want to kiss him so badly, but I don't want to push any further than I already have. He must see it, or maybe he wants it too, because he cups my cheeks, swiping the tears I didn't even realize had fallen. He brings our faces closer together, my eyes already falling shut with just the smallest brush of his lips against mine. "Only an angel could make me fall in love like you have."

His mouth is on mine before I can respond, which is good because there's nothing I can say. My mind has gone blank at his confession—what I think he's telling me. It really clears out when he kisses me, and when his tongue glides along the seam of my lips I let him in, easily. He kisses me like he needs me more than air. He kisses me like his life truly depends on it.

And I do the same.

I never thought we would end up here, like this, but nothing has ever felt so right, either. Especially when he lays me back on the bed, hovering his body over mine while he kisses me deeply. When he settles his hips between my thighs I feel how hard he is against me, and can't hold back a moan.

"You know what I really need right now?" he asks, keeping his mouth just out of reach as he pins my wrists down by the side of my head and I whimper in protest.

"Hm?"

"I need to feel your sweet pussy."

I try to arch up into him, but he's holding me down, so I nod. "Yes, whatever you need, it's yours. I'm yours."

He moves the neckline of my shirt, and I know what he's looking for, but it's not there.

"Why aren't you wearing the necklace I gave you?"

I swallow roughly. "Because I wasn't sure if you still wanted me to be yours and it felt wrong to wear it if I wasn't anymore."

"I'm sorry I made you question that, but I want to make something very clear to you." His voice takes a serious tone, the gruff, sexy one he usually has with me in bed. I try to clench my thighs together, but it only makes me feel him even more and I try not to get too distracted. "You've been mine, and you'll continue to be mine. The only one with the power to end this, is you. Because I'm yours completely."

I gasp, the tears starting to well up in my eyes again, and I can't hold it back any longer. I need him to know how I feel. He's been able to tell me so much more than I ever expected him to. He's confessed feelings for me while I've hardly been able to form a sentence.

"I'm yours, Wes. I love yo—" He doesn't let me finish before he kisses me senseless once again.

I'm not complaining. Everything has felt so heavy and with his lips on mine, I start to feel lighter. Or maybe it's from admitting what I've known for awhile now, actually putting it out there feels so good. Almost as good as it feels when he slides his hand into my pants and underwear, swiping his finger through my wetness and I'm already moaning for more.

He gives me exactly what he knows I need, rubbing tight circles on my clit that have me writhing underneath him. He groans into my mouth and pulls his hand away, causing me to cry out in protest.

He doesn't make me wait long before he's pushing my pants off my hips, but I want to scream as he removes himself from my body to pull them off completely.

"Take your shirt off, Angel, I want to feel every inch of your skin against mine."

I don't hesitate to do just that, watching him do the same so he's completely bare in front of me. I scoot to the end of the bed, looking up at him. I run my fingers along his skin, the indented V that leads like an arrow to his cock. Up his toned ab muscles, to his hard pecs, then down his toned arms until I'm taking his hands in mine, intertwining our fingers.

"Remind me what it feels like to be yours. Show me what your love feels like."

CHAPTER 48

Wes

I WANT to get lost in the control, to let go completely and fall into our primal habits when we're in bed together. I also want to savor every single second I can with her. I want to show her that I'll never let her go again, that this is real and that she means more to me than anything else in this entire world.

I don't want to think about how close I was to ending it. To never seeing her again, to never feeling this feeling. I cover her body with mine once more, kissing her roughly to drown out the what ifs. I want to be here—with her. I want to get better.

My tongue invades her mouth, licking and tasting her to remind myself how real this is. To taste the words she just said, and swallow them until they're ingrained in my very soul.

I run my hands along her body, feeling that she's really here with me, her smooth skin under my rough hands. I reach her thigh, hiking it up over my hip so I can angle my cock at her entrance, teasing her just barely.

"Wes," she whispers, and I have to stop myself from jutting forward to bury myself in her at just the sound of my name on her lips. "Tell me again."

"I love you," I tell her effortlessly, as I thrust forward and she moans at the sudden intrusion. My vision blurs at how tightly she squeezes me and I don't know if I'll ever see straight again. But it doesn't matter. I have her and that's all that does.

I don't let her say anything back, instead, pulling back and pushing forward again roughly because I don't need her to say anything else, I just want to make her feel good. I want her to know how important she is to me for as long as she'll let me.

It doesn't take long before she's clenched around me, and I know she's close. "Come for me, Angel."

She moans my name, digging her nails into my back while she detonates and it causes my own release to barrel through me. Neither of us move while our chests heave together with rough breathing. Our kisses slow but don't stop as our mouths move against each other. Even when I soften inside her, I don't want to move.

Rolling off her body, I pull her against me because I don't want to be more than a couple of inches from her at all times. I need her more than I need anything else. She saved me in more ways than one.

I hold her and she doesn't move away. Her fingers start tracing my skin and it lulls me into an unfamiliar calmness, until I end up drifting off to sleep.

We spend most of the day in bed, wrapped around each other, sometimes talking and sometimes we let our bodies do the talking. Bruno makes it known he needs attention, which is what causes us to get up. I'm reluctant to let Bailey leave, but she said she would be right back with Sadie. I don't think I've ever been so attached to another person, but I let her go, trusting she'll be back in just a few short minutes.

When she walks back through the door, both dogs are excited to see each other, and we let them out in the backyard. I pull her down on my lap as I sit on one of the chairs I have out here, keeping my arms wrapped around her as we watch our dogs.

"I heard Bruno is staying," she says with a small quirk of her lips.

"Yeah? How'd you learn that?"

"I went to the shelter to ask if you had been there and Gloria told me. I knew you were going to keep him. We all did, clearly."

I sigh. "Yeah, I really wanted him to have a better life than I could give him."

"Why do you think that? That dog is attached to you, and I think he's exactly what you need."

I hold her tighter. "Yeah, you both are."

"The three of us." She nods toward Sadie and I chuckle.

"Yes, all three of you."

We continue to sit in a comfortable silence while the dogs

play. Everything isn't better by any means, but I feel like maybe it can get there. Which leads me to something I've avoided for years. I know if I want to be worthy of the woman in my lap, the woman who says she loves me, I need to do something for myself. The very thing I've avoided because I didn't think I needed it, but the truth is I do.

I just needed to reach rock bottom before I could fully admit it.

"I'm going to start therapy," I mumble against Bailey's shoulder. She stiffens for a second and I regret telling her until she turns her head to look me in the eyes.

"I'll be here for you every step of the way."

I can see how much she means it, and it helps me relax because I know it's going to be hard. I know I'm not always going to be easy to love or the best partner, but I'll do everything I can to be the best for her.

"I'm going to as well," she admits, and I kiss her shoulder.

"Want to come with me for horse therapy sometimes? They *are* the best listeners," I tell her, remembering what Emily has said about the horses before. Realizing maybe she's right and Bailey would like it too.

"I'll try it, but you're not getting me on one," she says seriously and I chuckle, even though I have yet to get on one as well.

"Maybe that's something we can try together."

"I'll try anything as long as it's with you."

"Me too, Angel. We're in all of this together."

I mean it. Whatever challenges are sure to come up, the setbacks, but also the good and amazing things that are yet to come. We're in this life together.

Epilogue

BAILEY

TWO YEARS LATER

THE DAY I moved to Amity and saw my neighbor was the man I had sex with the night before who didn't seem to remember me, I never in a million years thought this is where we would end up. If you told me we would be moving into our new house together I would have laughed in your face. But here we are.

We found the perfect house when we weren't really looking, but it was too perfect to turn down. It's on three acres, with a two stall barn which Wes wants to get a couple horses to fill. I'm still getting used to the idea of sitting on them, let alone owning any. Regardless, Bruno and Sadie are already enjoying running around in the large area as we carry the first couple of boxes inside.

Wes takes the one from my arms after setting down the two he had in his, and then he pulls me into his embrace. "We're home."

I smile as he drops his lips onto mine, but we're interrupted when the sound of tires appear as other cars join us. Jameson's truck holds a lot of our things. Wes doesn't have much and didn't care to get rid of most of it. I didn't have much either, but we decided to keep my furniture at least for now.

We go outside to greet our friends and my family who all came to help, despite me insisting they didn't need to. It's weird having them around. During the hockey season they are all busy, but right now in the summer apparently they have nothing better to do than come help us move.

At least according to Brynn.

My sister who is wrangling her twin boys out of the car while Wes and the guys unload boxes.

Sutton walks up to me with her baby bump starting to show, and I glare at her. "You better not be here to help, you're not allowed to lift anything."

She waves me off. "Yeah, yeah, I already got a talking to from Jameson. I'm here for morale support and assisting with children as needed."

"Please assist me," Brynn pleads while Grayson tries to launch himself out of her arms while she tries to get his brother out.

I take my nephew from her arms and he laughs manically. "You would think torturing your mom is funny," I tell him, then whisper, "Me too."

"I heard that," Brynn calls out and I chuckle. "I swear, I told him I wanted one kid and he made it his mission to give me two at once."

"You make me glad this is the only one." Sutton smiles with a hand on her stomach.

"And you make me glad I won't be having any," I tease. "They're cute, but I like giving them back."

"Just wait until I send them to you for the summers and take a nice long vacation to Bora Bora," Brynn jokes.

"Very funny."

"No, I couldn't be away from you the whole summer." She nuzzles against Easton's cheek and he giggles.

Chandler joins us with Evie and Maya in tow while the guys join Jameson, Colton, and Wes with unloading and getting the house set up. It's weird having all this support around, but I can't deny it's nice to have all the extra help.

Wes and I could handle it like we handle everything ourselves, but not needing to is nice...different, but nice. A lot of things have been different this past year while we both started therapy, working through our individual issues wasn't easy, but it's helped more than I ever thought.

I never realized how much I harbored from my childhood. Obviously I had the nightmares and memories, but apparently having them be debilitating is not actually normal, who knew? Wes has been getting better with his own therapy. It was a struggle at first. He didn't want to go for a while, but once he got into a routine of it he started to see the positive effects.

It's been a journey, but having each other along the way has helped us both immensely. So has having Brynn and Brent back in my life. Bryson is another story, while he's out living his life, he reaches out every once in a while, but doesn't visit. I don't take it personally because I understand, I've been there. He'll come around if and when he's ready.

We bring all the kids to the open area of the property where the dogs are running around and they join in. Evie, the oldest, runs around easily while the boys and Maya waddle, falling but getting back up while they try to keep up with Evie.

"You excited?" Chandler asks Sutton, gesturing to her stomach.

"Terrified and excited."

Another set of cars pull up, and our large driveway can hardly fit everyone, but Lily announces her arrival with a loud, "Hey bitches!" She throws her hand over her mouth when she sees all the kids around. She just recently came back into town...with her boyfriend.

Parker joins in helping the guys, and I notice they don't say anything to each other. The tension is clear, and I'm sure he hates how much he has to see her and Aaron around. But I know their story is far from over.

"What'd I miss?" Lily asks, approaching us, watching the kids and dogs play around the yard.

"You tell us." Sutton raises an eyebrow.

Lily lifts her chin. "I don't know what you're talking about."

"Yeah, okay," Sutton scoffs.

It doesn't take long before everything is unloaded in our new house and everyone migrates inside. It's a tight fit to have everyone in here. Normally, I feel like I would be overwhelmed and uncomfortable by the amount of people around, but I don't.

It's kind of nice.

I slide up to Wes, wrapping my arms around his middle to check in because I know crowds can still bother him. He looks down at me with a smile and relief washes over me. "How're you doing?" I ask just to be sure.

"Great. How're you?"

"Tired," I sigh.

"Oh, are you? I didn't see you helping with many of the boxes."

"Hey, I did some, and I helped in other ways."

"Yeah? Entertaining your sister and friends?"

"Exactly." I give him a wide smile that has him pulling me against him even tighter and leaning down to whisper in my ear.

"You better behave, or I'll have to haul you away in front of everyone and lock you up in our bedroom."

I hum. "And what would you do with me?"

"You want me to tell you or do you want me to show you?" He raises an eyebrow.

"I mean if you're all talk, just say that. I know it can be a lot to handle me, maybe you aren't up for the job."

He lets out a growl, hooking his finger under the chain of my necklace, the one that claims me as his. "Sounds like you want a punishment, is that it?"

"Maybe," I taunt.

"Hey, don't be gross over there you have family in town," Brynn calls out, pulling us from our bubble.

I lean against Wes, smiling because those words aren't something I ever thought I would get to hear. I didn't think any of this was something I would experience, and it's safe to say I've never been happier. The best part is I know it's just the beginning.

The End

Memories of You is coming

Are you ready for Lily and Parker? Read their bonus scene before Memories of You.
READ IT HERE

Also by Madi Danielle

Amity

Small town romances

Embers of You - A firefighter romance

Scars of You - A neighbors enemies to lovers romance

Memories of You - A second chance romance

Denver Dragons Series:

Hockey romances

The Hat Trick - A why choose romance

The Power Play - A forced proximity cam girl romance

Cross Checked - A friends to lovers novella

The Break Out -An enemies to lovers brother's teammate romance

Uncaged Duet

A dark MMA why choose romance

Uncaged Desires

Uncaged Obsessions

Red Card Romance

Strike & Score - A dark soccer step sibling romcom

Foul & Fake by Octavia Jensen - A Fake dating soccer rom com

Bend & Break by Genna Black - A dark soccer murder mystery rom com

The Falling series

When They Fell - A friends to lovers romance

Who They Are - A cop romance

What They Feel - An enemies to lovers age gap romance

Acknowledgments

Where to begin? This entire series has already been such a journey. I want to thank every single person who has been on it with me. I hope I don't miss anyone!

Ashley - My booha and the reason most of these stories have come to be. Hot military neighbor (;)) wouldn't be here without you.

Sarah - Thank you for being with me since the very beginning. You are the absolute best and I appreciate you more than you'll ever know.

Chelsey - As always thank you for being everything! My PA, my bestie, my social media guru I don't know where I would be without you. I can never thank you enough!

Anja - Thank you so much for making my IG content you are the best. And of course our unhinged chats give me life. Even if you're bugging me for flower daddy...

Maeghen - Thank you for pushing me to write, for creating designs for me and for bearing with my (daily) crash outs.

Kim - As always thank you for this GORGEOUS cover! You kill it every time. Thank you for always doing the damn thing!

Kay - Thank you for being my editor, I can't believe how many books we've worked on together at this point. And how many more we have coming. You are the BEST.

Angie - Thank you so much for continuing to believe in me and my stories, I'll forever be so grateful for you.

MASSIVE thank you to Kristin and Daniel for the cover photo! I am obsessed with both of you. Thank you Kristin for reading an early copy for me.

Thank you to all my beta readers: Randi, Lanae, Courtney, Emily, Kelsey, Logan, Jane, Jessica, Katelyn and Leslie.

Thank you to everyone who has read and loved my books, I truly couldn't be here if it weren't for you all supporting me. Thank you doesn't feel like enough! I can't wait to share what's next because as you've seen Lily is...something. Lily and Parker are going to be so fun and I can't wait to share them with you all.

www.ingramcontent.com/pod-product-compliance
Lightning Source LLC
Chambersburg PA
CBHW071737110726
47908CB00006B/1621